To: Ron

Love

Ginny

Go Softly All My Years

Virginia Benson

All the characters in this book, other than historically known personages, are fictional, and any resemblance to actual persons, living or dead, is purely coincidental. Historical facts are, as such as could be determined by extensive research, authentic and true, and any misinterpretation of historical facts is the fault of the author.

The University of Chattanooga was not, to the author's knowledge, the site where any work was done on the nuclear project known as the Manhattan Project. It does have, at present, a campus in Oak Ridge, TN, but in the setting of my book, this was not the case.

Copyright © 2010 by Virginia Benson

Published by arrangement with www.lulu.com

ISBN: 978-0-557-28682-9

Cover Design: Virginia Benson
Cover Model: Lauren Benson

For Dana, Byron, and Eydie

6

CONTENTS

Part 1 September 1939—September 1941 9

Chapter 1 Coming Home 11

Chapter 2 Old Friends, New Teaching Position 21

Chapter 3 New Friends 27

Chapter 4 The Unexpected 37

Chapter 5 Another Vocation 43

Chapter 6 Friends of Britain Variety Show 49

Chapter 7 In Washington D.C. 55

Chapter 8 An Unpleasant Surprise 69

Chapter 9 Unwelcome News 79

Chapter 10 Breakfast with Edward 85

Chapter 11 Change of Heart 95

Chapter 12 Unenviable Meeting 103

Chapter 13 Riding the Rails Home 111

Chapter 14 Laying Out the Problem 117

Chapter 15 Encounter at Midnight 127

Chapter 16 Christmas at the Braddocks 133

Chapter 17 Catastrophe! 149

Chapter 18 Repercussions 157

Chapter 19 New Friends, Old Love 167

Chapter 20 Startling Arrival 179

Chapter 21 Revelations in a Quiet Talk 185

Chapter 22 "Good-bye" 195

Chapter 23 Phone Call *203*

Part 2 September 17, 1941—December 19, 1941 ...... **209**

Chapter 24 In Egypt *211*

Chapter 25 Looking for Reife and Col. Lowe *219*

Chapter 26 A Trek in the Desert *229*

Chapter 27 Astonishment! *233*

Chapter 28 Anxious Days *241*

Chapter 29 Golden Days Under Egyptian Sun *249*

Part 3 January 1942—Autumn 1944 .... **255**

Chapter 30 Phone Call From Cairo *257*

Chapter 31 Visit with Henrietta *265*

Chapter 32 Break-in! *273*

Chapter 33 Joy, then Calamity *281*

Chapter 34 More Bad News *289*

Chapter 35 Secrets *299*

Chapter 36 New Beginning *309*

Chapter 37 Persistent Love *319*

Chapter 38 Olaf Wins the Day *327*

Chapter 39 Loss *333*

Chapter 40 Journey's End *341*

Part 1

September 1939 – September 1941

Chapter 1

The Southern Railway train, spewing smoke, chuffed through the outskirts of Chattanooga past unpainted neighborhood grocery stores where a scattered few men, faces set in lines of dumb fortitude, lounged at doors. It had been almost a decade following those terrible days when one by one, they found themselves unemployed and starting a journey downward into a bewildering poverty.

The train passed sad little dry goods shops whose owners were eking out a living from a populace that had little to spend beside that which they could peddle on the streets. Men who had once held proud positions of responsibility and boasted of stellar work ethics were now buying produce from the farmers' markets, repackaging it, standing on street corners, and hoping to recoup their money with a tiny profit. It was September of 1939 in the worst depression in the United States' history and the train was on its way to the city's terminal. The homeward-bound students on the train were among the few whose families could still help them stay in college. Others had not been so lucky and had had to abandon their aspirations for higher education and support themselves by finding a job wherever they could. Some would return to their schooling later, but the vast majority would not, and so would become fathers and grandfathers of children for whom they would later make enormous sacrifices so their progeny would have the chance for a college education that they themselves had been forced to forfeit.

"Same old smoky, dirty town," Averill Lowe said to her seatmate as the train chugged through its last minutes on the Nashville to Chattanooga run. Averill and Henrietta Drayson had progressed from acquaintanceship to friends in the interval during the three hours, which elapsed from the moment Henrietta sat down beside Averill. They were both recent graduates of colleges in Nashville and both intended to look for work as elementary school teachers in Chattanooga. "But it's so alive," answered Henrietta. "Don't you always think of it being a great big, busy giant huffing, puffing, and pushing everyone else aside on its way to the top of the world?" She spoke in a state of excited breathlessness that Averill was to find was her almost constant state. Her gold-blond curls quivered with intensity.

Averill agreed, "You're exactly right. It's built on iron ore and manufacturing, heavy industrials, newspapers, and Society—all the necessary things for a cosmopolitan city. Nashville's been where I lived, but now I feel like I'm really home."

"I love it," said Henrietta. "I couldn't live anywhere else."

The two young women now stood waiting at the exit door. Averill's long brown hair spilled over her shoulders, parting at her neck as she stooped to settle her train case at her feet. Several masculine eyes showed appreciation at the sight of that slender form which was now in the process of un-doubling as she raised and steadied herself when the train shuttered with a sudden jolt as the brakeman applied the brakes. She lost her balance, plowed into a young man with a gold 'V' on his black sweater—an obvious Vanderbilt student—and he reached out willing hands to support her. His hands lingered and she pulled a tangle of hair that had wound itself around his glasses and said crisply, "It's okay. You can let go now."

"Sure you don't want me to hold on to you? Just think what would happen if somehow the cars came uncoupled," he asked hopefully, smiling.

"I'm fine, thanks," said Averill, turning her eyes, a tapestry of golden brown flecks against green flanked with impossibly long, black lashes, upon her eager benefactor. She smiled a slow, generous smile onto the bedazzled young man; but this picture of remote disaster did cause her to suppress a little frisson of fear. After all, the sheet of metal that bumped under her feet covered a cavern that yawned between two cars. What if it *did* suddenly collapse? She would plunge under the wheels. Hauling herself out of this morbidity, she wrenched her full attention to keeping her balance as the train rattled its way to the platform, but soon fell to studying the crowd waiting to disembark.

Many were college students who, like herself, had boarded the train in Nashville. Not without reason was Nashville called the Athens of the South. The city was chock full of colleges and universities and on the journey she and Henrietta had played the game of guessing which schools were attended by which students. Besides the Vanderbilt students there were two others she pegged as from Belmont. One she knew was from David Lipscomb because she had met her at a debate. Two rather serious girls stood quietly off to the side and she placed them quickly from the stickers on their baggage as Tennessee State University co-eds.

Many of the women were dressed as she and Henrietta were dressed, in their best clothes with heels, silk hosiery, tailored suits, she with a snood encircling and controlling her thick hair, Henrietta, a ribbon tied rakishly around her bobbing curls. Some of the men wore suits and ties. But there were a few who were dressed in their college clothes—men with lettered sweaters and light woolen slacks, women with saddle oxfords and socks, pleated skirts in plaid, woolen sweaters fitting small waists, and hair pulled from forehead and sides, rolled over mesh cylinders, and fastened with bobby pins. These rolls were known as 'rats' and were the feminine rage of the day.

Fall had come early in the bowl city of Chattanooga, Tennessee. Averill guessed the college students were coming home just as she was, having finished the school year by taking summer school. In her case, she had finished her college education in summer school because she had had to take almost a year off from studies to work as a sales lady in order to pay for college. Henrietta, she had found during their conversation, had gone through college 'on a check book'.

The L&N line of the Southern Railway screamed to a halt alongside the platform. Porters were already there with flat empty carts ready to load the baggage from the baggage car.

"Watch your step, little lady," the conductor said solicitously as he took each girl's hand and helped her descend to the concrete.

"Oh," breathed Henrietta, "there's Momma. Momma!" she screamed, waving an exuberant arm in the direction of a plump, matronly-looking woman hurrying as fast as her body, hampered by corsets, would allow.

Averill didn't look for anyone. No one but Mother knew she was coming, and Mother was sick in bed. She retrieved her baggage, became separated from Henrietta, and exited the station to look for a bus. Did the busses still run along here? She strained her eyes to find a glimpse of one.

She heard running footsteps behind her. It was Henrietta. "Averill! We can drop you off at your house."

"But isn't it terribly out of the way?" she asked.

"Not a bit of it. We're going up the Ridge. Your house is just off it, isn't it?"

"Yes."

"Well, that's settled. Momma's gone to get the car."

Averill looked around her at the familiar buildings. The terminal was in an industrial part of town and the railroad tracks ran right through it. Down toward the Tennessee River sprawled the main part of town. She couldn't wait to go to Loveman's and shop. She had dreamed for months of lifting gossamer silk hosiery out of their boxes, holding them up to the light marveling at their fragility, and buying a pair with her very first paycheck. She would delve through dressy soft calfskin leather gloves reveling in their elegant colors: white, chocolate, coffee-colored, soft dove-blues. Oh, it would be heaven.

"Here's Momma with the car! Momma, this is Averill Lowe. Averill, meet my mother, Camille Drayson, the worst driver in Tennessee. Do you want me to drive?"

"Hello, Worst Driver in Tennessee," grinned Averill, reaching across the passenger seat to pump Camille Drayson's hand with its firm grip in an up and down thrusting motion as hearty as any of her father's military friends ever performed. Mrs. Drayson's smile was almost as wide as her restrained hips and the plump face was covered with welcome.

"Don't you listen to anything Henrietta tells you about me," she warned as she shooed her daughter away from the wheel. Averill climbed into the back seat. "She'll make my grandchildren hate me. That is, if she ever gets any man to ask her to marry him."

"A lot you know," dimpled Henrietta and urged Averill with flapping hand to scoot over. "Come on, Averill, give me some room. The porter has put our luggage away in the trunk so we'll just sling yours in here," and she flung more baggage onto the back seat beside her friend, fortunately missing any of Averill's body parts. The DeSoto had a luggage holder like a steamer trunk on its back that opened from the top and where at present luggage erupted and threatened to cascade downward. This, Henrietta blithely ignored as she jumped in beside her mother and they set off with a crashing of gears.

Mrs. Drayson steered the car erratically down Market Street, turned left and headed east on Main Street toward Missionary Ridge. They swept past Three-Points Intersection where stood the liquor store that the repeal of prohibition in 1933 made possible. Deplored by many of the town's citizenry, it now did a bustling trade.

They reached the edge of the city and began to climb Missionary Ridge, which formed the eastern side of the bowl in which nestled Chattanooga.

"Turn right at the next road," Averill said and pointed to a small private road almost hidden among wild sumac, hickory, and pecan trees. After negotiating a breathtaking hairpin curve Mrs. Drayson propelled the car into a clearing whereupon a large white house hove into view, sitting with benign shoulders supporting a roof of chimneys and eaves. The car made a final turn and pulled up in front of the house. Averill sighed with pleasure when she saw its familiar screened porch winding its way across the front, curving around the edge of the house and disappearing somewhere in the back. The house itself rose to three stories and a fuselage of oak, beech, and willow trees embraced it protectively. Its gabled windows showed white curtains sparkling behind immaculate glass windows dating from the latter part of the past century and cupped on either side by slabs of emerald green shutters.

"Please come in and meet my Mother and have something cool to drink," suggested Averill, as the car rushed to its sudden stop, which sent an errant rooster scrambling for safety.

"Well, I don't mind if I do," said Mrs. Drayson. "Are you sure she will be well enough to have company?"

"She'd love to meet you. It will do her good."

"Mom! It's me!" Averill called out upon unlocking the front door.

"In here," her mother called from her bed.

Averill swooped down on her mother and enveloped her in her arms. "Mom, I've met the most fantastic people." She turned to face the bedroom door, "It's okay, Henrietta, Camille. She's decent."

"Oh, you poor dear," said Henrietta taking Mrs. Lowe's hand. "To get so sick with a simple little thing like a spider bite."

"I'm better now. I've been up this morning, but have to rest the remainder of the day, the doctor says," she said with a little *moue*. "Averill, can you make us some iced tea?"

Over refreshing drinks, the girls discussed their prospects for jobs. Averill had graduated from Spenser College and Henrietta from Eliza Woodruff Women's College and both had high hopes for teaching positions at the elementary school level.

"Oh Averill," said Mrs. Lowe turning to her, "isn't it awful about that madman, Hitler, marching into Poland? Now the English and French have been forced to declare war to honor their treaty with Poland and who knows where it will lead? Isn't it the most frightful mess? I remember you writing me that he bore watching because he was rearming Germany. If I were President Roosevelt," here she stopped to draw a breath.

Averill interrupted her hurriedly, "Oh, Mother. Let's not talk about that right now. Remember your blood pressure. You know you get all upset and then you'll have one of your dizzy spells," said Averill, patting her hand.

Mrs. Lowe switched topics with distracting suddenness and stated, "Both you girls should get jobs in places like Combustion Engineering or Hedges instead of teaching school. You'll only make a pittance teaching, and business is paying well these days because industry in Chattanooga is already planning for possible war."

Averill made another attempt to steer the conversation away from unsettling news of global affairs. Soon her mother would get on the subject of her father being overseas in an advisory position to the English military and other special assignments for the U.S. Army and the further they stayed off that subject the better off everyone would be. "Mother, if you can arrange to have Mr. Hedges call me and offer $10,000 a year for my expertise in riveting on a bolt, I'll go to work for him tomorrow."

"Now you're laughing at me," returned Mrs. Lowe and withdrew her hand. "Tell me, Mrs. Drayson, is your daughter this sassy?"

"All the time. And please call me Camille."

"And I'm Annie."

Talk proceeded on happier issues and at length, the two took their leave after Averill retrieved her luggage.

"Call me after you've had your interview at the Board of Education, next Monday." Averill called after Henrietta, "and I'll do the same. Let's hope we both get accepted."

When she returned to her mother's bedroom her mother was listening intently to her bedside radio. "I've tuned in H.B. Kaltenborn," she said in an aside to Averill. "Just listening to him makes you feel that the news is in good hands in this country."

"I'll leave you in his capable hands and go upstairs to unpack," said Averill.

Oh, it was so good to be home. She ran up the stairs to her room with the white Priscilla curtains and her soft bed. It was going to be so good to sleep in a comfortable bed. Spenser's had a way of being lumpy and uncomfortable. She ran a bath while she stripped off her hosiery and wiggled out of her dress. She threw her hat into the chair in front of a window alongside a bookcase of books. After long years she was finished with college and ready to take her place in the working world.

Chapter 2

Averill and her mother were among the last to be seated before Sunday morning service began at Covenant Church and Averill scanned the choir for familiar faces. Making eye contact with several friends, she nodded and smiled while they, in turn, smiled and tried to keep their places in the anthem. Then she turned her attention to the instruments. Sure enough, Edward Guinn was sitting in the orchestra pit with his slide trombone. She had known Edward since high school when he entered McCallie School the week after emigrating from England and started attending her church. He was older than she, had been a Rhodes Scholar at Oxford, and was now home in Chattanooga. She had sporadically dated him during high school without too much enthusiasm on her part; with not much interest one way or other, she wondered if he were going with anyone. She caught his eye and he smiled back at her with that wide, uninhibited grin that was his trademark.

She enthusiastically joined in the congregational singing but found her mind wandering during the sermon and thinking about her coming interview with the school board. Would she get a teaching position? Oh, God, let me get a job, she prayed.

Averill drove her mother home. "You're sure you'll be all right? You don't mind my going to the restaurant with Edward?" she asked. "There's a casserole in the oven and I made a green salad and whipped up that dressing you like so much."

"Averill, I'll be fine. You go on and have a good time."

Averill drove to the restaurant where she had promised to meet Edward and saw him waiting outside. She parked the car and, ducking a little to save her new hat, she stepped out of the driver's seat and bent to garner her gloves and handbag from the passenger seat. She turned from locking the car and found he had silently made his way to her side.

"Hi," he said, grinning, his face inches from hers. It was a nice face, she decided, and his brown crisp, curling hair with its blond highlights from the southern sun emphasized a healthy tan.

"Hi, yourself. Have you been waiting long?"

"Just got here. How is your mother? I hope church did not tire her too much."

"Frankly, I think it wore her out, but she'll never admit it."

"You look great," Edward said, as he reached forward and tucked a stray wisp of hair behind her ear. "I've missed you."

"I've missed you...and all the rest of the gang," she finished, distracted by the hopeful expression that leaped into his brown eyes. Momentarily confused, she turned and would have tripped had he not steadied her by taking her elbow. Wordlessly they made their way down the path through patterned sunlight filtering through the golden maples, red-purple-leaved elm, the ubiquitous green southern pine, and queenly lushly leaved magnolia trees surrounding the rather small red-bricked Town and Country restaurant that squatted on the banks of the Tennessee River. The wind was cool and there were no diners sitting at the outside tables even though striped blue and white awnings that whipped in the strong breeze might possibly shield such clients.

Entering the restaurant, they were led to their seats by a pert little hostess who looked to Averill to be young enough possibly to have finished junior high school. Their seats had a view of Lookout Mountain, but Averill saw at once that a view of the river was not visible. "Oh, I wish we could sit outside," she whispered to Edward.

The hostess was still near enough to hear. She turned and said, "Would you like to? We have seating available."

"Oh, yes," breathed Averill. "It's not too cold for you, is it Edward?"

"Of course not. Let's do it," he answered, and they followed the hostess to an outside table with a spectacular view of the water and were immediately serviced by the waitress carrying tableware and a young man who threw a white linen tablecloth over a table.

"This is perfect," said Averill. "Now tell me what you've been doing with yourself since we last talked. It's been ages."

"Dare I hope that it seems ages because you haven't seen me?"

"Of course," Averill said, automatically, and a little surprised. A flirty Edward she had not expected. She looked at the curls springing up all over his head and saw that his freckled face with the square chin had a look of maturity she had never observed. "Wasn't it last spring you got your masters from the University of Wisconsin?"

"With the ink on my diploma hardly dry, I started work as a teaching assistant at the University of Chattanooga teaching engineering and doing the odd consulting job for Combustion Engineering.," he grinned.

"Engineering? Why, Edward, how clever you must be! Just the other day Mother suggested I go to work for Combustion Engineering now that the country seems to be gearing up for possible war with Germany."

Edward brought his hands up in mock consternation. "What? Well, so much for our diabolically secret plans. If every housewife in the city knows about a coming war, can the Germans be far behind? Seriously, if you ever want a position within Combustion, I have a few contacts that might help you—especially in the accounting department."

"No, thank you," she said, visions of Bob Cratchit sitting on a stool in Ebenezer Scrooge's office day after day springing to mind.

As Edward talked of his work She listened and thought how perfect it would be if she could fall in love with him. She supposed both sets of parents would wish it. She thought that perhaps Edward himself did. Steady, dependable Edward; he would never send her pulse madly racing, but he had been her friend for donkey's years. As she listened to him talk she was seized with…lassitude? No, it was more familiar than that. Could it be boredom? Surely not, but during their long lunch there were times when she had to exert tremendous willpower to restrain herself from looking at her watch. Would it never end? Finally the air grew uncomfortably chilly and even to the relaxed Edward it became obvious they must take their leave.

In bed that night Averill thought Edward would ask her out again and she would have no good excuse not to go. She fell into a restless sleep.

She was ushered into the office of the Superintendent of Elementary Schools, and upon crossing the threshold of his office, a tall man with a kindly smile rose to greet her. Dr. Thurston reminded her—a little—of her father and she felt suddenly assured and confident.

He looked over her college testimonials and records that she had previously mailed and she learned, to her great embarrassment, that she was supposed to bring something called a résumé. Dr. Thurston waved this aside and instead told her that if she could start by the beginning of the next week he could place her in a fourth grade class at a school just three blocks from her home; he seemed far more interested in the history of her childhood.

"I read here that you spent your first twelve years in Egypt. Was your father in the military?"

"Yes, he was and still is."

"Do you speak Arabic?"

"Yes, I speak it very fluently, as a matter of fact."

"Excellent. Perhaps you will find a way to introduce a little Arabic into your teaching."

"I'll certainly try; the school location you suggested is ideal. My father is overseas with the army, and my mother's health is not good and she is alone all day. This way, I won't have to spend a lot of time traveling to and from work. It's just perfect, as a matter of fact."

Dr. Thurston smiled at this enthusiasm and said, "I think you'll fit into the slot quite splendidly, so that makes two of us who are happy." He smiled his transforming smile, and she had a wild desire to kiss his baldhead in gratitude. Prudently, she restrained this doubtful behavior and concluded her first job interview with a resounding success—which she supposed must have set something of a speed record for the Hamilton County Board of Education until she learned that Henrietta had been hired on her first interview and at the same school as she.

Chapter 3

Averill and Henrietta arrived at the conference room at Oak Plains Elementary School for a pre-school staff meeting, dressed wildly different. In deference to the sudden downturn of the mercury, Averill wore her woolen Highland plaid and a rust-colored sweater, her shoulder-length brown hair firmly controlled with sides pulled back and anchored with a tortoise clip. She wore low-wedged heels. Henrietta, on the other hand, tottered on extremely high-heeled sandals wearing a severely cut business suit and a rather matronly shawl flung over her shoulders. Averill privately thought she was dressed as if she expected to attend a party, a business meeting at City Hall, or a chat in rocking chairs.

Averill looked around for faces she might recognize. There was Pris Quigley, looking much as she did that day long ago when both lounged on the grass in front of the high school making plans for the weekend between feverish spasms of finishing their assignment for the next period. Pris's hair was as she remembered it—flying in all directions but distractedly attractive. She was talking quietly to a fellow teacher beside her at the long table when Averill caught her eye. Pris's eyes opened wide and she threw back her chair and flew across the room to greet her.

"Averill Lowe! Are you teaching here?"

"Yes. Isn't it going to be fun? Oh, and here's my friend. It's her first year in teaching, too," and Averill turned to Henrietta and pulled her forward.

"Marvelous. This is just going to make my year," Pris said, drawing a breath of pure rapture after introductions. "I've been dreading it, you know. Last year was so dismal. Now then, there's someone I want you to meet." Pris beckoned to the young man to whom she had been talking when Averill entered the room. "Klaus, I want you to meet Averill Lowe. Averill and I have been friends forever. And this is Henrietta, her friend. This is so fabulous, I just can't believe it."

The young man, Klaus, stood, leaned forward, and said gravely, "I'm glad to meet you." He took each of their hands in a formal and slightly foreign way, looked at them steadily, and repeated each name carefully.

Pris said, "Klaus may not stay on for very long. He's been telling me his plans for joining the army now that Germany has invaded Poland."

"War will come to the U.S., too. It's just a matter of time," Klaus stated, rather didactically.

"Oh surely not," protested Henrietta.

"Mother never ceases talking about it," Averill groaned. "When Germany marched in to Poland the first of the month, she called me long distance and vented two dollars worth of hysteria."

"Well, I think we should stay out. It has nothing to do with us," said Henrietta, firmly.

Klaus stared at her in an unfriendly way and answered, "There you are wrong, Miss Drayson. Our legislature has opened us up to great peril with their budget cuts for the military. England is finding this out, too. Last year their Prime Minister came back from his meeting with Hitler and held up a piece of paper signed by Hitler promising peace. Of course, England and all the world has discovered Hitler never planned to abide by any treaty; he is a liar and thug. The U.S. will find this out, also," he finished nodding significantly.

"Wasn't that Prime Minister Chamberlain who did that?" asked Pris.

"Yes." He paused to give her an approving glance. "He arrived after meeting with Hitler and waved a paper in front of the reporters and announced, 'Peace in our time.' What a fool!"

"Germany is miles away," said Henrietta, comfortably. "It won't attack the United States."

"We're not only threatened by war with Germany," the solemn young man continued, shaking a warning forefinger back and forth in the air, "Imperialist Japan is running out of room for her population, and is already waging war with China for more land. She'll eventually look to U.S. protectorates in the Pacific for her dreams of expansion,"

"What an odd man Klaus is," thought Averill. She opened her mouth to reply and then realized the principal was standing at the lectern looking at their little knot of conversationalists with something approaching irritation. Hurriedly she took a seat as did the rest of the little group.

The meeting began and Averill was caught up in all the plans for the new school year. Words such as objectives, curriculum, motivation, and discipline were tossed around with suggestions to accomplish them all. Teaching was going to be more arduous than her practice teaching had led her to believe. Here she would be responsible for the welfare of some thirty children for a big share of their day. They depended on her. The parents depended on her. The school system depended upon her. An invisible yet weighty cloak fell on her shoulders that she found she was never to dislodge for the rest of her teaching career.

Autumn shed her purple, orange, and rust leaves onto yellow carpets and the days grew shorter and colder. Averill was finding that war overseas was affecting her everyday life. The school was limited in coal, and teachers and students were forced to dress warmly; on many days, they needed their coats. Averill had stood too near a radiator and had burned a hole through a stocking and made a burn on the side of her knee that made wearing hosiery difficult, but she dealt with the problem by painting lines down the back of her legs. Seamed stockings for the women were a part of the dress code that no one dared flout. Cafeteria fare was nourishing but uninspired with the lowly vegetable soup becoming the staple on the menu. This soup, a carton of milk, and a tiny cup of half-orange sherbet and half-vanilla ice cream were Averill's daily fare. Sometimes the mothers volunteered to make sweet yeast rolls, rich with margarine and cinnamon and these became red-letter days for students and teachers. On even rarer days suspect beef—fatty, gristly, and mostly bone—was offered which Averill invariably declined.

She enjoyed lunching with the staff. The teachers' lounge had been requisitioned for a classroom, so they ate in the cafeteria with the students, but at a separate table. There were lively debates over cafeteria food, school discipline, crowded classrooms, but most of all—the war in Europe.

"This soup tastes like dishwater to me today, but I couldn't bring myself to order roast beef. What they serve for beef here would make a goat cry," said Henrietta on a blustery early-December day as she plunked her tray down beside Averill who shared the table with Klaus.

"Actually, goat tastes rather good. I ate it in Jamaica when I was on vacation with my family one summer," Averill commented.

"No, thank you. I'll stick with dishwater."

"The Soviet Union has attacked Finland," Klaus remarked, rattling a newspaper as he held it with one hand and ate with another.

"Both Germany and England have been rather quiet the last few weeks. Some are calling it the 'phony war'," observed Averill who, after her first brush with Klaus Ernst, had made it a daily habit to keep up with current events. It also had the happy effect of assuring that her fourth-grade pupils were well versed in what was going on in the world.

"Germany is biding her time," said Klaus. "This quiet time won't last. She'll eventually go for France. Hitler hates the French more than almost anyone else because they wouldn't forgive Germany her war debts after World War I."

"And because of France's pact with Poland to defend her in case of invasion," added Averill, ashamed of showing off for Klaus, but doing it, anyway.

Klaus raised his head quickly and looked at her as he might have looked at a pupil who had given a right answer to a question on a quiz. "That, too," he smiled, a gesture that transformed his rather cold good looks.

On Saturday, Averill entered the kitchen and saw that Annie was sitting holding a letter in her hand. "Letter from Dad?" Averill helped herself to coffee and sat down at the table across from her mother.

"Yes. It's a strange letter. He doesn't sound like himself," Annie said thoughtfully. Then she changed the subject. "What are you planning to do with your day?"

"Klaus and Henrietta are going to see Ruby Falls with Edward and me," she answered. "Klaus has been in Chattanooga three years and never seen it."

"One time was enough for me," said Annie.

"I know, Mother. But you have claustrophobia. Not everyone is afraid of caves and other closed spaces. Anyway, there are lights. They don't leave you alone."

"Except for the time when they turn out the lights to show you how complete the darkness is. It's so dark it's got weight. You can feel it."

"M..m..m," answered Averill as she opened the morning newspaper. "I'm so glad we take both the *Times* and the *News-Free Press*. I want to know every scrap of news going on in the world these days. My students are becoming very interested in current events."

"It says a lot for their teacher," remarked Annie.

"Thank you for the pretty compliment," Averill reached for her mother and gave her a quick hug. "There's the doorbell. That will be Edward."

When Edward and Averill pulled up in front of Henrietta's house, she was sitting in the front porch swing, bundled against the wind with Klaus seated beside her, his arm curved around her shoulders.

"How long have you been waiting?" asked Averill when the two piled into Edward's back seat.

"Not long," said Henrietta. The enraptured look on Henrietta's face told Averill everything she wanted to know about how things were between her and Klaus. Averill knew she herself did not feel that way about Edward and—just for a minute—she felt a tinge of sadness. Because of this guilt she moved a little closer to Edward who reached down, took her hand in his and squeezed it, not letting go of it until they approached Lookout Mountain where he needed both hands to negotiate the roadway's winding turns.

The road was bounded on one side by high rocky terrain reaching into the sky and on the other by a guardrail that had been constructed by the Civilian Conservation Corps, which was created in 1933 by President Franklin Roosevelt to give work for unemployed men. Beyond the guardrail the land plunged into space where at its depths was industrial Chattanooga with its thousands of chimneys roiling thick black smoke from the coal fires blazing within hundreds of grimy buildings where crews of men gladly worked overtime on this Saturday to make up for long years without work. News from across the Atlantic had spurred Washington to begin awarding contracts for armaments to Chattanooga factories. Beyond this landscape of factories the Tennessee River curved and buckled in upon itself as it flowed in and out between Missionary Ridge, and Lookout Mountain. Signal Mountain, farther to the north, had pushed it into changing its course once again into a hairpin turn called Moccasin Bend and thus carved out an area of land which was almost an island within the city.

"It's the most beautiful place in the world," breathed Averill, looking down from their aerie in the rocks as their car climbed upward into the sky.

"Ah, but you have never seen Switzerland and Bavaria," said Klaus.

"Is that where you lived before coming to the States?" asked Edward.

"I have traveled there," said Klaus. "My father was a diplomat in Berlin and took his family with him sometimes.

"Oh, tell us about your family," said Henrietta.

But Klaus would not talk further about his family. Their questions met with resistance and the tone of his answers closed the subject and admitted no possibility of more probing questions.

After the trip to Ruby Falls cave inside Lookout Mountain—so-named because of a waterfall inside that shone ruby red in certain lights—the foursome drove to a little restaurant nestled on a jut of land that overlooked the city. Averill looked at Henrietta with concern. She had suddenly become very quiet.

"Are you all right, Henrietta?"

The face that before the tour of Ruby Falls had colored with glowing happiness was now pale. In response, Henrietta shook her head and angrily brushed away a tear. Klaus looked ill at ease and wordlessly looked out over the city below.

Edward said easily, "Let's order, shall we? The city looks even better on a full stomach."

Averill looked at Edward in gratitude and steered the conversation to early history of Chattanooga and its vital role in the War Between the States. Edward held up his end of the conversation and Klaus, by virtue of his inquisitive nature kept the questions flowing. The meal ended with an uneasy constraint, and, by mutual accord and with profound relief, they headed for home. Edward dropped Henrietta and Klaus off at Henrietta's house.

"Edward, stay a minute. I want to see if Klaus goes inside with Henrietta," Averill said plucking at his coat.

"It's their business, Averill," but he drove slowly away from the curb and, by craning her neck backward,

Averill could see Klaus walk Henrietta to her door. She saw him speak somewhat stiffly to her, walk purposefully to his car in the driveway, and accelerate with a burst of exhaust and furious energy.

"Something happened, Edward."

"I know."

That night Henrietta refused to move when Camille Drayson went to her dark bedroom and told the almost indistinguishable lump on the bed she was wanted on the phone. "All I know, Averill, is that Klaus is joining the army," Mrs. Drayson told her upon returning to the phone, "and he has said he thinks it best that call it quits."

Chapter 4

On Monday morning Averill took her children out to the playground for their physical education classes; while the physical education instructor took them through their paces, she ducked into the cafeteria. Teachers had been instructed to stay with their P.E. classes and help, but Mr. Roland, it turned out, preferred a lone hand with his classes.

"Care for a cinnamon roll, Miss Lowe?" asked the cafeteria manager. "Mrs. Beresford came in this morning and they're just out of the oven."

"Oh, yes please, Mrs. Druggett. I didn't eat breakfast."

Mrs. Druggett lifted out a roll, drizzled icing over it with a spoon, and handed it to her on a napkin.

"Heavenly," said Averill as she bit into it.

Behind her, Henrietta walked through a door from the hall over to the cooler and pulled out a carton of milk. When she turned, Averill saw her face. She was crying.

"Morning, Henrietta," Averill said, moving over to pull her into a hug. "How 'ya doing?"

"I'm fine. No, I'm not. Averill, do you have a minute to talk?"

"Let's sit here."

Seated, Henrietta said, "I made such a fuss Saturday. I'm sorry."

"It's okay. Is Klaus still determined to join the army?"

"Yes. He'll join after Christmas. He wants to make a complete break with me. Said it was the fair thing to do." Henrietta said quietly.

"Fair?"

"Yes. Isn't it silly? He's got the idea that we should not 'tie ourselves down'," and Henrietta's eyes darkened with bitterness. "It's just an oblique way to say that he doesn't care for me as much as I do for him."

"Henrietta, I'm so sorry. If the roles were reversed would you break it off?"

"Of course not. I'd want to get married right away and follow him wherever he's stationed. He doesn't love me, Averill, and I love him so. I'll die, I'll just die," sobbed Henrietta.

Averill rubbed her shoulders and said slowly, "He strikes me as being deliberate and methodical. Being cautious is an attribute of that. Perhaps he just needs more time."

"No, if he loved me he'd take the chance. It's been tearing me to shreds over the weekend. If you want to know the truth, part of me is glad it's over."

Spring of 1940 showed a swelling population as rural farm workers left uncertain working conditions and made their way to Chattanooga to join with the local workforce in factories suddenly inundated with government contracts. Children from these families found their way into the city schools and the school board discovered qualified teachers scarcer each day, for, alongside this, teachers were leaving poorly paid educational positions to go into office and factory jobs that paid more.

Averill arrived home one day to find Edward sitting at the kitchen table eating cake and drinking coffee. He pushed the half-eaten cake aside and rose.

"How was your day?" he asked.

"It was busy. Edward, something's happened. What is it?" Instinctively, she reached for the knob of her mother's bedroom door where they could both hear Annie on the telephone. She pulled the door closed and turned to face him. He moved to face her, reached for her hands, and pulled her to him. She studied his long narrow face and saw that his brown eyes, always so calm and steady, were excited. A tiny tic pulled at one corner of his mouth.

"I have about seventy-two hours to pack and leave for England. The University is sending me to London for research and I may be gone for several weeks…months—it's indefinite and I want you to go with me. I don't want to be away from you that long. This isn't the way I planned to ask you but Averill, I love you. Say you'll marry me."

Averill stared at him in astonishment. "I can't just throw up my job, Edward. It wouldn't be fair to the school board. It wouldn't be fair to you…to me…Edward, I can't." She struggled to release her hands and thought of all the things she might say; they sounded dismayingly similar to what Henrietta reported Klaus as saying when he called an end to seeing her. With a flash of insight she knew that Klaus had not loved Henrietta.

"The school can get a permanent substitute to replace you. We can rush visas and passports through. I don't want to go without you. Say yes, my darling Averill."

"Oh, Edward, I can't…I'm not….I don't feel that way about you," she stammered, the brutal truth out in the open. "Edward, I'm so very, very sorry."

"You mean…when you say you don't feel that way about me…you don't love me? But I thought…I mean, I just took it for granted…"

Averill wondered if it had been willful blindness, or was Edward one of those individuals who, seeing life only from a narrow viewpoint, was constantly surprised by reactions from those who entered his world? She said feebly, "It's just friendship, Edward. You don't want to settle for that."

"Yes, I do. Friendship often turns into something more lasting than romantic love. Averill, we can be so very happy. Please say 'yes'."

"This is ridiculous, Edward." Averill's voice was abruptly steely. "Whatever were you thinking? I don't have the slightest desire to marry you or anyone else. Please go. If you stay it will just be more painful." She lifted her suddenly freed hands, looked with forced impassivity into stormy, baffled eyes, and walked out of the kitchen. She had reached her bedroom when the front door closed with a bang.

Averill ran downstairs after dumping her attaché case and school gear on her bed. She went into the kitchen, opened the refrigerator, pulled out a milk bottle, and reached into the cabinets for a tumbler. Through the window she could see her mother laying out seedlings in the garden. Draining the cold milk, she placed the empty glass in the sink and passed through the screen door to the back porch where she sank onto the wooden step leading into the backyard. The grape arbor nearby was active with bees; there was a smell of fresh clover and new-grown grass in the air. The clouds were so high they seemed blurred. The earth had sprung to life once again.

"Hi, Honey. There's a letter from your father on the mantel in the living room," called her mother.

"To me?" Usually her father wrote to her mother and expected her mother to tell her the news.

She ran into the house and found the letter.

Dear Averill:

This has been an evening of the unexpected. As I was returning to my quarters, I literally ran into a boy from our church back home that I think your mother told me you were dating. His name is Edward Guinn and he is in England on business for the University of Chattanooga. He said to give you his greetings.

He was with a fellow named Klaus Ernst. They were leaving the hotel as I was entering and we collided. They introduced themselves, and Lt. Ernst said he was acquainted with both you and your friend, Henrietta. He said he had taught with you at Oak Plains Elementary, had recently graduated from officers' training school, and had been posted to England.

Averill, I want to ask you to do something that you will not understand at all and for which I cannot tell you the reason. Please trust me in this. You will receive a visitor in the next few months—a Mr. Reife Braddock. He will offer you a job. I want you to take it. It will not be something you will dislike, I think. I'm sorry this will cause you to have to leave your teaching for a while, but it is vital to the success of the European war effort. Please do not ask me to explain further. I cannot, except to re[eat that it is vital.

I hope you are well. Tell your mother that I will write her a separate letter and you keep this one under your hat. Just remember the name—Reife Braddock. Sorry to sound like a character in a paperback spy novel.

With fondest love,
Dad

She dropped into a chair and stared into a cold fireplace. She didn't want to give up her teaching job. Her father had no right to ask this of her. Another thought chased this one away. He would not ask her to do this unless it was important. That much she knew.

Chapter 5

Averill sat at her desk outside Reife Braddock's office in Braddock Engineering Inc. sorting the day's mail that she had picked up from the post office. The languid tang of autumn creeping through the hills this September of 1940 and reaching the city bisected by the curving Tennessee River prompted Averill to buy chrysanthemums from a stall on her way from the post office, scout out a vase in a storeroom, and arrange the flowers on a credenza in her oak-paneled office. The muted bronzes and bloody rusts portended the coming of winter with its gathering storms. Inside her was a disjunction of quickening gladness for the approach of autumn and its promise of the holidays and an apprehension born of muted warnings from overseas.

Averill wore a long-sleeved yellow sweater that fell to her hips where the plaid yellow and brown pleated woolen skirt continued the line and came to rest just below her knees. Her shapely legs were clad in sheer silk and her feet clad in low-heeled brown court pumps. The sweater and skirt were redolent of schooldays and looked out of place here in the exquisitely corporate office of Reife Braddock, young scion of a family recognized throughout the south for heavy industrial engineering.

Several weeks prior to today, she had arrived home from shopping with Henrietta to find an awkward-appearing, angular man with a shock of dark brown hair sitting in the living room talking with her mother. When he unfolded and stood for the introduction, she saw that he was quite tall, and when he spoke she saw that height was not the only attribute she had misjudged. He was not awkward at all; the squat chair had perhaps given an illusion. He rose with the command and ease any sure-footed mammal might give when movement was necessary. He introduced himself as Reife Braddock and offered Averill the job she had known was coming—that of his assistant in his father's engineering firm.

"I have never before recruited workers for my firm like this, and I'm sure you have never been so recruited," he said with a smile that made Averill wonder how she would have found the resolve to refuse the job, had she been so inclined.

"Please sit down, Mr. Braddock," she said with an answering smile. "My father wrote that you would be contacting me." Her mother gave a startled movement that told both of them that all of what was taking place was a surprise to her. "But for quite a while nothing happened and I almost forgot that I might be approached by you, to be quite honest."

"I'm sure you must have. Nevertheless, it has not been forgotten, just taken a little time to get rolling. Our firm is engaged in the federal government's program of Cash and Carry, a program to help England wage its war against Hitler's Germany. Their ships pay cash for supplies in our ports and pick up the armaments the U.S. manufactures for them. But you perhaps know that. We have gone to three 8-hour shifts and are working around the clock. My father has capable employees, but more and more I am being called onto the factory floor to help oversee these exacting government contracts. It makes for long days, as I'm sure you can appreciate." He smiled again and the gesture displayed an engaging small gap between his two front teeth that Averill had long noticed in men with English ancestry.

"I appreciate your making the effort to call on me personally," responded Averill. "It was very kind of you."

"You said your father, Colonel Lowe, wrote you that I would be contacting you?"

"Yes, he did."

"My secretary has taken an unexpected retirement and I very much want you to fill the vacancy, Miss Lowe. As to qualifications, you are literate; anything else you need to know can be taught to one who has your aptitudes and education."

She smiled just a little at his stilted, though sensible, presentation of the situation. It suddenly appeared to her that it might be fun to work for a man such as Reife Braddock and she said, "You understand I must contact my principal and tell him I will be leaving. He will be forced to hire a teacher to take my teaching position. School starts in three weeks, so I may have to start the school year until a replacement can be found. But I will join Braddock Engineering as soon as possible. Is this agreeable to you?"

"Perfectly," Reife Braddock said. Rising, he reached for his soft velour hat and turned to shake Annie's hand. He followed Averill to the door and held out a hand with square, trimmed nails betraying smudges of grease. The cobalt-blue eyes gave the lie to any stodginess when he commented, "I have the feeling you and I will get along fine, Miss Lowe," and his chiseled face suddenly changed with his wide smile that in turn exposed laugh lines putting his age to be somewhat older than she had first estimated. He turned, took the front steps two at a time, and entered a waiting taxi.

"Well!" said Mrs. Lowe, looking a trifle dazed. "You and your father are a couple of oysters. I had no idea. You might have told me."

Averill hugged her mother and said, "I need to type my resignation. My principal is going to be less than jubilant about this," and ran up the stairs to her bedroom.

Now, two weeks into her new job, the door to the Mr. Braddock's office flew open and that same young man peered out and mumbled something about coffee. She poured a cup from a coffee pot on a little table tucked into a corner by the stairs and took it into his office. While he drank, he dictated the first of the day's correspondence. At intervals, he stopped to rub his eyes that were dark with circles. It had been another long night at Braddock Engineering, Inc., she guessed. He could have told her that he climbed into bed at three o'clock that morning.

Reife Braddock paused and reached for a document lying on his desk. "Miss Lowe, take a letter to the Friends of England Organization. Tell them we will participate in their fund-raiser. Poll our employees and find every amateur singer, actor, piano player you can find and book them to perform. If someone plays the spoons or guitar, put them down for a slot."

Averill grinned at Reife. "You may be opening up a can of worms, Mr. Braddock."

"I don't care if I'm opening up a can of sharks. We've got to help Britain. They're fighting for their lives over there."

Averill had seen the newspaper accounts of the Battle of Britain where the Germans, thinking the western war was won with the rout of the English from Dunkirk in Occupied France, had started daylight bombings of southern England military air fields and boldly went on to bomb civilian London.

She made a foray into the factory the next day and made a list of employees who were willing to perform at the *Friends of England Variety Show*. Enthusiasm ran high and she soon became caught up with arrangements for the printing of the program and tickets. Word had leaked out that she was quite an accomplished pianist herself, and she found herself promising to perform.

Chapter 6

Averill finished a run-through of *Rachmaninoff's Prelude in C-sharp Minor* with the Chattanooga Symphony Orchestra while keeping one eye on her 'To-Do' list. The night of the *Friends of Britain Variety Show* was at hand and the volunteer workers and performers were jousting backstage for peeks at the audience. She hurried from the piano bench to check off the last item on her list by making sure the boxes of American and English flags were open and the flags distributed to the waiting chorus now filing into place on their risers. Holding up her long skirt, she conferred with the perky high school coed in charge of the distribution of the programs and met with the maintenance crew responsible for setting up and afterwards cleanup. She had lined up students to help with each of the variety acts and they appeared prepared to help with anything the amateur performers might need for their acts.

At last relieved of the nuts and bolts of keeping the night's activities on track by a skillful delegation of responsibilities, she joined the performers backstage. Henrietta was alone in a corner studying the script of a radio sketch in which she played Eleanor Roosevelt. Reife was deep in conversation with Chattanooga's mayor. The backstage clock was reaching toward eight o'clock when Russ Higgins, a foreman at Braddock's who would act as Master of Ceremonies, stopped his pacing, and glanced at his watch.

"Showtime, folks," he said and, from behind the curtains, he cued the leader of the orchestra. It swung into the beginning bars of *The Star Spangled Banner*. The curtain was raised to disclose bleachers lined with members of the East Side Community Chorus dressed in red, white, and blue waving tiny American flags as they led the audience in the national anthem. A prayer was offered, and the remarks of the city's mayor who had the reputation of saying in a hundred words what could be said in three, were mercifully brief, whereupon Russ strode onto the stage and announced the first of the evening's offering: a magic act.

Averill had no time for pre-performance jitters; she was too busy attending to others who experienced them. She found herself scrounging about for a waste can for an eight-year-old juggler when his last meal came up just before he was to go onstage. Reife deftly slipped the next performer into the sick child's slot and the night's performance rolled on without missing a beat. Henrietta and Pris Quigley were a hit with their comedic Vaudevillian back and forth dialogues of the president's wife and Clementine Churchill, and it was soon time for Averill's piano prelude. Seated at the Steinway grand piano furnished by Braddock's and moved from the firm's glass-enclosed conservatory, she began the flourishing beginning notes while her wine-red velvet dress moved around her legs with the energy of the majestic opening bars. Although she had secured her abundant long dark brown hair with tortoise-shell combs, her passionate technique added picturesque unrest to her coiffure in addition to that already wrought backstage by managerial duties. When during a pause in her playing, her eyes alighted on Reife standing in the wings off the stage and she saw the look of a man as if awakened from sleep, it distracted her and she lost her place for a heartbeat before recovering with a desperate discipline. She emerged from the strife of the music's first movement and finished the piece with the calm that the music demands.

She stood up, bowed to the applauding audience, and, dazed by the spotlight, she walked blindly off the stage into someone's arms. They held her tightly and she looked up to find Reife smiling down at her. Only when she smiled shakily and a bit self-consciously did he appear to become aware of others onstage and loosened his grip. Averill walked free and returned to the stage to acknowledge the continuing applause with a smile and gracious gesture toward the orchestra.

The chorus led the audience in *Rule, Britannia*, this most rousing song of England, and the singers skillfully segued into *God Bless America*, which the entertainers gathered onto the stage to join, after which there was the usual hubbub of departure and the dismantling of music stands.

"Ready to go?" called Henrietta to Averill who was chatting with the conductor of the orchestra while the members gathered up music and instruments.

"I'll give Averill a lift home," Reife said, coming up behind Averill and resting a hand lightly around her waist.

"I'll get my wrap," murmured Averill, casting a bewildered look at Henrietta. An enigmatic smile hung on Henrietta's lips as she turned to make her own way through the crowd.

During the short trip to her house Averill kept the conversation flowing despite an unusually quiet Reife.

He pulled into her driveway, switched off the ignition, opened his door and walked around to help her out. He took her arm and tucked it into his, patted it, and said simply, "Thank you for tonight." They climbed the stairs to her porch and at her door he took the keys she pulled from her purse, reached past her and unlocked the door. Upon entering the entryway he removed her coat and hung it on the coat rack. Then he turned and with both hands pulled her to him.

"Thanks for everything," he said against her hair, released her, opened the front door, and turned to look at her.

"Sleep late tomorrow," he said, then ran lightly down the steps.

Well! He had certainly dealt well with the usual awkward hesitation after a show of intimacy between a man and woman who had, with one giant step, moved from that of employer and employee to something more. Shaking off a feeling of schoolgirl awkwardness, she wondered if she should chalk up the first round to suave Reife Braddock.

The next morning he asked her into his office. Russ Higgins was there with a hawk-nosed man with huge black circles under restless, and oddly watchful, eyes. He wore an English army uniform and his sleeves bore four gold stripes. The visitor rose and brushed back his graying hair as she entered. Reife introduced him as Group Captain William Blake of the Royal Air Force.

"You are Colonel Lowe's daughter?" the man asked Averill.

"Yes."

He gave a nod but didn't comment further.

"Averill, we'd like you to sit in on our discussion this morning. Would you please take notes?" Reife asked.

She took a seat against the wall and for the next two hours she wished she had worked harder at shorthand in high school. The discussion was technical, filled with logistics concerning various armaments that Reife's company would build, and, afterwards her shoulders and neck muscles would ache from the tension of keeping up with all that was said.

Averill left them to type up her notes and soon the two men were making their way out of the office pulling on overcoats on their way to 'a blasted conference' according to Reife's rebellious mutterings as the door closed behind them. Night was drawing in when she deposited her typed transcription of the afternoon's meeting in the in-basket on Reife's desk, turned out the lights, and left.

It was dark when she arrived home with the shortening day, but her mother had left lights on for her. A letter from her father bearing an APO postmark of New York City was propped against the sugar bowl on the kitchen table.

Dear Averill:

You should soon get a letter from Edward asking you to meet him in Washington, D.C. He'll arrange for your room and travel. I'm trusting that you will have enough confidence in me to agree to meet him. The reason you give to ask for a week's vacation is entirely up to you. I think you'll find that if you tell Reife Braddock I have asked you to travel to Washington that will be sufficient, but use your own judgment.

May I ask you not to share this letter with your mother, for now? I will explain later.

With fondest love,
Dad

She folded the letter and reinserted it into the envelope, turned out the light, and climbed the steps to bed. There she thought upon the letter from her father and wondered, rebelliously, if he weren't arbitrarily stretching his habit of command into her life long after the point where he should.

She turned on the news with H.V. Kaltenborn. The situation in Europe was grave. MacArthur was requesting troops from the U. S. to help defend the Philippines from a possible Japanese attack and Congress was deliberating on an oil embargo of Japan which would no doubt bring the wrath of the Japanese Empire upon the U.S. She wondered how long her country had before it would be plunged into war.

Chapter 7

Early in November, Averill arrived home to find Edward's letter postmarked with a return address of a New York City post office box number.

Dear Averill,

How's the new job at Braddock Engineering? It has been almost a year since I've been back in the states and I'm looking forward to seeing you. My work in England is finished for the present and now I must go back to the business of becoming a university professor.

I believe your father has told you I would be writing you with a request. I am returning home from England via Washington, D. C. and wonder if you will come to Washington to meet me? My travel arrangements call for me to arrive in D.C. on Wednesday, November 13. I am booked at the Hay-Adams Hotel and have taken the liberty of reserving a room for you in the same hotel for the week of November 18-23.

You may find it perhaps irritating that I have told you so little of the reason for this trip and I'm sorry that I can't say more until I see you in Washington. In the next post you should receive a voucher for the expenses for your travel. May I suggest that you make train reservations soon? Your arrival time will coincide with the week of Thanksgiving and seats will be at a premium, I expect.

Regards,
Edward

P.S. I understand that Klaus Ernst corresponds with Henrietta. It would be unwise to let her know you are coming to Washington to meet me. Sorry to sound cagey. Please trust me on this.

Thoughtfully, Averill consulted the calendar.

"Reife, do you have a few minutes to talk?" she asked the next morning upon entering his office.

"Shoot," said Reife, laying down a report he had been studying. His eyes locked onto hers and she was troubled at the tired lines that had appeared in his face over the past two months.

"I would like to have several days off the week of November 18. My father has asked that I travel to Washington on business for him."

He studied her then smiled. "I know. I'm going with you."

"You're going with me?" She stared at him. "But why?"

"Sit down, Averill. Didn't your father hint that I might go, too?"

"No," she answered, and perched on the edge of a leather wing chair. She tucked her pleated cream woolen skirt under her and leaned forward, with a perplexed air. She thought a little light began to flicker far back in Reife's eyes as he watched her but it was just for a second and just as quickly, his eyes reflected their usual composed expression. He rotated a pencil between his fingers and in a mild tone he said, "It so happens I must go to Washington on a matter not unrelated to that of your father and must be there that same week. I thought perhaps we might travel together." He sat back in his chair and she thought a smile lurked.

Averill gaped at him. He placed the pencil carefully on his desk and waited. Finally she stammered, "My father suggested—rather cryptically I might add—that perhaps I would have no trouble getting the time off, but he said nothing about your accompanying me."

"I wouldn't go so far as to say that he knew I might go with you, but he knows that I am to be in Washington during November. I'm booked at the Hay-Adams Hotel for Thanksgiving week," here he paused when she gave a startled movement, "...and yes, I know that Edward Guinn has made reservations for you there." He gave a quick, rueful smile as she stared at him wordlessly. "It may annoy you that I have already booked train tickets for both you and me for Monday, November eighteenth. I hope not."

Averill jumped to her feet. "You're quite right I'm annoyed. What right do you have to treat me as a child who can't book her own passage?"

Now it was Reife's turn to look startled. He held out appeasing hands. "Whoa, Averill. No one is treating you as a child. If I considered you a child..." He stopped, thought differently about whatever he was about to say, and looked at her thoughtfully. "On the contrary, I will need you in D.C. — at least part of the time. Even if your father and Edward hadn't asked you to go...yes, I know about their plans," he broke off, responding to her reflexive grip of the armchairs as she registered an astonished reaction. "I'm sorry you were kept in the dark for a period. It wasn't my decision." He waited but she said nothing. "Be that as it may, I was going to ask you as part of your job. It's one reason

I hired you in the first place. I'm sorry if you think all this was too high-handed. Please hear me out."

Averill sank down into her chair and tried to keep her tone from being sulky as she spoke. "I don't have a clue as to why Edward asked me to meet him there so would you be good enough to tell me?"

"I can only guess at the reason he's in D.C., but he must tell you that himself; I'll tell you at least part of the reason I'm going—and it's also part of the reason why you're going. The company has received an order from the United States government for a new tank that will be partially assembled in the field; something that has never before been done. It's classified and I don't have to tell you that it is highly confidential."

She answered with a quiet, "Of course."

He nodded, and continued. "I have conferences scheduled with the Army Chief of Staff's representative that will be technical and will require extensive notes. I need you to help do research and sit in on the meetings."

"Oh." It was all she could think to say.

"I booked sleepers. There's no reason to arrive worn to a frazzle."

"I see. I'm sorry. I was out of line to lose my temper."

"No you weren't. It's quite to be expected."

As she left Reife's office later to resume typing letters, from the entryway a woman sailed into the office and shrugged out of her fur-trimmed jacket worn in occasion of a colder than normal autumn day. Averill took in the designer suit at a glance, the expensive coat chucked carelessly on a credenza, and the saucy hat tipped forward over the woman's appraising dark blue eyes and guessed this was a woman completely at ease in her surroundings.

"Mr. Braddock, please. He's expecting me. Tell him it's Joan Conover," there was a trace of imperiousness in her manner, and the eyes were more indifferent than unfriendly.

"Of course," said Averill, and buzzed Reife's speaker. "Miss Joan Conover is here to see you."

"Mrs.," the woman murmured.

"Send her in," Reife said over the intercom.

"You may go in," Averill said, smiling at the frosty Mrs. Conover, good manners coming to the fore.

For the next hour she fought to keep her mind on transcribing her shorthand notes into a coherent letter. Reife's office door suddenly opened and the woman appeared with Reife following behind her. "I'll call you," he said, reaching forward to kiss her cheek.

"Yes, darling, do," Joan Conover said, raising a hand and resting it on his cheek. She nodded at Averill, scooped up her coat and before Reife could help her had wrapped it around herself—she carried no handbag—and slipped out the door. Reife quietly returned to his office, leaving Averill to chastise herself as a fool for thinking that the night of the variety show had meant anything to him. He had this delicious female in his sway, why should he want her? Seven times fool! She hammered the keys.

During a telephone chat with her that evening Henrietta let fall the comment, "Averill, I received a letter today from Klaus postmarked a month ago…yes, he asked to write to me. Isn't that a shocker?" she interrupted herself to say. "Anyway, it had been misdirected. I can't think why. My address hasn't changed. He wondered where Edward had gone and said he used to see him quite regularly in England, now suddenly he's gone. Have you heard from him?"

Averill answered carefully. "I only hear from Edward now and again and his letters always have a New York City return post office box number."

"Klaus wondered why," Henrietta went on, "if Edward was still in England, he didn't run into him. After all, it's not as if there are all that many Americans in England sashaying around with a war on."

"I know. It's odd, isn't it?"

The next day she mentioned this to Reife and he asked gravely, "Averill, how well do you know Klaus Ernst?"

"We taught together. He dated my best friend but broke off their relationship when he enlisted in the army but still writes her."

Reife lifted his brows and the subject was dropped.

In those weeks preceding the trip to Washington, Group Captain Blake came to the office almost every day. Some days they were on the factory floor; other days were given to the two closeting themselves in Reife's office with blueprints. On the Sunday before Averill was to leave for Washington, she looked over in church to see Blake sitting across the aisle. After the service, he approached her.

"Would you join me for lunch, Miss Lowe?" Impeccable manners accompanied an upper-class British accent.

"I'd be delighted," answered Averill. She took him to her favorite place to eat. Mrs. McLaughlin was a recent widow who took in boarders and welcomed any of the church families who wished to join them for Sunday dinner. It was family style and serving bowls were placed on Lazy Susans down the long table. There were meat dishes covered with her caramel-colored brown gravy, and the table groaned under its load of vegetables and salads. Mrs. McLaughlin's signature dish was a casserole of creamed pasta, cheese, and green peppers. Bowls of this sat at either end of the table. There were platters of buttered carrots and squash, turnip greens swimming in bacon grease, cut-glass relish dishes of fresh green onions and radishes from her garden, and always pie and cake for dessert.

Halfway through the meal, Averill realized she had made a mistake in her choice of eating-place. It became obvious that Blake wanted to talk with her privately and she had hampered this with the family-style dinner. Afterwards, she suggested a visit to the Lookout Mountain Incline. They drove across town to St. Elmo only to find it closed for Sunday. The empty track soared into a steep climb up the mountain from its valley-floor station. Midway up the ascent one could see double tracks enclosing a small concrete island where the ascending and descending cars paused for the respective conductors to change cars and return to their Lookout Mountain and St. Elmo docks. The two sat in his rented Packard in the parking lot and talked. He had seen her father not four weeks ago, he said. He was well but very busy in London. He talked about bumping into her friends, Edward Guinn and Klaus Ernst, there. "You know them well?" he asked.

"I grew up with Edward. I don't know Klaus extremely well, but you don't work with a fellow teacher without learning a bit about them," Averill explained. "I know that he lived for a while in Berlin. His parents, I believe, live there still."

"Why did Ernst come to America?" he asked, casually flicking a gold cigarette lighter on and off, although there was no sign of a cigarette.

"I have no idea. I believe he said he has an uncle who immigrated to the States early in the thirties."

"There is quite a lot no one knows about Klaus Ernst, but I do know his father was a former German diplomat who is now a leader in the Nazi Party," said Blake who had now taken to tossing the cigarette lighter into the air and catching it.

"Surely Klaus wouldn't be allowed by the military to be in England if he was dangerous to security," Averill said.

"Perhaps. You leave for Washington tomorrow, do you not, Miss Lowe?" he asked, suddenly pocketing the lighter and reaching for the ignition.

She wondered if Reife had told him this. "Yes," she said frostily, irrational anger attacking her at this incursion into her private life.

Blake started the car, backed out of his parking place, and drove in the sparse Sunday traffic to her house. They said little else on the way. When they pulled up into the driveway he said, "Please allow me to help you, Miss Lowe," and before she could reach for the inside latch he had leapt from the driver's seat and was opening her passenger door. Ashamed of her childish spurt of temper, she allowed him to take her arm as they walked to her front porch. They had walked only a few steps before the front door of the Lowe house opened and the Lowe's third-floor tenant, Fortuna Medina, emerged. Thinking back to it later, Averill was almost sure Medina hesitated a fraction of a minute in confusion by the sight of Blake before he headed down the steps, but he said only, "Good afternoon," to her and nodded to Blake's courteous greeting as he continued his way to his parked car.

When the two reached Averill's front door Blake looked after him with a thoughtful air and asked, "Who is that man?"

She told him his name, adding, "He boards with us."

"I see."

"What do you see?" she asked, picking up on an edge in his tones.

"I thought at first I recognized him, but perhaps not." He added stiffly, "It has been most enjoyable talking to you. May I see you again?"

"I'm sure we'll see one another at the company," she said, gently establishing that she was not interested in seeing him socially.

"As you say," Blake said, dismissively, but she noticed a small, angry pulse surfacing in his temple. He slapped his driving gloves against his thighs, descended the steps, and drove off. Averill watched him leave, her mind busy. Something about Blake did not ring true, but, after all, he was Reife's friend. She dismissed it from her mind with a shrug and entered the house.

The train was waiting in the station when Averill and Reife arrived at the Chattanooga railroad terminal on a blustery November morning four days before Thanksgiving. Passing quickly through the terminal they reached tracks upon which numerous trains were being stoked as they hissed and belched black smoke into the air. She and Reife passed several such raring-to-go trains, found their own, and were directed to their seats by a Pullman porter with skin the color of creamed coffee and a jovial manner peculiar to such men the world over. Reife brought work from the office and was soon immersed even before the train departed the station. Averill found her place in Richard Llewellyn's newly published *How Green Was My Valley*. All her life Averill was to remember the contentment she felt sitting across from Reife closeted in their private world that November just before Thanksgiving of 1940.

First seating was called for dinner and over a spotlessly white, starched damask tablecloth, they sampled a cheese appetizer bathed in olive oil and herbs, enjoyed an entrée of rack of lamb with fresh green beans *à la noix*, twice-baked potatoes, and Cherries Jubilee with coffee for dessert. The yeast rolls were so light, Reife said, he had to hold his down with his butter knife before it floated to the ceiling. Generous bowls of butter and real cream arrived in silver plated bowl and pitcher.

The Pullman porter led them to bunks made up with fresh, sweet-smelling white sheets ironed to perfection. A lullaby of train wheels click clacking along their rails and sporadic hootings of its horn sounded in the distance and she drifted asleep with the smell of old leather, sweat-stained velvet—surprisingly inoffensive— and stale pipe tobacco wafting over her.

Sunrise was still an hour ahead when the porter awakened her. "Miss Lowe, we will be arriving in Washington in an hour." Reife was already dressed and in the lounge car when, after a quick dress and pack, she joined him there. He hailed a taxi upon debarking and the driver stashed their luggage in the trunk on the back and secured them with thick leather straps. They were navigating the busy streets and Averill was idly looking out the window when she stiffened and cried, "Stop!"

The driver applied the brakes. Reife shouted, "What is it?"

Averill said, pointing back to the sidewalk. "Back there, that man, it's my father!"

"Your father? Isn't he in England?"

"Let me out." Before anyone could stop her, she threw open the door of the taxi, sprang onto the street, and ran across the street to where passers-by were congregated at a stop light. Pushing through the crowd she looked for the military coat and dark wavy hair that was her father. He was gone. She looked around at the shops and ran into the nearest one. It was a shoe shop.

"Did a military officer come in here?" She panted. The question was ludicrous. The shop was very small and there were two customers, neither of which was her father. They stared at her.

Behind her she heard Reife ask, "Did he perhaps pass by on the street out in front?"

The proprietor said rather crossly, "I've been busy this morning; I haven't had time to watch the sidewalk outside."

"I'm sorry. I'm from out of town and I thought I saw a friend from home. Please excuse me," said Averill.

Reife took her arm and they left the shop. There was a bookstore next door to the shoe shop, a leather goods store on the other side; beyond these was a doorway where steps climbed to a law office above the street. She entered the bookstore and looked around. It was a small place with books piled in every available inch of space. There was no one visible except a woman who was examining a tray with books tumbling on it every which-a-way. A small, stooped man entered from the back through curtains. "May I help you, Miss?" She shook her head and withdrew. Out on the sidewalk Reife was coming out of the luggage shop. "Nothing," he said. She indicated the stairs to the law office. "I'm going up there." Determinedly, she climbed the steps to the law office, opened its door, and entered.

The room contained a desk, two or three chairs, and a battered sofa resting against a wall with yellowing wallpaper. An elderly man was standing before tattered volumes of books in the glass-fronted bookcases that lined the room, holding an ancient book. He turned his head at her entrance. "Yes?" he inquired, in a light, high voice that could have been a shuffle of the dry leaves on the grounds outside.

"I'm sorry," said Averill and plunged back down the stairs where Reife waited. "Perhaps I was wrong," she said. "What possible reason could my father have for being in Washington? His letters certainly never hinted he was coming to the states. And anyway..." She was thinking of the beautiful woman who had been holding on to his arm and leaning in to him.

"I think you may have seen someone who looked like him," Reife said gently.

The taxi stood waiting and the driver opened the door for her. His look was impassive, and she was grateful that neither he nor Reife said anything else for the rest of the journey to their hotel.

The bellhop set her bags inside her room at the Hay-Adams Hotel and turned, "Will there be anything else, Miss?" Distractedly, she handed him rather more coins than she had planned, and the young man was excessively solicitous while she made polite noises wishing him gone. Throwing her hat into a nearby chair and kicking off her heels, she lay down on the bed and pondered how one's mind can imagine such ridiculous things. She drifted...

There was a knocking somewhere. She opened her eyes and looked toward the door. Reife's voice came through the door. "Averill?"

She jumped off the bed and opened the door.

"Hey, how about some food?" He stood there wearing a fresh shirt, his suit pressed by the hotel valet

"Gosh, I'm starved," she said, running her fingers through her hair.

"Nothing like a night on a train to bring out a longing for bacon and eggs," Reife said, as if their ride from the terminal had been uneventful.

"And biscuits," Averill added. "Give me five minutes and I'll meet you in the dining room."

Thirty minutes later after washing her face, refreshing her makeup, and changing into sweater and skirt they were seated at breakfast. Reife pulled out a letter. Studying it he told her, "I'm to meet the military brass in an hour. When are you to meet Edward?"

"At ten." She consulted her watch. "We have time to enjoy the breakfast and music. I've never had breakfast music played for me before."

"Some European hotels provide it, but I've never experienced it in the United States."

"Have you traveled overseas much?"

"Yes. Most of my life was spent accompanying my father to Europe. Sometimes my mother would come along; sometimes she would stay home with my sister."

"Is your sister younger than you?"

"You've met her. She was in the office the other day."

"Joan Conover is your sister?"

"Um-huh. Who did you think she was?"

Averill blushed and, noting his amusement, said with defiance, "I thought she was your girlfriend."

Reife raised his eyebrows. "Why would you think that?"

"She called you 'darling'."

"Ah, yes. I have four brothers and she loves us all to distraction, but she and I being the youngest are especially close. "

"Why doesn't she like me, or is she always rude to your secretaries?" Averill asked.

He raised an eyebrow. "Was she rude? That sounds unlike her."

"Most rude."

"I'll speak to her about it."

"No, just forget it."

"All right, we'll forget it. I admit Joan can be imperious sometimes," he said. "Tell me; is this your first visit to Washington?" From across the room in the doorway, Edward had spotted them and was weaving his way between the tables.

"May I join you?" he addressed Averill who looked up, startled, but Reife was already on his feet, gesturing to an empty seat beside her. "Please," he said, politely.

"Edward, I am glad to see you," she said. "Reife, have you met Edward Guinn?"

"Yes, I've met Mr. Braddock," Edward nodded at Reife and gave the proffered hand a short, jerky shake then pulled out a chair.

"Yes, indeed. How are you, Edward?" Reife asked, resuming his own seat. The air was suddenly chilled, Averill thought, though both men seemed scrupulously polite. She studied Edward and decided he had obtained a large measure of self-confidence since he had been abroad. *Has it been just nine months?* She wondered what he really had been doing in England. Presumably, she was to find out.

Chapter 8

"Will you have coffee?" Averill asked Edward.
"No, thank you," he replied, drumming his fingers on the table softly.

Abruptly, Reife stood up. "You must excuse me. I have an appointment. Edward, will you join Averill and me for dinner tonight?"

Edward appeared to be hanging onto his temper with great effort; Averill thought she knew why. Edward was the one who invited her to Washington and in his eyes Reife was the intruder. Edward replied icily, "Thank you, I was going to propose that the two of you join me."

"Well, that's settled then," said Reife, smoothly. "We'll meet later, it seems. I must leave you now. Excuse me." He picked up the breakfast check, wrote a sprawling signature and a room number, and handed it to the waiter. He gave them both a nod, turned, and headed for the outside door.

Averill lifted her cup, took a sip of the coffee and, after placing it in its saucer looked at Edward and said, "It's good to see you, Edward; you're looking well. Are you sure you won't have coffee?"

"No, thanks. If you're finished I'd like you to take a little walk with me," Edward said, scooting his chair back. "Do you need to change your shoes?"

"My, you're in a hurry. No, my shoes are comfortable ones, and yes, I'm finished." Averill gave him an inquisitive sidelong look as she gathered her short grey leather gloves from the table and picked up her purse but his face showed nothing. He was instantly beside her to help her into her coat. They exited onto a street filled with blaring horns and jaywalking pedestrians and Edward hailed a cab. "Let's go see old Abe Lincoln," he suggested.

"Great idea. I've been looking forward to seeing the Lincoln Memorial."

The taxi let them out in front of the memorial and they threaded their way through the onlookers and found seats on the steps in front of the giant figure. There was a cold, brisk wind blowing, but they hardly noted it. They were sitting in the shadow of a man who had changed history, whose personal life had been unfulfilled, but who had triumphed through iron will and a sterling character to serve his country.

After some minutes of silence she asked bluntly, "You seem so grim. What's wrong, Edward?"

He sat very still, then said, "I apologize for my behavior but you can hardly expect me to be dancing with joy at seeing you in love with Reife Braddock."

"In love with Reife?"

"Did you think I wouldn't notice?" Edward waved aside a pigeon that appeared to select his head for his target and reached for her hand. "Averill, I love you," he said softly. "I've never stopped loving you and to tell the truth I'm having trouble being civil to Reife Braddock right now."

"Edward, I'm sorry. And I'm not in love with Reife."

"That's unworthy of you, Averill. At least you could be honest with me."

She made an angry motion and withdrew her hand while she studied the tourists who walked up and around the monument or stood to gaze at it wordlessly. *I shall go softly all my years*, she thought, echoing King Hezekiah's despair in the Bible when told his illness would be fatal. For she knew she would never marry Reife without God's blessing. But—God changed his mind and healed Hezekiah, she remembered, and her heart lifted. She withdrew her hand, turned to him, and asked gently, "Why did you ask to meet with me in Washington?"

He brushed off his coat and pulled it out of the Lincoln Monument traffic where an unobservant sightseer had stepped on it, shifted his body where he sat on the step, and asked, "How well do you know Klaus Ernst?"

She hadn't known what to expect but this was the last thing. "Ernst? I don't know him at all except for teaching with him a few months. Come to think of it that's the second time I've been asked that question recently."

"Who else asked you?"

"Reife."

Edward's face tightened, and then he asked, "Does Ernst write to Henrietta?"

"Yes, he broke off their romance, but he still corresponds with her. I don't think it's been a happy experience for Henrietta to be involved with Klaus. I've always thought he's the kind of man women should avoid; he appears he may be one of those men who sow broken hearts wherever he goes. I would guess he had a woman in every borough of London."

Edward seemed to consider this. "I never saw him with women but after all, he has broken up with Henrietta so would that be such a crime?"

"Perhaps not," she said reluctantly.

"Do you think she would reconsider her attachment to him if she knew that he is under suspicion of diverting goods meant for the war front for his own personal gain?"

"What? Klaus Ernst a thief? I don't admire the man but I would never have believed that of him."

"It hasn't been proven, but he's sitting in the brig right now awaiting trial for siphoning U. S. supplies to a black market outlet for resale. The army has arrested about ten men who are part of the conspiracy to defraud the U. S. of goods that were to go to England's fighting troops through our Cash and Carry policy."

"This will kill Henrietta."

"Perhaps it is better that she not know. He hasn't been convicted yet and if he's innocent you will have made her unhappy for nothing."

Averill wondered if she were in Henrietta's shoes would she want to know. She decided she would. But she and Henrietta were different. Averill lived in reality—gritty though it may be. Henrietta was an idealist; she saw things as she wished them to be. Averill could not help but think it was a recipe for disaster. Such women never saw the consequences coming and were constantly thrown into turmoil by unexpected pay-offs. Perhaps they had a kind of happiness with the constant expectation, however. She shivered suddenly with the cold, clasped her hands around her knees, and said, "She did mention that he had become interested in Chattanooga's economy since he joined the army and asked her endless questions about it in his letters."

"Such as?"

"Oh…I dunno…he asked about the factory work load, were factories on three shifts daily, were the majority of people supporting the war against the Nazis in Europe? Trivia like that."

Edward became thoughtful. Suddenly he said, "You're going to catch cold. We need to keep moving. Let's just walk."

"Let's walk over to the Capitol."

"Can you continue walking in those shoes?"

"Don't fuss, Edward, there're very comfortable. Come on, let's go."

Averill linked her arm into Edward's. How horribly treacherous she felt wishing it was Reife walking beside her instead of Edward; as a result she spoke with a false bright lilt as she made conversation, and to her own ears it sounded like the voice of Judas. "Will you have to register for selective service when it's put into effect next year? Or will your teaching defer you?"

"I'll cross that bridge when I come to it," he said briefly, and his manner told her that for him the subject was closed. They walked on. Averill glanced at Edward from time to time but he seemed lost in thought.

"A penny for your thoughts," Averill finally said.

"What? Oh, it's nothing. Well, yes it is something, Averill. It will wait."

She stopped and blocked his way. "Edward, what is it?"

"Averill, let's wait until lunch. After that, I'll tell you everything I know," he reached for her hand and tried to walk on.

She saw his face and suddenly felt the strength go out of her legs. "Everything? Everything about what? Is something wrong with my father?" She stumbled a couple of feet to a park bench and sat down heavily.

"Oh, it is. I can tell from your face. My father. Something has happened to him. Is he ill? Is he… dead?"

"Averill, you're father was perfectly well when last I spoke to him in England." He sat beside her and pulled her against him. "He's fine, really. Let's keep walking. It's too cold to stop."

Her first thought was that it couldn't have been her father that she saw as she rode to the Hay-Adams hotel from the train terminal and her heart suddenly lifted. She got onto her feet, brushed a fallen leaf off her skirt, and pulled Edward up. "Well, then, I can bear whatever it is. Let's go. It's just another block or so."

They had headed northeast from the Lincoln Memorial to Constitution Avenue, past the reflecting pool where winds swirled the leaves, the pool mirroring the memorial with a background of reflected trees; they progressed north on 17th Avenue, past the White House, and followed Pennsylvania Avenue southeast until it joined with Constitution Avenue and thus to Capitol Hill. A squirrel peeked out of dying foliage above their heads as they reached the Hill; there was still a cold breeze. The warm weather which had swept over the north central states earlier—Billings, Montana had registered a record 72 degrees—was slowly moving east and, although it was going to be a mild Thanksgiving in the nation's capitol, the warmer weather hadn't arrived yet. "The Capitol Building is magnificent," exclaimed Averill, "I had no idea. Can we go inside?"

"I think so. Let's go and find out."

They entered through the historic Columbus doors and with other sightseers wandered through halls where power was king. They stood on the second floor rotunda and contemplated the beauty of the polished floors, statuettes, and portraits. They stood transfixed by the ceiling painting on the dome that according to the brochure, depicted the Apotheosis or crowning of George Washington as a god in the heavens and had been painted by the Italian painter, Constantine Brumidi, in the 1860s. At length, Edward laughingly pulled her out of the center of the walkway. "Come on, little Country Mouse, let's move someplace where you can gape without being run over."

Later, after a lunch in a tiny restaurant just down from Capitol Hill, they finished a lunch of sandwiches and soft drinks in the crowded café where Edward had managed to steer the conversation away from Averill's father. Finally she said, "Edward, you're avoiding talking about my father. Tell me."

Edward pulled her up out of her chair and said, "Come on. We'll walk over and see how the construction of the Jefferson Memorial is coming. With all the controversy about its design and the environmentalists screaming about the uprooting of cherry trees, the project may be shut down. I promise to tell you about your father on the way."

They headed northwest again to an area south of the White House where they could glimpse cranes above the treetops. Edward reached for her hand and tucked it under his arm. "Washington is certainly a contrast to what London looks like these days."

"Edward, quit stalling. Tell me about my father."

Edward said gently, "Averill, I wish I didn't have to tell you this. Your father has written to your mother and she should have received the letter by now so I can tell you. As a matter of fact, your father gave me a letter to give to you which I imagine explains things better than I can." Edward reached for his coat's inside pocket and brought out an envelope. "Let's sit down here," he pulled her over to a bench lining the construction site. "You read it and then ask me any questions you like."

Averill took the letter slowly. "It must be bad," she said.

"It's not the end of the world." With that, she wondered if Edward were already beginning to prepare her.

The letter was written in her father's customary scrawl.

Dearest Averill:

As you will know from the radio and papers, the war is brutal here in London. We are bombed nightly by the Germans. The people here are as brave as you will ever see but they need U.S. help. They are praying daily that Roosevelt and America will come to their aid. My staff—some of which are Londoners—has members who come to work every day not knowing if their houses will still be there when they go home.

I am such a coward, Averill. Even now I'm circling the purpose of my letter, not wanting to tell you outright. It's simply this: there is a woman who has been my personal driver for almost a year. The sad truth is, I have fallen in love with her and want to marry her as soon as possible. I am hoping your mother will give me a divorce. Please believe me when I tell you that this was the last thing I ever expected to happen. I know you will find this hard to forgive. The only thing I can say in my defense is that war has a way of bringing truths—long submerged—shooting to the surface.

I take a lot of the blame; I have no doubt neglected your mother to advance my career and dragged her all over the world when she would have preferred to stay home where she was comfortable. I will not say more at this time. I know you will do everything you can to comfort your mother.

With fondest love,
Dad

Averill folded the letter slowly. Then she looked at Edward and said quietly, "I hate him. I will never see him or speak to him again."

Chapter 9

Averill was face down on her bed when she heard a knock at the door. She ignored it. Whoever it was she didn't want to see them. The door opened determinedly, there was a rustle of soft footsteps on the carpet and she sensed someone standing by her bed.

"Averill," Reife's voice said, "Edward told me about your father. Come now, you'll make yourself sick. Sit up and dry your eyes. You've cried long enough." He pulled out a crisp white handkerchief and pushed it under her out-flung arm.

"How do you know when I've cried enough? Please go away, Reife. I'm going home. I promised myself that after I packed I'd let myself cry. Well, I'm packed and I'm crying, and I'm going to keep on crying until every tear in me is gone. And then I'm going home." Averill pounded the pillow furiously, but to her surprise her crying subsided.

"Fine. Go ahead. Cry. Just remember if you go home you'll make it harder for Braddock's to build the armaments the government is asking for. It'll mean that if the United States goes to war, we won't have that extra edge that those tanks and artillery might provide. I need your help in wrapping up this contract. That's the truth, whether you like it or not."

Averill sat up and looked at Reife. His face was flushed and his eyes angry. She had seen that anger but never before had it been directed at her. She snatched the handkerchief and scrubbed her eyes as if she could wipe out every word she had read in her father's letter. She sat very still as Reife reached over and smoothed down her hair.

"That's a brave girl. It's a bad blow but you'll weather it," he said, his eyes smiling at Averill. "Why don't you wash your face and comb your hair and come down to the dining room downstairs. Group Captain Blake is there and I need you to sit in on our discussion."

She cried, "Don't treat me as a small child and don't patronize me!" She jumped to her feet. "Group Captain Blake? What's he doing here?"

Reife stared at her. "You're surprised? Surely you know that our firm is working with him in finalizing the contract for armaments."

"Of course I knew. I didn't expect to find him in Washington."

"I can see you don't care for him. So...the Sunday you spent in his company did not cause you to fall in love with him. He's unmarried, you know, and quite taken with you." Reife teased, a smile in his eyes.

"He's a tiresome man," Averill said, crossly.

"Maybe so, but he's dropping a good word in Uncle Sam's ear for Braddock Engineering," Reife said, lifting her chin and smiling into her eyes. He leaned and brushed her lips with his. "I'm counting on you." With that, he reached for the door, opened it, and was gone.

Averill changed into a green plaid woolen dress with white collar and cuffs, applied fresh lipstick, and brushed her hair until it shone. Instead of waiting for an elevator she elected to take the stairs from her fourth floor room. She entered the dining room, flushed, but with some of the anger exercised out. She spotted them at once. Group Captain Blake looked up first and scrambled to his feet. "Good evening, Miss Lowe. How very beautiful you look tonight."

"Hello, Group Captain Blake. So nice to see you." She heard the false note in her voice and thought how manners were sometimes the means of covering one's feelings. She forced herself to smile through rigid muscles.

"Sit down, Averill," said Reife. "The Group Captain and I are having a drink. What will it be for you?"

"A soft drink, please. Ginger ale, I think."

Group Captain Blake raised his eyebrows but Reife replied, "Of course. Waiter, a ginger ale for the lady, please."

"Yes, sir," the little Filipino waiter gave a slight bow and left with the order.

"I see you brought your steno pad. Very sensible," said Blake, smiling at her with an exaggerated appreciation that seemed excessive since she was Reife's secretary. Did he think…? Oh, she couldn't help it. He was an odious man. And she didn't like the way he looked at her. So knowing. So oily.

"Of course," she coolly replied.

Reife noticed the slight shift of her body away from Blake and interposed, "Blake, is June a firm date to ship those armaments? I'm not sure we can meet that deadline. I'm running two shifts seven days a week with a skeleton crew on the third shift. My foreman, Russ, is working the day and I've promoted an excellent employee, Thomas Cain, as the second shift foreman. I need to hire one other and they're not easy to come by."

"Who is foreman of the skeleton third shift?" asked Group Captain Blake, managing to shift his silverware so that his hand touched Averill's. She quietly moved her hand to her lap.

"My father came out of retirement to do it. I'd rather not count on him for too much longer. He just had his seventy-first birthday and I'm not willing to put his health in jeopardy," Reife answered. "I'll scout around for foremen. There are plenty of good men who are underemployed out there."

The little waiter returned with Averill's drink. Blake half turned in his chair and addressed the waiter, "How long has it been since you left the Philippines?"

The waiter straightened up and said, "A little over a year, sir. When Lt. Col. Eisenhower left to be stationed in California, we went with him, but when he was transferred to Washington State we came to the Capitol. My wife now works for Mrs. George C. Marshall," he finished, not without a flush of pride.

Reife commented, "Whoa! The wife of the U.S. Army Chief of Staff. Very impressive." A smile was beginning at the corners of his lips. "Eisenhower was aide to General Douglas MacArthur, wasn't he?"

"Yes sir. But those of us who know him well think it won't be long before he'll be a general, too."

"I see." The smile became a wicked grin and he said, "I hear that someone asked Eisenhower if he had ever served under MacArthur and he said yes, and he'd studied dramatics under him, too."

The waiter smiled uneasily, as if he was betraying his esteemed former boss by his response, and he chose his words carefully. "Yes, sir. That sounds like him."

"Perhaps Lt. Col. Eisenhower will soon be in Washington D.C.," Reife suggested, with an uplifting of eyebrows and a conspiratorial grin.

"Perhaps," ventured the waiter, returning the grin.

"We'll order after awhile. You don't mind if we sit and talk for a time, do you?"

"Not at all, sir. Please, take all the time you need. My name is Manuel. When you're ready to order I'll be glad to serve you."

"Thank you, Manuel."

Reife returned to the discussion that was interrupted. "Now, another question, before I commit to hiring more personnel: if we can hit the June delivery time, will the army give us further orders?"

"If the goods are satisfactory, I don't see why not," replied Blake.

The talk became technical and the evening wore on. Averill watched Reife's quick mind cover salient points and pin down possible difficulties. Further, his conversation was interspersed now and again with drawling recollections of his astonishing family's travels with a family of five sons and a daughter; and long afterwards, she remembered that evening as strewn with glowing, almost palpable sparkles and a pulsating aliveness. It was well into the evening before she gradually became aware that underneath Reife's light-hearted approach to the evening's business there was a studied, even grim side to his discourse. She suddenly wondered if he disliked Blake as much as she did.

Back in her hotel room, she prepared for the night. She would stay the time she had promised to stay. She would put her father's treachery and her mother's predictably anguished reactions on the back burner of her mind. Despite this resolve, when later she put her lights out and prepared to sleep, she wept. She was dropping off to sleep when abruptly she sat upright in her bed. She had found it easy to dismiss as impossible that the man she saw on the sidewalk from her taxi to be her father, mainly because the possibility of his having such a companion was so incomprehensible. He had been holding the arm of a woman and was looking at her with the unmistakable gaze of that of an enraptured lover. Now after learning about her father's love for another woman, she wondered if she had been right and if she had not seen her father on the streets of the Capitol, after all.

Chapter 10

The next morning Averill was still in her dressing gown when her phone rang. It was Edward. "Will you meet me for breakfast? I'm in the café now."

After the waitress had left their table with their orders he asked with concern, "Are you all right? Your eyes have dark shadows underneath."

"No, but I'll survive."

"I would have done anything to spare you that bit of news from your father yesterday, Averill."

"I know. Let's not talk about it. Tell me, when did you meet up with Klaus Ernst in England?"

"He looked me up when Henrietta wrote him that I was coming to England and suggested that we meet at the Officer's Club for breakfast as his guest. He's in a high position of responsibility with England as the liaison procurement officer of the U.S.'s Cash and Carry program. You probably know that as a neutral country we can only supply England with military armaments if their ships come to our ports and pay cash for them. Cash and Carry supplies are helping England wage war but in time it will inevitably bankrupt them unless the U.S. can find a way around their having to pay cash. Roosevelt's idea of Lend-Lease where we extend them credit is now being purposed but he is facing pressure from an unsympathetic congress and a mostly isolationist populace."

She said thoughtfully. "If Klaus is somehow involved in diverting some of the armaments that Braddock, and other manufacturers are producing, this is high treason, isn't it?"

"It's extremely serious." Edward stared into space for a few minutes, then shrugged his shoulders and spoke. "Averill, you might as well know because you're going to find out anyway. The journalistic hounds are getting nearer and nearer and the news will break by the weekend at the latest. I'm over here by military subpoena to testify at the trial of Klaus Ernst. It begins next week. As a matter of fact, I won't be seeing you much after today because I need to spend the rest of the week meeting with lawyers and preparing for testimony."

The waitress appeared with a tray. She handed a plate of scrambled eggs and bacon to Edward and set Averill's coffee and poached egg before her.

"But why ask me here? Why did my father encourage me to come? What's going on, Edward?"

"Your father wanted to see you without your mother being present. He asked me to deliver the letter I gave you yesterday and probe about and see how you'd feel about talking with him here in Washington if he should come." He looked as if he might say something further but turned again to his food.

"Well, I don't want to see him."

He gave a shrug and said, "It's just as well. He may not have elected to come after all. We men get cold feet easily. If he were in Washington, I wouldn't know where to find him. He was supposed to get in touch with me and didn't."

She pushed back her half-eaten egg and sipped her coffee while Edward finished his eggs and bacon and consumed several pieces of toast. "Shall we do a little more sightseeing?" he asked, throwing his napkin onto the table and reaching for the check. He scrawled his room number and they went out into the crisp morning.

At the corner, he picked up a paper and read the headlines. "Benito Mussolini's war against Greece isn't going too well. I see that the Greeks are pushing the Italians back into Albania. The Nazis will have to release troops to pull Italy's chestnuts out of the fire, and that'll be all the better for England."

"How that will humiliate that pompous Mussolini," remarked Averill.

"He'll wish he had stayed with his journalism career, and as for Hitler, it'll send his jackboots hopping all over his quarters. Germany will have to divert manpower they weren't expecting to spare," Edward said.

Averill forced herself to stay off the subject of her father for the rest of the day as they toured the Smithsonian's various museums. Arriving at their hotel with aching feet she called at the desk and the concierge handed her a telegram. She glanced at it, saw it was from her mother, read the terse plea, and lost any desire to eat. In her room, she kicked off her shoes, dropped into an easy chair, and thought about the telegram. She could read the frantic message between the words, COME HOME STOP PLEASE STOP MOTHER.

She was awakened by the sound of knocking on her door. She had fallen asleep in the chair. She stumbled to the door, smoothing her rumpled dress as she did so, and Reife stepped inside as soon as she opened the door. The telegram had fallen from her hand as she slept and now rested on the floor. He bent over, picked it up, flicking a look over it as he did so, and handed it to Averill.

"Will you go?" he asked, simply.

"No. I believe you're the one who made it clear that some things are more important than one person's temporary suffering."

"I'm going to bathe and dress for dinner. Will you join me?"

"When do you wish to dine?"

"Let's shoot for forty-five minutes."

"I'll drop by your room."

She took a long, soaking bath, dressed, and reapplied her makeup; then she knocked on Reife's door. He was dressed except for his shoes and knotting his tie. "Come in. I'll be a minute." She looked around at his room. Books and papers filled the table in a little alcove in front of a window looking out over Lafayette Square. While Reife laced his shoes, tied his tie and gathered up his things from his dresser—keys, wallet, handkerchief—she stepped over to look at this magnificent city built on the Potomac River with numbered streets running north and south, alphabetized streets running east and west, and diagonal streets bearing the names of states radiating, spoke-like, from the White House. She thought she remembered from a long-ago history lesson that George Washington had almost certainly played a big part in its design. The French, who had come to the aid of the struggling colonies during the Revolutionary War, had contributed architects and other artistic influence to its design and had helped make it the artistic city it was.

"Ready?" asked Reife behind her. As she turned, she saw that he was standing absolutely still. She had the impression that he had been standing there a good while watching her look at the scene outside his window. There was a warm drowsiness in his eyes that sent her heart to her stomach. He broke the spell with what appeared to be a force of will and stepped to the door saying softly, "I'm glad you decided to stay."

Seated in the dining room Reife looked around and said, "I was last here a little over ten years ago. My father and I came in 1929 shortly after the hotel opened. He was grooming me to take over the business someday and I met quite a few politicians that year. We spoke privately to President Hoover and I remember my father trying to tell him diplomatically that we needed to build up our armies and navies and warn him of the United States' increasing isolationism. It would have been to our own advantage, of course, but Hoover, I think, took it as simply self-serving and showed us the door."

"Did you always know that you would be head of Braddock's someday?"

"I think so. I was the youngest of five brothers, none of whom wanted the job and my sister, the baby of the family, couldn't have cared less about anything other than running with the international set she met through her husband. I loved it from the very beginning. I used to follow our old foreman, Jimbo, around when he supervised, so I had the advantage of learning, little by little, the company from the inside out."

"Tell me about your brothers," said Averill leaning on her elbows and looking at him over the platter of mussels, shrimp, and lobster set in the middle of the table.

"The oldest is Dale who is divorced and quite the ladies' man. He owns a photography studio and writes novels in his spare time—none of which are ever read, I suspect. Next is Bill who is a lawyer. He's married and has a son and daughter. Frank is a surgeon and has a son and daughter and Jim is just older than I. He's in real estate development and has two daughters."

"Did your dad take over the business from his father?"

"No, he worked for my grandfather who owned a lumber mill but it went bust after which my father enrolled in Baylor Military Academy in Chattanooga. He was twenty-three. After graduating, he enrolled at Georgia Tech and worked as a machinist part-time. A lot of students did this in 1895. He never earned a degree—Georgia Tech was little more than a trade school then—but came back to Chattanooga and opened up his own small machine shop. He had an excellent business head and had the good fortune to marry my mother who had inherited quite a bit of money. The business succeeded beyond his wildest dreams."

"Your mother seems a fascinating woman," observed Averill. "You look more like her than your father."

He smiled at her. "I'll take that as a compliment. Mother has a good brain behind that façade of Southern Belle persona. She kept the books for Father the first few years. Now she devotes her business skills to Erlanger Hospital. She sits on its board among other duties."

A duo of U.S. military colonels entered the restaurant and nodded to Reife as they were led to their seats. Reife twirled the stem of the glass with his fingers that held his cold drink, and Averill studied the phenomena of the moisture in the warm air of the room meeting a cold surface, condensing into droplets, which coalesced into rivers, and finally ran to the base of the glass where it deposited a ring of moisture on the tablecloth. He changed the topic abruptly and asked, "Did Edward tell you what he was doing in Washington?"

"Yes," answered Averill, becoming aware of the admiring scrutiny of the two military officers who were seated at a table not far from them. She shifted in her seat to where she didn't feel so on parade, flattering though it was. "He's here to testify in the trial of Klaus Ernst."

"I suspected as much."

"I thought you did," she said with a sudden upturned look under long lashes.

He held her gaze, smiled, and said, "Blake told me about the scam Ernst is accused of setting up and the fact that the trial starts next week. He mentioned Edward being a prosecution witness."

"How do you think Blake knew?"

"For quite a while now, I've suspected he's the one who exposed Ernst to the authorities," said Reife grimly.

"Where would he get his information?" Averill persisted.

Reife reached for his glass and drank a long draught, placed it on the Damask tablecloth, and was silent. He avoided Averill's eyes by helping himself to another lobster tail and working at it with his lobster fork. "I'm not sure," he said, with some evasion, while he concentrated on freeing the meat from its shell and depositing the crustaceous remains on a plate with the rest of the lobster's carcass.

"Blake told me the first day I met him in your office that he knew my father. For an Englishman, he seems to have known a lot of what is happening at the U. S.

headquarters in London," Averill commented after a pause.

"We are in England under their military auspices. He is, in a way, your father's boss."

"I see. There's something you're not telling me about Blake. Why? There's something wrong about that man. I know it. I feel it."

"Woman's intuition?" He said lightly.

"Yes, if you want to call it that."

The waiter stopped at their table and asked, "Would the gentleman and lady like to look at the dessert menu?"

"Not for me. Averill?"

"No."

Reife signed the room check account and Averill reached for her handbag.

"Wait," he said placing his hand on top of hers. "There are two things I'll tell you about Blake."

Averill waited. Reife lifted his hand from hers and ran it over his eyes in the gesture she had seen so often when something unpleasant had to be faced.

"Tell me."

Reife again reached for her hand, pressed her fingers, and said, "The first thing I will tell you is that Blake is the brother of the woman your father wants to marry."

Her grip on the handbag convulsed, loosened, and the bag fell to the floor. Reife bent to pick it up and placed it gently, almost reverently in her lap. She drew a deep breath, "And the second?"

"This one is a bit more sticky." He reached out a hand and gently stroked a petal of the lone red rose in a long crystal tube on their table. The sight of those long fingers with the square nails scrubbed clean of the grease that sometimes was caught underneath, momentarily diverted Averill. Strong hands, yet brushing the velvety smoothness with a feather-like touch. He continued, still gazing at the flower. "England's intelligence agency shared with our Army Signal Intelligence Service a surveillance photo of Blake in the company of a known Nazi agent in England. My source in the War Department says this agent may have passed to Blake information detrimental to the operations of Allied intelligence, possibly the identity of an agent known only as 'Valiance' whose undercover work during the Battle of Britain had a good deal to do with the rout of the German Luftwaffe."

Averill replied exultantly, "I knew there was something wrong about that man!"

"Averill, listen to me carefully. We must proceed in our acquaintance with Blake the same as usual. If he is what our SIS suspects he is and senses any question being raised as to his loyalty, I'm sure you know it will do a lot of harm."

"And my father? Does he know this?"

"Yes. Because of Jo Blake, the SIS has rigorously grilled him. In their opinion, Jo Blake's relation to Blake makes her a great risk; your father has not had an easy time of it these past few months."

"Does he still believe in Jo?"

"Oh, absolutely. Won't hear a word against her."

Averill digested this in silence and a thought assailed her. "Does Edward know that Blake may be an enemy agent?"

Reife's tone was bland. "You might ask him that yourself." Upon this ambiguous note he rose and, in silence, escorted her out of the dining room.

Chapter 11

Reife spent long hours in meetings and Averill spent the days doing research for him in some of the libraries found in Greater Washington D.C. She copied documents from the District of Columbia public library and Georgetown University Library, and made trips to the libraries of Alexandria and Arlington Counties. On Thanksgiving Day, he worked and Averill played tourist, meandering through the streets of the Capitol. Trapped in the wintry winds blowing off the Potomac, she couldn't help but think, was a ambiance which might have been the result of a convergence of Northeastern bustle and a deep tenaciousness of purpose, overlaid with a deceptive Southern languor.

Reife took time off to meet her for the Thanksgiving dinner the Hay-Adams Hotel prepared for its guests, and Friday she typed up notes for Reife. That evening found her packing her bags to be ready for the early morning train departure on Saturday when a knock sounded. It was Edward who wanted her to go downstairs for a farewell coffee. After seating themselves in a couple of plum plush chairs in the John Hay Room—a room named for Abraham Lincoln's private assistant, John Hay, during the dark days of the War Between the States—Edward ordered coffee, cheese, and crackers.

"You look exhausted, Edward," said Averill. "How do you think the trial will go next week?"

"There's so much evidence against Ernst, I don't see how he can be found not guilty. Testimony will show that he stole at least a quarter of a million dollars from the Cash and Carry program. We expect him to claim he was duped."

"Duped? By whom?"

"That would be simply conjecture on my part, and I'll not say. If they find him innocent of the charges, in time the government will go after these people and their names will be released. If he's found guilty his accusations will be discounted," he answered, avoiding a direct answer.

Averill looked searchingly at Edward. "What do you personally feel about his innocence?"

He said reluctantly, "My gut feeling is that he's guilty."

"Henrietta will be devastated."

Edward sat looking into the flames of the fireplace. She watched him and an awful thought assailed her.

"Edward, is my father one of those Klaus will accuse of duping him?"

Edward's mouth tightened. "Averill, don't ask me that."

Averill sat back in her chair, frightened as she had never before been in her life. If her father had been accused that would answer why he was possibly in Washington at this moment. He would have to be if he were to defend himself in the trial next week. Anticipating this, he had arranged to meet Averill here away from Annie. All the pieces were coming together.

Staring into the fire and ignoring Edward's conversational gambits, she said in a flat voice as if mesmerized by the flames, "The day I arrived in Washington, Reife and I were driving to our hotel and I thought I saw my father. The man was holding the arm of a young blond-haired woman. When I stopped the cab and jumped out to run to where I last saw them, they were gone. I persuaded myself that I had been mistaken. Now I wonder if the man I saw was indeed my father."

Edward said nothing and turned the cup of coffee around and around in his hands. Averill put her untasted coffee on a table and rose. She had made her decision. She said, "I'll be here a few more days. If my father is here and is under a cloud of suspicion, I want to see him. If you won't tell me where he is, I'll have to find another way to discover if he's in town. Please excuse me."

"You're angry."

"Yes, I'm very angry."

"Please believe me, Averill. If I could tell you more, I would."

She nodded and walked out of the room. At the receptionist desk she told the night manager that she wished to place a telegram. She wired her mother that she would be staying on. Then she climbed the steps and knocked on Reife's door.

He came to the door in his dressing gown.

"Come in, Averill."

He led her over to the little alcove overlooking Lafayette Park and said, "Have a seat. I was just finishing up some paper work." He motioned her to a chair at a table that held a briefcase, a stack of folders with spilling-out papers, the remains of coffee, and a bottle of *Quink* for his fountain pen. She caught the glimpse of a document stamped 'Top Secret' in red letters lying face-up before Reife casually raked it into the open briefcase, snapped the clasp, and swung it onto his bed. Then he sat down across from her.

"Shall I order something to drink?"

"No thank you." She sat quietly gathering her thoughts.

"What is it?"

"I have reason to believe that my father has been subpoenaed to testify in Klaus Ernst's trial next week. I suspect, no I'm almost sure, he's here in Washington and I'm not leaving for Chattanooga tomorrow." Tears that she had been holding back all evening welled up in her eyes and threatened to spill over. Reife sat very still and seemed to be making up his mind.

"What makes you think your father is here other than the fact that you saw a man who looked like him on the street?"

"Reife, how much do you know about the trial that is taking place next week?"

"Averill..."

"Klaus Ernst is in a military prison here in Washington awaiting trial on fraudulent dealings relating to U.S. funds. I'm almost sure he's prepared to implicate my father. Did you know this?"

"Yes, I have heard talk."

"Why didn't you tell me my father was being accused of fraud?"

Reife made a dismissive gesture. "Your father's appearance is merely military posturing. A formality. No one believes he's involved. It's a defense that has already backfired against Ernst. Blake is coming in thirty minutes to discuss some matters. If anyone knows where your father is, he does. I'll ask him about the matter if you like."

"I do like; he may very likely lie, but I want to be present when you ask him."

"Very well. In the meantime, let's expect to leave tomorrow as planned. Russ sent me a wire that makes me itch to get back."

"Has something happened at the plant?"

"Some employee became angry and attacked the bookkeeper."

"Viola Smetts? Was she badly hurt?"

"She seems to be recovering is all Russ said."

"Oh, we need to get back; but I've sent my mother a wire that I'm staying on."

"Just sit tight until we talk to Blake."

In her room, Averill paced up and down, trying to take in the fact that her father might be only a few blocks from her. Childhood memories swirled in her head. Annie Lowe had not taken kindly to foreign life, had preferred her native Tennessee, and had seen no reason not to voice this preference often. Averill was not too young to observe that her mother and father had fewer and fewer words to say to each other. Over the years, unhappiness like carbon dioxide had crept into a chamber where blazed the candle that made up the life of her home, and, little by little, the joy and buoyancy of both of her parents was no more. With a flash of adult insight she saw how desperation could have made her father ultimately ripe for reaching out to another woman. And then he had been posted to England.

Now, sitting with Blake and Reife an hour later she listened as Blake admitted that her father was indeed in the city and that he was to testify in the trial of Klaus Ernst. "Where is he staying?" she asked Blake.

"With some friends of his in Georgetown," Blake told her. "But he's moving to a hotel tomorrow."

"What hotel?" she asked.

"Let him contact you. He knows you are here and wants to see you."

Averill battled to keep her impatience under control. "Very well," she said rising. "Tell him I'm staying on for a few days in order to see him." She didn't look at Reife for his approval. Even if she lost her job she was determined to see her father and find out the depth of trouble he might be in.

"I'll postpone our train reservations a day or so. We should know something soon," said Reife.

"You'll stay on?" Averill looked at him in astonishment.

"Yes."

She nodded and left the room.

It was midnight and she had gone to bed, but not to sleep. Softly through the door Reife spoke, "Averill, it's me."

She opened the door and Reife said, "Did I awaken you?"

"No, come in."

"I cancelled our train reservations. I'll come for you and we'll have breakfast about nine tomorrow morning. We should have heard from Blake by then."

"Reife, you don't have to stay in Washington with me. I'll be all right."

"I know that. Your father's presence in Washington touches Braddock Engineering because it involves our contract with the U.S. government's Cash and Carry program. Go to sleep, now, and we'll talk about it in the morning. We should know by then if your father will agree to see you, despite his earlier instinct to ask you here for that very purpose."

"Agree to see me? Of course he will agree to see me."

"You know better than I that your father can be somewhat unpredictable. Let's hope he's not too panicked."

"My father is never frightened."

"This could be worse for him than facing an enemy's bullets. Goodnight, Averill."

Averill sat on her bed and the thought that her father would not want to see her struck her in its import. No matter that when she had found out that he wanted to divorce her mother she had said she never wanted to see him again. The knowledge that he was in possible great danger had changed that. She knew any charges that he might have defrauded his country were preposterous. Her father's integrity in finances was impeccable. She fell asleep after she covenanted with herself that she would be at her father's side throughout this whole nightmare, even if it meant that his mistress was on the other.

Chapter 12

She and Reife were finishing up breakfast when Blake appeared at the doorway. He came swiftly over to them. Reife indicated a seat and asked, "Will you have breakfast with us, William?"

"No, thank you. I've already eaten. Good morning, Miss Lowe. I hope you slept well."

"Thank you, Group Captain Blake. Yes, very well." She wasn't going to discuss the tossing and turnings of her restless night with this odious man.

"What do you have for us?" asked Reife, getting to the point rather abruptly. He had been watching Averill's face and knew the suspense about her father was almost unbearable.

"Your father wants to see you," said Blake, turning to Averill. "He is staying at the Willard Hotel. He'll meet you in the lobby. He's there now."

"Thank you," said Averill quietly, "I'll be ready to leave in ten minutes."

"I'll go with you," said Reife.

They entered the Willard Hotel's lobby with its massive marble pillars. "He doesn't want us going to his room," said Averill, "which means he is almost certainly not alone."

"Perhaps," Reife said, noncommittally.

A man dressed in a jacket with open shirt collar jumped to his feet and with easy strides, walked toward them. Averill went into her father's arms rather stiffly and extricated herself almost immediately.

"How are you, Dad?" she asked in a voice that was colder than she meant because she struggled for self-control.

"Fine, fine. Sit down." Colonel Lowe indicated upholstered wing chairs grouped around a low table. A newspaper spilled from the seat of one. A cup and saucer with the remains of coffee and a small silver tray holding a cream pitcher and sugar bowl sat on the table. "Good, good. Will you have coffee?" he asked, as a waiter materialized.

"Yes, please," she answered, settling herself uneasily in the proffered chair, unaccustomed to seeing her father nervous.

"Wonderful. And you, Reife?"

"Yes, please," Reife said as he sank into the embrace of the oversized chair.

After the waiter left with their orders, Averill said, "I was surprised to find you in Washington, Dad. Group Captain Blake said you're here for Klaus Ernst's trial."

"Your young friend has proved to be a liar and a cheat, Averill," Lowe said, then added, "I'm sorry to have to tell you that."

"It's hard to believe," replied Averill.

Lowe said gravely, "Yes, it is. The military charges that Ernst, acting as a liaison officer for the Cash and Carry program between England and the U.S., used his position to divert English sterling into his private bank account. He's countering with the allegation that I was the one who rerouted the money and that he was an unsuspecting victim in this transaction."

"What nonsense," Averill said, firmly.

"Yes, it is nonsense. Ernst is the one who had access to the money, not I. Depending on how the trial goes, I may be exonerated by testimony, but if they find Ernst 'not guilty' there's a chance they'll come after me, but I think it most unlikely. So far I have not been accused by anyone but Ernst. However, I have been subpoenaed by the prosecution as a witness."

The waiter approached with a silver tray on which rested two cups and saucers and a silver carafe from which he refilled Lowe's cup and filled two others.

"I knew it," Averill cried, her face paling as she reached clumsily to take the coffee from the tray. Reife's hand shot out in time to steady the rocking cup. "No one would say, but I just knew you had been accused. I don't know how. Just this gut feeling,"

"Don't worry, Averill. I don't," her father said, reaching over to pat her hand. "Ernst will be seen as what he is—a thief struggling to escape the consequences of his crimes by deflecting the guilt elsewhere,"

Averill shrank from her father's touch. "I hope so," she said awkwardly.

Lowe turned to Reife. "Blake told me that your business here in Washington is finished," he said in a low voice. "I'm glad you got old Harry Stimson to award you the contract."

"If all goes well, my factories will have a fairly large shipment for England by mid-1941," Reife responded.

"Maybe by then Roosevelt and Congress will decide to grant England credit. England's exchequer is already dangerously near the red ink." Col. Lowe had decided to ignore his daughter's puzzling mood changes. He pointedly talked across her to Reife. "They have to buy the fuel to send their ships to our shores and then pay cash for the supplies before they can be loaded. It's pretty murderous on a country which has spent millions of pounds trying to defend itself from Nazi aggression."

"Are you able to say what your mission in England is?" asked Reife. "If you can't, that's fine, but Averill and I have wondered."

"I'm a military observer," Lowe answered briefly. A short silence followed this.

Averill determinedly brought the subject back to her immediate concern. "I was supposed to leave this morning for Chattanooga, but wanted to see you before I left. I want to tell Mother how you are."

"I'll be fine. The evidence against Ernst is overwhelming. There is only a slight chance I'll have to stand trial," Lowe said smoothly.

"I'm concerned that you're all alone here in Washington. You need family with you." Averill's emotions were seesawing up and down and, after initial shyness, she searched her father's eyes and, as the Biblical Job in the Old Testament, she knew that the thing she feared had come upon her. Somewhere… in this hotel… there was a woman who was making sure he was not alone. Lowe cleared his throat and looked discomfited. She dropped her eyes to hide the anger that she knew flared in them. From the corner of her eye she could see that Reife was moving restlessly with embarrassment. Averill ignored him. She said bluntly and in a harder tone, "Is your mind still made up to go through with the divorce from Mother?"

Lowe shifted uneasily in his seat and then said, "I'm sorry, Averill, but yes, I want a divorce as soon as it can be arranged."

"Mother is not well. This may kill her," she said, accusingly.

"What's wrong with Annie?"

"She had bronchitis rather badly two or three years ago and she's never been the same."

Lowe fidgeted again in his seat then offered weakly, "I'll see to her financially, of course."

"Dad, can't you please reconsider?" Now Averill was almost begging.

"No, no. I want to be happy, and the only way I shall ever be happy is to marry Jo."

"Why should you be happy and Mother unhappy?"

"Someone has to be unhappy, Averill," he said simply.

"I want to meet her. She's here, isn't she?"

Lowe looked down at the table, reached to his collar to adjust a tie that wasn't there and a tic at the edge of his left eye appeared, familiar to her from childhood days as a sign of discomfiture. His hand was unsteady as he reached for his coffee cup—this was a man who could always call up reservoirs of composure in tight spots, she remembered—and asked in a voice that fooled no one, "Who are you talking about?"

"You know who I mean. This other woman. May I meet her?" Averill pressed.

After a pause he spoke so softly she had to strain to hear the question. "Are you sure you're ready for this?"

"Yes, that's another reason I stayed on in Washington."

Lowe bowed his head in defeat; then rising from his chair like a very old man, he offered feebly, "Let me see if she's available."

Lowe headed toward the elevators. Reife leaned over and took Averill's hand. He murmured, "Just stay calm."

"I'm not a child, Reife. I'm not going to throw a tantrum."

He said dryly, "I have never once thought of you as a child."

He leaned forward and folded his hand over the one he had enclosed, and his voice was infinitely gentle. "You're lashing out like a cat at a dog. Slow and easy, Averill." They sat in uneasy silence until Averill suddenly said, "They're coming," for over Reife's shoulder she could see her father enter the lobby holding the hand of a slender woman. As the woman drew nearer Averill saw straight brown brows and an unmistakable English complexion. Through long flowing blond hair her violet-blue eyes peeked out and shyly rested on Averill. She thrust out a small hand and said so softly it was hardly audible, "I'm Jo Blake. My brother has told me many nice things about you, Averill."

Averill said coolly, "I've heard about you, also."

Reife half rose, retrieved his overcoat from the fourth chair in the group, and indicated the chair to Jo, "Please sit down."

She hesitated. Lowe nodded reassuringly and said, "We can only stay for a few minutes. We have business with my attorney in an hour."

"Your attorney?" Averill asked, alarmed.

"In relation to next week's trial, Averill," Lowe said.

"I want you both to know the heartbreak you've brought to me and my mother." Averill said, bluntly.

There was silence. Then her father said softly, "We neither of us wanted this to happen, Averill. Can't you wish us happiness?"

"No, I can't. Mother isn't happy," said Averill. Then she turned to Jo and asked, "Excuse me, but I couldn't help but notice that you're limping. Were you injured in the blitz? Will you always be a bit of a cripple?" She was being abominable but she didn't seem to be able to help herself.

"Yes. The Germans bombed our house while we were sleeping. My parents were killed but I was pulled out," the woman said so low Averill had to strain to hear her.

"I'm sorry." Averill said, ashamed now.

"My leg is practically healed. The doctor says the limp should not be permanent."

Averill watched her father reach over and take Jo's hand. She pointedly looked at their clasped hands, and her father abruptly released the hand. He signaled to the waiter for more coffee.

"Are you a witness for the prosecution, also?" Averill asked Jo.

"No."

Averill was stabbed. No, of course she wasn't. She was here to provide comfort and support for her father: a role her mother might otherwise have filled.

"Tell us about England," Reife suggested. "How are your people holding up during these air-raids by the Nazis?"

"Morale is very high," said Jo. "And of course we have Winston Churchill. He is splendid the way he inspires our people. I don't know where England would be without him."

"Oh, yes. He succeeded Chamberlain when Parliament repudiated him, didn't he?" asked Averill, making a gallant effort.

Lowe answered, "Yes. The English like to recount the dramatic scene in Parliament last May where Leo Amery quoted Oliver Cromwell, who—as the meanest education in England does not fail to teach—dismissed Parliament in 1653 by crying, 'Depart, I say, and let us have done with you. In the name of God, go!' and turned against his friend, the pacifist Chamberlain." He laughed ruefully. "Long on tradition—the English. Chamberlain resigned shortly afterwards."

"England now appreciates that the only person who told them for years that Germany was rearming and preparing for war is Churchill," Jo said in her soft voice.

"It's lucky for England that we have a friend in Roosevelt," added Lowe.

"He has to be very diplomatic about any aid the U.S. gives Britain," replied Reife. "There's still a good many people who feel that this war doesn't concern us." He turned to Averill and asked, "Will you have more coffee?"

Averill childishly lifted her chin while thrusting a vagrant curl behind her ear. "No, I want to go home," she said. In the last few minutes, she had changed her mood like quicksilver and her voice held the whimper of a small child. "Perhaps we can catch tonight's train for Chattanooga." Suddenly, she couldn't get away from her father and this woman fast enough.

"I'll grab us a Pullman," said Reife, his voice soothing as if in the nursery.

She fumblingly felt for her coat that draped the back of her chair. "I'll send mother a telegram," she said, deliberately looking in her father's direction.

Her father blinked nervously and looked at his drink. Jo looked over at him with concern, then turned to Averill and said, "I'm glad you came by. Thank you."

As Reife and Averill stepped out into the cold morning, Reife slipped one arm around her and, with the other, pulled her head onto his shoulder as they made their way back to the Hay-Adams. "That was not an easy hour."

Chapter 13

Averill and Reife boarded the train in the early hours of Sunday and were shown to their Pullman berths which were made up and waiting. The swaying of the train lulled Averill to sleep immediately.

The next morning found them clacking past farms and small towns where traffic stopped at the crossroads and waited for them to chug past. In the dining car they were shown to a table with a snow-white cloth replete with a little vase of freshly cut flowers in its middle. They ordered freshly squeezed orange juice, eggs with bacon, hash brown potatoes, and buttermilk biscuits with a bowl of fresh dairy butter that melted into a flow of thick yellow nectar the minute they smoothed it on the hot bread.

Averill sipped the hot coffee and studied the scenery outside the window where, set back from the tracks, modest houses drifted past, a few with unpretentiously decorated Christmas trees already in their windows. She found herself, for the first time in her life, dreading Christmas. The thought that her father would be spending Christmas with another woman was almost unbearable.

"What are you thinking?" Reife asked, studying her.

"Christmas." It was partially true, anyway.

"Ah, Christmas. Which reminds me: Mother will be giving her annual Open House on Christmas Day. The whole family will be there. Will you come?"

"How lovely. Of course I will."

"Good. That's settled. You're an only child, aren't you?"

"Yes. I've always hated it. I would like to have a brother or sister—or both."

"Were you lonely as a child?"

"Sometimes. Before we settled in Chattanooga we were always moving so I never made any close friends. I was always saying goodbye to any friends I made."

Averill stared out the window, remembering. "It wasn't so bad, though," she added, turning back to Reife, smiling, "Fortunately there was always music. We'd arrive in a new locale and before we unpacked Mother would find a piano teacher for me. I've always missed having a brother or sister but I'm glad I took the music lessons."

"Oh, I don't know. You might have had a big brother who bullied you. Or a sister who was jealous of you because you were prettier and took away all her boyfriends."

"Or was a raving beauty who stole all mine," she dimpled.

"Inconceivable."

They smiled at each other and locked eyes a fraction too long for mere friendship. A little flustered, she dropped her eyes to her plate and moved her eggs from one side of her plate to another.

"Something wrong with the eggs?"

"They're cold."

"Would you like to send them back and get fresh?"

"No, I'm through. Just let me drink my coffee and stop hounding me about my food. You're worse than my mother."

Reife laughed and signaled the waiter for a refill of coffee.

Averill settled back in her seat and looked out at the passing pastures. They were in Kentucky now, and horse farms with stallions kicking up their heels on the faded blue grass underneath dark and restless clouds—reminiscent of Turner paintings—sped by. Trees, denuded of their leaf clothing, stood sentinel over the bucolic scene. She turned to Reife. "The telegram from Russ. It was bad news, wasn't it?"

"Yes." He looked beyond her and said, "If you're finished, let's give someone else our table. There's a line forming."

Seated in their compartment, Reife said no more about the telegram but took out his briefcase and began making notes on a long yellow legal tablet. Averill opened her train case and pulled out the book she had begun on the trip north. She methodically turned its pages but soon came to realize she was taking nothing in and laid it aside. She rested her chin on her hand, drank in the passing scenery, and mentally reviewed what she knew about the man sitting across from her.

He was at least ten years older than she, maybe more. He came from a large, close family and was especially fond of his sister, Joan, with whom he had lunch at least once a week. He had spent a recent vacation in Canada with his father where they had shot three deer. He liked jazz, was punctual and neat in his personal habits. He was on the board of the Hunter Art Gallery, rooted for the Chattanooga Lookouts baseball team, and had never been married. Sundays were for golf.

She picked up her book, tried to focus on the print again, gave it up, tossed it aside, and rested her head on the seat. From under lowered eyelids, she watched Reife. She must not be so stupid to fall in love with this man, she told herself. This was madness.

They arrived at the Chattanooga terminal at midnight. Glancing outside as she gathered her belongings, she saw faces trained expectantly toward the cars that turned a sickly green underneath the thin yellow lights of the platform. A sudden onrush of outside air brought a smell of smoke and burning oil, a nearer smell of stale coffee, old sandwiches and the unmistakable odor of humanity too long stored together. Reife, with black shadowed eyes in the sudden bright light of the car, wrestled luggage from the overhead carrier. Why was arriving at a train station so much more depressing than leaving it?

"I'll get these two. Can you manage the other one?" he asked.

She nodded, and, sodden and stupid from a cramped sleep she gratefully caught sight of Braddock's foreman, Russ Higgins, wearing a wide smile waiting on the platform and leaning on a trolley piled with luggage.

Stumbling, she followed Reife and gratefully hung on to his supporting arm as she descended the iron steps. "Russ, old man, we could have called a cab," Reife said, throwing an arm around his foreman.

"Yeah, well, I was in the neighborhood. I found some of your luggage; is there more? How do, Miss Lowe, I found one of your bags, too. Let me help you with that."

"Oh, Russ, you're an angel. I'm missing my large black calfskin. What about you, Reife?" Their luggage was soon all accounted for and they made their way outside to a city whose smokestacks were pouring smoke into the chill late November air. Most of Chattanooga's manufacturing plants were now operating on Sundays.

Reife and Russ talked in the front seat as she half-dozed in the back. Despite Russ's flippant talk at the station, she knew they talked of the crisis at the factory. Russ pulled up in front of her house and Reife, a suitcase in each hand, saw her into her front hall where Annie had left a light burning, and then turned to plunge down the steps to the waiting car and drive off into what was left of the night.

The rest of the house was dark as she turned to mount the stairs with her train case. A light switched on in the kitchen. Annie Lowe appeared at the doorway into the living room in her nightclothes.

"Averill," she said.

"Oh, Mom," answered Averill, and ran to envelope her in her arms.

"Averill, your father...."

"I know, Mom."

"You know?"

"Yes. I saw him."

"You saw him?"

"Yes. He's in Washington. Can we talk about it in the morning?"

"Can't you just tell me why he's in Washington?"

Averill relented. Her mom had lain in the darkness, sleepless, waiting for her to come home. "Sure, Mom." She hugged her mom to her as they walked into the kitchen.

Over a fresh pot of coffee, she told her mother about seeing her father. She didn't mention that he wasn't alone and that she had met the woman he now wanted to make the new Mrs. Lowe. She dare not even hint that he was under suspicion for both fraud and treason.

"I just can't believe it, Averill. That after twenty-five years he would want to leave. What did I do?" Her cry was the timeless one of all the rejected ones. "What am I to do? Averill, help me, help me."

It was almost three in the morning when she settled her weeping mother back to bed with a hot water bottle and she sat in the darkness on the side of the bed until Annie said in a steady tone, "Go to bed, Averill. I'll be all right."

"Oh, Mom, I wish I could have spared you this."

"I know, darling. I know. I'm glad you're home. It helps," said Mrs. Lowe and kissed her forehead. "Go to bed, now. I know you're exhausted."

Averill drug herself up the stairs, threw off her clothes and after a quick brush of her teeth, got into bed. The room was cold. Their boarder, Fortuna Medina, who rented the attic bedroom, had taken it upon himself to take charge of the coal furnace in the basement but he had banked the fires for the night. Sometime during the night, she staggered to the old armoire that stood in the corner, got another quilt, and spread it on the bed. She fell back asleep and woke to warmth seeping into the room, the indescribable smell of fresh-brewed coffee, sunlight asserting another day through the Priscilla curtains, and her mother calling from the bottom of the stairs.

Chapter 14

"Averill, Mr. Braddock is on the phone," her mother's voice pierced through the mists of sleep. She reached for her bathrobe, raced down the stairs, and took the phone.

"Averill, it's Reife. I know we talked about your taking the morning off, but I need you here. Friday one of the factory workers—Nick Fahrenheit—breached the glass enclosing Miss Smetts's office, and attacked her with a hammer. She's in critical condition at Erlanger Hospital. I need you to finish payroll; it must go out today."

"I'll be right there, Reife," and she placed the phone in its cradle.

"What happened?" her mother asked.

She told her, and Annie said, "You get dressed and I'll fix you a quick breakfast."

Averill ran up the stairs and dressed hurriedly. Her mother had eggs, oatmeal and toast ready for her. "How could this have happened?" Her mother asked, seating herself across from Averill and sipping at her coffee.

"I don't know the details, Mom. Reife got a telegram in Washington about an attack on our bookkeeper, but it didn't seem to be serious. I heard Russ and him talking in the front seat last night as we drove home, but I was half-asleep when they discussed it and just caught phrases. Now it seems our bookkeeper is seriously injured and he needs me for payroll. I'll know more about it when I get there." She finished eating, grabbed her coat off the coat rack beside the door, and went out into the chilly weather.

When she arrived at the factory, she went into Reife's office. "Good morning, Reife."

"I'm glad you're here, Averill. We're in trouble. Viola took a turn for the worse last night. It looks bad. In addition to attacking Viola, Fahrenheit put sand in the motors on some of our machines. One line is completely shut down. They've been working around the clock to fix it, but it looks like it will be down for the rest of the week."

"I'm so sorry about Viola. Would you rather I attend to the mail or start on payroll?"

"Start on payroll; I'll do the mail," he said, glancing up at her and then down to a police report. As she started to leave, he said, "I almost forgot. 'Friends of Britain' has asked us to do another variety show. They want it to be sometime in January. Just keep it in mind. I'm depending on you to coordinate it." He lifted his head again with a quick smile. "That okay?"

She smiled back. "You've got it." She turned to leave and caught his reflection in a mirror on the approaching wall. His eyes were following her.

The staff had done what they could over the weekend to clean up. The glass around the accounting office was gone, leaving it as open as a county fair booth, but the wreckage had been cleared. Pris Quigley, who had been persuaded to leave teaching and come to work at Braddock Engineering, came up from below and hugged Averill. "It's just too awful," she moaned.

Averill said. "Poor Viola. Why did Nick do it? Do they have any idea? Was it something about his paycheck?"

"He claimed he was shortchanged on his overtime. Viola checked the records and told him that his check was correct. Then he demanded to see Mr. Braddock. When they told him he was out of town, he left, went to his workstation, and came back with a hammer and started swinging at the glass. Then he forced his way into her office. She took several brutal blows to the head before they could subdue him. Half the plant was in here trying to pull him off her. He just went mad. It's hard to believe that she was still alive when they wheeled her out of here."

Averill, together with Pris, finished the payroll at five o'clock. At home, she was reading the evening paper when the doorbell sounded. It was Reife.

"Let me take your coat," she said reaching up to take his scarf.

He caught her arms and said, "I've just come from the office. I haven't eaten. Let's get something to eat."

She lifted her coat from the coat rack and Reife held it while she thrust her arms through each armhole. He wrapped her scarf around her neck. Only then did she know how exhausted he was. The shadows were darker under his eyes. For a minute, she experienced an insane desire to kiss them. He held her by her scarf for an infinitesimal second and she saw an answering impulse in his eyes. He turned, opened the door, and ushered her out, his hand firmly on the back of her waist.

Seated in the restaurant, Averill asked, "Is there news about Viola?"

"We're hopeful. She lost a lot of blood. They've given her transfusions. She's not allowed visitors except family."

"I know. I went by Erlanger's after work and was turned away."

"Can you do accounting until I find someone to replace Viola?"

"Of course, but how will you manage without a secretary?"

"The unimportant stuff will just have to pile up. It won't be for long. I've already advertised for another accountant."

"Reife, I just thought about something. Mom took in a boarder some time ago. His name is Fortuna Medina and he's looking for a job as an accountant."

Reife lifted his eyebrows. "A boarder? How old is this boarder?"

She dimpled. "Oh, be serious. He's about forty, round as a bowling pin, and wears coke bottle glasses. He came to America from Italy in 1935 when Mussolini declared war on Ethiopia. The depression has hurt his chances to land a job as an accountant and he is working as a custodian for Oak Plains Elementary School. I gather from what he's said that he had a promising accounting career in Italy, but he despises the current government."

"Send him in to me tomorrow afternoon. Say, about two o'clock."

"I will. I don't know if he's what you want, but I know he's a hard worker. He's been indispensable to mother around the house since he moved in."

"I heard from Blake today. The trial began, but nothing much has happened of importance. They still expect Klaus to deny wrongdoing."

"That means he'll try to bolster his defense by accusing my father of his crimes."

"Perhaps. How's your mother?"

"It's broken her heart."

Reife finished his chicken fried steak in silence. Then, in a change of subject, he said, "There was a newspaper article in the New York Times about the desperate position England is in. She's all alone since France fell."

"Time is running out for England unless America enters the war."

"I think she will. Roosevelt is certainly for it."

"Most of the people I know are vehemently against it."

"Yes." Reife put down his coffee cup carefully and said, "Every woman or man who has a son, brother, or husband of age to fight, will march on Washington."

"What do you think?"

"I think you're looking a little tired. Shall we go?"

"You dodged that very neatly," she said, smiling up at him.

He threw money on the table, gathered up their coats and scarves, his hat and her gloves. He squeezed her shoulder as he helped her with her coat and they walked out the door to his car. As they approached the car he gently turned her around by the shoulders and leaning her against the car, kissed her. She relaxed into him and then slightly tensed against him; he quickly released her.

He leaned past the door and helped her into the passenger side, walked around to the other side, got in, and pushed his key into the ignition, but didn't turn it. He looked over at her and asked, obviously nettled, "What was all that about?"

She didn't pretend she didn't know what he was talking about. "Reife, we need to talk." She plunged in desperately, "You and I are so different…"

"Well, thank God for that," he said with a cynical lift of an eyebrow.

"No, that's not what I meant," she said. "Oh, Reife you're not making this easy for me."

"Sounds serious," he said, his voice neutral.

"I've never talked with you about my relationship with God. You see…oh, this is so hard. You see," she stammered, desperately wishing she was anywhere but where she was, "I've been struggling so with my feelings for you. I can't, I mean I want to but, oh Reife, I'm sorry. You'll never know how hard this is to say."

He seized on her mention of God. "What makes you think I don't believe in God? Most people would call me a good, moral man."

"I know you are. I'm sorry, this is all sounding so judgmental, and I'm sorry. I'm stating this so badly. For now, let's just be good friends, shall we?"

"I see. Good friends. All right, I think I can handle that." He turned the ignition, started the motor, and in silence drove the short distance to her house.

On her porch, she said, "Reife, you're angry."

"No, I'm not angry, just confused. I thought you liked me."

"Oh, Reife, I do, I do. You don't know."

"No, I guess I don't." He encircled her waist and pulled her to him as she opened the door with her key. He murmured into her hair with a hint of laughter in his voice, "Good night, Averill. Don't worry about it. I'm not asking you to marry me, you know."

"Good night, Reife," she said, and, turning with an annoyed movement that was almost a flounce, she entered her house, irrationally pricked that she had made her point in a matter that apparently didn't need to be made. Long had she thought that when the time came to make the little speech she had just delivered, Reife would be either hurt or angry. To be honest, she had hoped he would be as distressed as she felt herself to be. Instead, he had seemed amused more than anything! Her face burned as she climbed the stairs to her bedroom. Was she turning into one of those hateful women who led a man on and, when his ardor flamed, dampened it with rejection? Or equally as bad, a vain, silly egoist who thought any man who enjoyed her company was dying to marry her? What an idiot she had been to make so much out of what was for Reife just a passing flirtation, nothing else. Well, he'd certainly run from her now and that was what she wanted, wasn't it?

She went to bed, but not to sleep. Scalding tears soaked her pillows and she angrily flopped them to their dry sides. Had her heart been seriously wounded or was tonight's scene simply a bruise to her pride? In college, she had seen several young men distraught after she broke off a relationship after a month or so. She reached for her bedside lamp, sat up in her bed, and opened her Bible. She found the scripture in Second Corinthians. *"Be ye not unequally yoked together with unbelievers: for what fellowship hath righteousness with unrighteousness? And what communion hath light with darkness?"*

She wondered why this brought no comfort.

The next morning, headachy and unable to eat breakfast, she arrived at the office having girded herself to face the mockery she would surely see in Reife's eyes after her presumptive little speech last night. Pris was weeping at her desk.

"Pris! What's the matter?"

"Viola died during the night," Pris replied, pulling a tissue from a box on her desk.

"You can't mean it!"

Reife passed Pris's office on the way to his own. He nodded at them both, but didn't stop. His face looked like death and Averill knew that he had heard the bad news.

After lunch, Fortuna Medina came into the accounting office for his interview. She ushered him in to Reife's office and had just returned to her work when the switchboard operator rang her, "Hey, Averill. You have a caller who's holding until I can find you."

"Put it through."

"Hi Averill. It's Henrietta. Your Mom told me you were back. I can't wait to see you. Can you have dinner tonight?"

Averill thought guiltily that all thoughts of Henrietta had vanished in the past day's events.

"I have to work late tonight. Is nine too late for you?"

"Of course not. Shall we meet at The Toddle House?"

Averill thought that an event that should have brought her pleasant anticipation was now a dreaded prospect. She knew she ought to tell her about Klaus's treachery before someone else did.

At the restaurant Henrietta rushed over to hug her. "Averill! I haven't seen you in ages and I have so much to tell you. The afternoon's classes just seemed to crawl. Then I had after-school activities. My class is planting a vegetable garden in back of the school and I was covered in dirt. After running home for a quick shower, I had a PTA meeting. I'm starved." Henrietta jumbled everything together but Averill got the picture.

"You're planting a garden?"

"Oh, it's a bee in the superintendent's bonnet. He thinks we should teach our students how to plant and cultivate food in case there's war. Actually, he got the idea from Britain where food rationing is making it absolutely necessary."

"Sounds like fun."

"Actually, it is."

"Speaking of England," Averill said, "our company is sponsoring another Friends of Britain Variety Show in January. Can you and Pris get up another script?"

"Oh, what fun! I'll get to work on it tomorrow."

"How is school going otherwise?" Averill asked, picking up the menu.

"Oh, Grimes is having us sell bonds, collect tin cans and other metal; and can you believe this—the students bring the cans to school and the teachers have to be in charge of keeping track of them. We're about to revolt. I'm willing to help Britain in the Variety thingy, but I draw the line at checking sacks of tin cans to see if they've been washed out and flattened."

Averill laughed and pushed the unpleasantness of Klaus Ernst to the back of her mind. She wouldn't even raise Klaus's name.

The pit of Averill's stomach had relaxed too soon; for Henrietta took a bite of salad and announced, "I got a letter from Klaus today. It sounded like the ones he wrote before we broke up. Maybe he's having a change of heart."

"Henrietta, just go slow about Klaus."

"Why do you say that?"

Averill sat very still and looked at her lap.

Henrietta laid her fork beside her plate. "Tell me, Averill. It's bad, isn't it? Has he been killed?"

"No. Oh, Henrietta. Klaus is standing trial in Washington this week for defrauding the government of Cash and Carry supplies we've shipped to England."

"That can't be. He wouldn't do that."

"He's not been found guilty," she said encouragingly. She was on no account prepared to tell Henrietta that he had turned the blame against her father.

"I want to go to Washington to see him," Henrietta said.

"Why would you want to rush up and possibly have him turn a cold shoulder?"

"Didn't you hear me? He's writing again and his letters have changed, Averill. I think he's in love with me again. I want to be with him in Washington."

"You probably won't be allowed to see him, Henrietta."

Henrietta was still for a minute then took Averill's hand and said, her voice soft, "I know you're skeptical about Klaus loving me, but you'll see. He does."

Chapter 15

During the train trip south from Washington, she asked Reife to attend church with her during the Christmas holidays. Today on this first Sunday of December, he sat beside her and joined in the singing of the carols. The church was warm and fragrant with pine and scented candles. The stained glass window over the chancel, outlined in electric candles, filtered red, green, yellow, and blue lights onto the creamy gowns the choir was wearing especially for the Christmas season. Averill looked around her and caught the eyes of a family across the aisle. She smiled at the younger child, a girl of about nine, who had assumed a grown-up air with her chin held high and wearing an mien of importance held half of the hymnal she shared with her mother while she sang *O Come All Ye Faithful* in a clear soprano that reached across the aisle. Averill let her eyes continue to drift over the people and wondered how many were struggling to pay their rent. Who among that sea of faces had spent their last dollar for groceries and would eke out the following week living for another paycheck? Her dream the night before returned to her.

She had woken shivering with cold but, reluctant to leave her warm burrow such as it was, drilled even deeper into her feather mattress, attempting to put off the evil moment when she would have to get out of bed into the icy air and fetch another blanket. She fell into a troubled sleep and dreamed she was gliding past lines of quivering men standing in freezing cold. She moved to the front of the line and saw a man awaiting a stamped paper. She knew—as is the way of dreams—that he would be the only to be given a job while the rest would be turned away. She glanced back at the rejected men and exchanged a glance with one near the end of the line. His eyes reminded her of a scene she had witnessed some years before. A dog, tail wagging gleefully, was reveling in a pile of garbage by the side of a road. Unexpectedly, a car in front of her swerved onto the slope and there was a sickening crunch as the bumper met the unfortunate animal full on. She saw dumb suffering and acute bewilderment in its eyes, followed swiftly by an expression that seemed to ask, "Oh, wonderful world, what have you done to me?" as it slowly crumpled to the ground.

She pulled her car onto the shoulder and walked back and stooped beside the dog, reaching out to lay a tentative hand on its flank. She had no water to offer, but it was too late, anyway. She watched with the dog as his sun darkened and was snuffed. She never forgot those eyes—and now she was seeing them in the face of a fellow human.

She awakened once more with the realization that the cold she had experienced in her dream was being visited upon her restless body. She twisted and turned on her bed seeking warmth. Still she dozed without rising to put another blanket on her bed. Gradually, she had the feeling she was not alone. She looked for her mother in the doorway, but instead saw a Presence dressed in light approach the foot of her bed. The Presence held out hands with two horribly scarred wrists. She raised her eyes to look at the Presence and the light blinded her. She fell from her bed onto the floor and knelt before the figure and trembled. He spoke and His voice sounded like far-off bells and the trickling of water, and a soft, sweet wind swirled throughout her room. "Come unto me, all ye who are heavy-laden and I will give you rest," the beautiful voice said. She looked with adoration at the Presence and knew He was Jesus, the Son of God. A scrap of verse that she remembered from Sunday School came to her mouth and she replied, "My Lord and my God." The Presence raised a hand in a sort of blessing and left. She was suddenly awake and there was only the dark of her room and the shadow of the familiar objects. The cold drove her to add another blanket and in warm contentment, she fell back into sleep.

She had awakened to the sound of church bells and carillons. The words of the old hymn, *Holy, Holy, Holy*, ebbed and flowed within her as she bathed and dressed and prepared to meet the Presence in worship. Now, during the Recessional, Reife reached over and placed his hand on hers. She grasped his fingers as she silently breathed a prayer that Christ might reveal Himself to this man who had walked so imperiously into her life.

At the Lowe house, Annie served a Sunday dinner of roast beef, browned potatoes, carrots, and green beans. For dessert, there was peach crisp, hot and bubbling with spices. The talk turned to Christmas.

Reife said, "Averill is coming to our Christmas evening party, Annie. Will you come, too? My mother is looking forward to it."

"I'm so terribly sorry. My Mah Jong group is having a special party Christmas Day and I've promised to help cook. It's not just a club of women who meet for Christmas, you know, we join other groups in cooking for a downtown mission."

After dinner, Reife left to do some work at his office and Averill washed up the dishes while Annie napped. When the kitchen was once again tidy, she pulled out her plans for the *Friends of Britain Variety Show* and spread them on the table. The date she set was in a month's time since Reife had wanted it as soon as possible: England was becoming financially depleted and desperately needed help. She worked up a draft program and began making telephone calls.

The next day Fortuna Medina began work as the company's new accountant and Averill gratefully surrendered her payroll duties and returned to a backlog of work as Reife's secretary. Group Captain Blake materialized before her.

"Good morning," she said, civilly.

"Good morning, Miss Lowe. May I see Reife?"

"Certainly. I'll see if he's free." She flipped on the intercom. A minute later, she ushered him into Reife's office. Toward the end of the day, she looked up to see him studying her from in front of her desk. "It is good to see you again, Miss Lowe. I have something for you from your father." He pulled out a thin envelope from his inside pocket.

"Thank you. How kind you were to bring it to me."

"Not at all. Well, I'm off to Washington. Happy Christmas."

"Merry Christmas."

Alone, she tore open the envelope. A check fell out. There was a short letter:

Dear Averill,
The trial for Ernst is over and he was found guilty and has been sentenced to eighteen months in the brig at Fort Sill. I'm exonerated of all charges and am winding up my affairs here and will sail to England after the holidays. I was touched that you delayed your plans to see me at the hotel. I had hardly dared hope you would ever want to see me again for I know how hurtful my actions have been for you. I am spending Christmas with Grandmother Lowe if you need to get in touch with me.
Merry Christmas to you and your mother.
Dad.

As she was thoughtfully folding the letter, the phone rang. It was Henrietta. She had received a letter from Klaus telling her he was being assigned to Fort Sill, Oklahoma.

She sat, her eyes pensive, scarcely conscious of the bird that pecked at the birdseed she kept in the feeder outside her window. The sky was lead-colored with dirty clouds sifting through in patches. She could hear thunder in the distance and now and again, she saw the jagged blaze of lightning.

"Bad news, Averill?" Reife asked behind her, gesturing toward the folded letter she again held in her hand.

"Blake brought a letter from my father. Klaus Ernst has been sentenced to eighteen months in prison."

"I know. I heard the news from a friend in Washington. Bad news for your friend, Henrietta."

"She's talking of visiting him this spring."

Reife's eyebrows rose. "I hope she's not being shortsighted." He placed a stack of letters in front of her.

"Will you write answers to all these? You know what to say."

"Of course."

Reife disappeared into his office and she inserted letterhead into her typewriter and began typing as, outside, a winter thunderstorm moved in.

Chapter 16

Christmas morning dawned with a cold rain falling. Fortuna Medina descended the steps, passed the Christmas tree in the big entryway with gifts lying open where Averill and her mother had celebrated their own quiet Christmas morning an hour earlier, and entered the kitchen of the Lowe home.

"Oh, Fortuna, we were hoping you would decide to eat breakfast with us. Your place is set and the sweet rolls are hot from the oven." Annie Lowe indicated a plate with gifts resting beside it.

"You are too kind," he replied. His brown eyes flashed with childlike delight at the two women. He opened the shopping bag he carried and produced two gifts. "These are for you." he said with a Continental flourish.

"Shall we eat and then open our gifts?" asked Annie.

Averill had noticed his crestfallen look at this suggestion and she declared, "Indeed not, Mom. Fortuna and I want to open ours now."

Fortuna opened his with unabashed eagerness. "What a beautiful tie clasp. I shall wear it with much pride." They all laughed when he pulled out his tie from under the sweater, clipped the tie clasp on and let it hang on top. He patted it proudly. "Now open your gifts," he commanded.

Averill and Annie unwrapped perfume and much was made of passing the vials around to be smelled. They both applied it then and there and so breakfast began with a festive air. It was a spare breakfast as American breakfasts go: orange juice, hot sweet rolls, and coffee. "...to save room for Christmas dinner," said Annie.

Averill and Fortuna seemed loath to leave the table, and Annie soon excused herself and went into her bedroom and closed the door. Averill knew her mother would sit at her grandmother's antique desk in her large bedroom and write a long letter to her own mother, who lived in Maine with her only son, Annie's brother.

Fortuna and Averill lingered with coffee at the kitchen table and Fortuna talked of his childhood in Rome where his family had always attended the Pope's Christmas morning greeting in St. Peter's square.

"Such wonderful Christmases in Italy!" he exclaimed. "Never will I forget. And Christmas dinner. Mamma Mia! Food enough to feed an army. Now it is all different. Italy is fighting on the wrong side and they are losing. Such disgrace. Such dishonor this fascist pig has brought upon our people."

Fortuna then launched into a recital of how Mussolini had risen from obscurity, become a newspaperman, clawed his way into the political system, and had become the dictator of the fun-loving, deeply religious population of Italy. He had revealed his latent militaristic ambitions by launching a reluctant army at the kingdom of ancient Abyssinia, now called Ethiopia, in Africa. To Fortuna's delight, they had been beaten.

He was cynical about the friendship of Mussolini and Hitler, convinced that Hitler was jealous of Mussolini's early victories and wished to draw him into the war to further his own dream to annex lands that made up the old Holy Roman Empire. The tragedy, Fortuna said, was that after Mussolini's token first victories he had failed miserably in his further military exploits. On the other hand, Hitler's military machine had achieved brilliant victories because he had had the foresight to plan his propaganda. With psychopathic cunning, Hitler had overlaid a mantle of stirring pomp and ceremony upon his military machine. The twisted Nazi cross with its dreams of world conquest had been superimposed onto the true cross of Christianity and pious Germans had been swept along with the tide of the rhetoric from a genius devil. The humbled but still proud nation— smarting from the terrible consequences laid onto them by the victors of the First World War— had followed Hitler into his maniac's world.

Averill, who had spent her childhood in Egypt on the continent of Africa, was able to speak firsthand of some of the internal reasons Ethiopia had been ripe for picking by the military might of the Italian leader. An hour had passed before both realized the day was wearing on.

Fortuna took his leave by leaping up the stairs with great energy to dress for his lunch with an ancient great aunt, and Averill opened the closet door in the hall and pulled out her wrapped presents for Reife and his family and carefully began to pack them for transport to the Braddock's that evening. She had painstakingly shopped for gifts for his brothers' children, for his mother and father, and for Reife. She had bought him a pair of antique bookends which she had scoured the shops for days to find. She piled her gifts into two big shopping bags and went upstairs for a leisurely bath.

She lay in the bathtub with her hair piled high on her head while the herb-laden bubbles from a jar of bath salts and the candles she had bought especially for Christmas made the room redolent with the Christmassy smells of pine, eggnog, and cardamom. She meditated upon the life of Christ and what happened on a night almost two thousand years ago and what it meant to millions of people now living. She thought of Reife and how things might be different if she could only feel that his relationship with Christ was uppermost in his life. She forced herself not to think of his cobalt blue eyes and how they looked at her sometimes with a tiny fire blazing behind their cool depths turning them into a new kind of blue. She wouldn't go there, she told herself, for what was the use? She was plunged again into the doubt which had begun to assail her as to whether or not she should have accepted this invitation for Christmas but assured herself that he and his family were her employers and it was Christmas. Again, the deep honesty of her nature caused her to look at this for what it was—a circumvention of the fact that she wanted to spend this evening with Reife. Was this so wrong?

She descended to earth with a thump when Henrietta called from the hallway.

"I'm in here, Henrietta," and she leapt from her bath and grabbed her robe as the door opened and Henrietta stood there holding a package tied with cascading ribbons.

"Merry Christmas," Henrietta said and stepped forward to hug her friend.

Averill produced Henrietta's present and they sat on the bed, ate salted almonds, opened their respective presents, and exchanged news. Henrietta had received a letter from Klaus insisting upon his innocence and awaiting departure to his place of detention for eighteen months.

"I want to go be with him. I want to live there in Fort Sill somewhere. On the base. In an apartment. I've got to be near him, Averill. You don't know Klaus as I do. He can't be guilty!" Henrietta pounded the bed and paced the room. She saw that Averill was about to speak and she cried, "No, don't tell me I'm wrong. I'm not. I know I'm not. Please, please be on my side, Averill. No one else is. Mother cries every time I mention it. Pris thinks I've made a big mistake. I love him! I can't eat, sleep, or do anything other than to think about him and want to be with him."

Averill made soothing sounds. She knew Henrietta was in no condition to look at Klaus Ernst with unbiased eyes. And who was she to judge? Sometimes the heart saw more clearly than the eyes.

"I am on your side, Henrietta. I want you to be happy. If Klaus is essential to your happiness, then I'll support you. All I ask is that you pray about it. Will you?"

"Oh, Averill, what do you think I've been doing all these months? Of course I've prayed."

"Forgive me, Henrietta, but have you then sat back and listened?"

"Not really." Henrietta was willful, determined and reckless but completely open and honest. "I am so afraid that He'll say 'No'," she said grinning sheepishly.

They both laughed at this frankness and Averill thought that in her way Henrietta was being more honest with herself than she was. Averill said, "At least you know you're not playing fair with God. You've given him permission to say 'Yes' but not 'No'."

"I think He's saying, 'Yes'. I really do," insisted Henrietta.

"I hope so," said Averill and changed the subject. It was too uncomfortably close to the way she was rationalizing her feelings about Reife. Later after Henrietta had left for home, Averill pulled out a long forest green silk dress and spread it on the bed. Reife had said his mother and father were 'ridiculously old-fashioned' when it came to Christmas Day. Upon her probing, he admitted that his mother would probably be wearing a long dress. She washed her hair, piled it on top of her head, and fastened it with a clip, set with semi-precious stones that had belonged to her grandmother. Her black sandals with their ridiculously high heels had been with her all through her college years but she had retrieved them from Mr. Allen's shoe shop the day before and they had been rejuvenated. She pulled on the dress that caught her waist, reduced it to nothingness, then skimmed her hips, and fell in a straight line to scan her shoes. She applied a light makeup, misted the back of her ears with Fortuna's exquisite perfume, and surveyed herself in the long mirror that hung on her closet door. The dress had been given to her by her parents after her first year of college when she made the Dean's list and the cut of the dress was good enough that it would never be out of date. The dull silk caught the light from her bedroom's fireplace and quickened to life the green winter firs in her eyes. The glow of youth, health, and happiness was reflected from her floor-to-ceiling mirror on her bedroom wall. The girl in the mirror smiled back as she held her black velvet cape and miniscule evening bag and pulled on black calfskin gloves. After adjusting her jade necklace—a gift from her father—she turned off the light and descended the stairs.

The winding drive up Lookout Mountain always thrilled her. To look down at her city where people worked, lived, loved, and sometimes broke their hearts always moved her. No matter that for most in those toy houses, each day was a battle to survive the worst depression the country had ever had; the majority were living and loving with courage, hoping with bravado that tomorrow would bring an end to suffocating poverty. Today, Christmas of 1940, found the smokestacks free of the black smoke which belched into the air seeping into every building and causing the Chattanooga housewives to hoard their rags to scrub and dust and fight the intruder only to come back to fight the coal soot the next day. But today was Christmas and all cleaning had been done. Wooden floors were waxed and shining, windows were brilliant after being rubbed with ammonia and newspaper, coal stoves had been burnished and were red hot with fires that had cooked the turkey and baked the hot biscuits and cornbread for its stuffing, and somehow a Christmas tree had been purchased and was decorated. She had driven past myriads of homes with electric candles in the window and thought of the long hours those men and women had spent in Chattanooga's factories and machine shops in order to give their families this day and her heart sang at their courage.

Now on top of the mountain she reached Reife's house and drove in through open, hospitable gates and turned into the curving drive. The house was built around 1890, she judged, and was designed after the lovely antebellum houses more common farther south. It was white brick and there were Greek columns atop posts, and both the first and second floors had porches, or galleries, as some of the occupants of such houses called them. Behind them were sets of windows that reached from floor to ceiling. There was a gabled roof with dormer windows and chimneys set on both sides of the house. She imagined parties in warmer seasons where late-night guests would pour out the doors onto the galleries with windows open and every light ablaze; but today, although there were cars parked in the circular driveway, no one was outside in the cold rain. She rang the doorbell and heard chimes. The door was opened and she was greeted by a young girl whose maid's dress was covered by a white organdy pinafore who took her cape and her two bags of presents. "This way, Miss Lowe," she said and led her into a large room with a fire burning in the grate with about twenty people milling about.

Russ Higgins saw her first and came to greet her followed by the senior Mr. Braddock who said, "Averill, my dear, how grand to see you. Mother, here's Averill."

Mrs. Braddock glided over holding her long skirts and drew her to herself so that cheek met cheek. "Averill, what a lovely dress! We're so glad you could come. Oh, here's Reife. Your lovely Averill is here, Reife. You look cold, my dear; come over by the fire. Findley, get Averill a drink."

"Of course, my dear," said Mr. Braddock.

"Something non-alcoholic," Reife told his father. "Averill, come meet the family." He approached a tall bald man who whirled as Reife said, "Dale, I'd like you to meet Averill."

Averill looked into blue eyes that its owner was trying to focus on her as he placed his drink on the mantelpiece. He was balding and tall and had to bend to take her hand. In his alcoholic fog, he was courtly as the stateliest of gentlemen and his eyes were kind, if a bit remote. "How do you do, Averill? How grand that we at last get to meet you." He took her arm and said, "Let me introduce you to the Braddock gang. There's five sons and only one black ram in the litter—Reife." He laughed uproariously. "Thought I was going to name myself, didn't you?" As they circumnavigated the crowded room, Dale, uncertain in gait, almost upset a tray of canapés as he made his way past a laden table; Reife, following behind, caught it as it was sliding over the edge.

A boy, about seven, tugged on his arm. "Uncle Dale, you promised to play a game of chess with me."

"And this manner-less young rascal is Frank Junior. Frankie, this is Averill, a friend of your Uncle Reife's."

Frankie said shyly, "Hello." Then, obligations fulfilled, he tugged again at Dale's sleeve. Come on Uncle Dale. You promised."

"So I did. Well, I must keep my promise. My dear, it seems that Reife must introduce you round. So good of you to come," and he allowed himself to be led by the youngster to another part of the room.

Reife led her past a folded screen that in less busy days was, Averill guessed, extended to provide a divider to the large room. "Frank and Ellen, meet Averill." Two figures, one a tall, thin man with graying hair and an almost childishly upturned nose oddly coupled with sharp, observant eyes turned, as did a cozily plump woman with untidy hair wearing a rather bilious green dress. The woman held out her hand and said in a warm voice, "How lovely to meet you, my dear." The man, belying his stern appearance, smiled a dazzling smile that transformed his face and held out a long, fine-sculpted hand and said, "How do you do, my dear?"

A young girl of about twelve came up and handed Averill a drink saying, "Here's your drink, Miss Lowe."

Ellen echoed Averill's thank-you with a warm smile for the child. "That was sweet of you, darling." She placed her hand lightly on the girl's shoulder and a cluster of thin, golden bracelets on her arm moved toward her elbow. "Averill, this is Bill's daughter, Evelyn," The girl smiled shyly. Ellen's other hand caught at Averill and pulled her forward saying, "Oh, and I want you to meet her father and my brother-in-law, Bill—and his wife, Leona."

They approached a man and woman who were watching a Chinese checkers game between two young girls in a corner. The man, of medium height whose suit could not quite hide his tendency to embonpoint, stuck out his hand as soon as they reached him. "Hello," he said gravely. "Glad you could join us. This is my wife, Leona."

Leona was a slender woman who Averill later was to find always had a cigarette in her fingers and exuded a haggard kind of beauty, with languid eyes that Averill was to learn appeared to be half-closed much of the time. Her crooked smile showed wrinkles that proclaimed her to be nearer fifty than the forty she appeared from a distance. Averill guessed her to be older than her husband.

"How do you like Chattanooga?" Leona asked.

"I love it. I've been away at college, though, and a lot of things have changed."

"Oh, I understood that you went to the University of Chattanooga," exclaimed Ellen beside her.

"Momma, that isn't her," piped up a child, one of the players of checkers.

"Shut up, Ruth," warned her checkers partner.

Ellen opened wide distressed eyes. "Oh, I'm so sorry. I must have confused you with someone else…oh, dear

I mean…well, someone said… sometimes I don't listen very carefully," she finished in a fluster.

Reife smoothly turned the talk to the new bridle path the residents were proposing for Point Park on Lookout Mountain. Ellen said to Averill plaintively, "Now we'll talk about the other topic of conversation in Chattanooga other than the war in Europe. It's another thing the Braddock brothers can disagree on."

Averill sipped her soft drink and replied with a skillful duck of the controversial subject, "How lovely this room is."

Laughter erupted in the direction from where Gertrude Braddock was seated. Averill looked over and saw Reife's mother convulsed with laughter. A young man seated on the arm of her chair said, "Careful, you'll spill your drink," and put out his hand to steady her.

"Yes, it is a lovely room, isn't it?" responded Ellen. "Come, I want to introduce you to Reife's sister, Joan."

"I met her once in Reife's office. Isn't she the one in the silver dress talking to the tall man?"

"Yes, that's Joan. The man she's talking to is my brother-in-law, Jim. His wife, Colleen, is the small, dark woman over by the French doors. Let's meet Colleen first and then I'll introduce you to Joan." Ellen bustled away, pulling Averill along, the picture of a gregarious, friendly woman who liked to see others happy. She was duly introduced to Colleen, and Averill was reminded of a small bird sitting in a nest afraid to fly. "It's nice to meet you," she said timidly to Averill.

"Now, let's say 'hello' to Joan," suggested the ebullient Ellen. "Joan, dear, Averill has arrived."

It wasn't Joan who said 'hello'; it was Jim turning from Joan and fixing friendly eyes on Averill who said, "Hi, there. Reife told us you were coming, but try as we might we can't be on our best behavior." As if to verify the truth of this statement, boisterous laughter broke out and a crash was heard followed by the dying tinkle of glass on marble. All eyes looked over to where Findley Braddock and Russ were brushing the liquid from their respective suits. Gertrude was first on the scene with several napkins to clean up. "That will teach you to argue with full drinks and not too steady heads," she said as she scrubbed the hearth place.

After watching the scene in amusement, Averill turned back to the woman Ellen had been introducing. Joan stared at her frostily. "Good afternoon," she said.

Before Averill could reply there was a screech at the scene of the accident. "Dear, oh, dear," said Ellen as she abandoned her hostess duties and ran to fetch towels. One of the children had dropped her doll into the sudden flames that had sprung out when droplets from the alcoholic drink had splattered into the flames. Averill watched the family respond to the crisis. During the confusion, Joan moved judiciously away, and this left Averill free to roam the room and look at the pictures. An angry-looking man with tufts of white hair peeking out behind each ear stared down at her disapprovingly above a table set against a wall.

"Rather an intimidating old gentleman, don't you think? Said to be the kindest soul alive but you wouldn't believe it from his portrait, would you?"

Averill turned and looked into the eyes of the man who had been perched on the armchair laughing with Gertrude Braddock. "Hello. I'm Peter Conover," he added, reaching for her hand.

"I'm Averill Lowe."

"I'm not going to pretend that I don't already know your name. The fact is, the whole family knew you might be coming," he smiled. He was older than he appeared from a distance, and when he smiled, there were deep wrinkles at the corners of his eyes.

"So I've gathered," Averill said dryly.

"In any case, I saw you perform at the variety show. I enjoyed the Rachmaninoff very much. Have you ever thought about making the concert stage your career?"

"No, never."

"Why not?"

"I'm not nearly that good," said Averill without false modesty.

At that moment, dinner was announced and Reife appeared at her side. "Hello, Peter. I noticed Conover stock was up yesterday. Your re-organization seems to be paying off."

"It was hard to get the old man to change his ways, but he finally agreed," Peter replied. "Guess I'll round up Joan and sample some of Bessy's turkey and dressing."

"Averill, shall we go in?" asked Reife.

"Who's Bessy?" She asked as they made their way to the dining room.

"She's our cook. Been with us since I was a little boy about Frankie's age."

The dining room with its holly, candles, and fir was the focus of everyone for the next hour. Conversation was lively and as a matter of course ended with the war in Europe. Beside various plates on the white linen tablecloth, the Braddock men sketched battles and campaigns with the tines of forks. The harassment of incendiary fires from German bombs over Europe was thoroughly dissected and discussed and then turned to Britain's pitiful monetary state. "It is absolutely essential that this country loan Britain money in the way of ships, airplanes, and armaments," Reife declared, emphasizing his statements with vigorous motions of his fork. "England—to put it bluntly—is broke. Halifax admits it himself," alluding to Lord Halifax who was England's Ambassador to America. There were differing opinions on how best to help England financially and multiple plans on how to defeat the Nazis. The women, with the exception of Colleen, were as vocal as the men. At length, Gertrude rose, her husband followed, and gradually everyone made their way into the living room.

Peter Conover led Averill over to a black baby grand piano. At once, voices which had been raised in schemes England might use to win the war were raised in begging Averill to play. She obliged with a medley of classical and jazz then ended up playing Christmas Carols in which everyone joined in singing lustily, if not tunefully. Presently, the crowd drifted to the Christmas tree where a mound of gifts rested, among them those that Averill had brought. Gifts were passed around and everyone ended up with a pile in front of his or her chair. The Braddock adults were as excited as the children.

Reife professed himself pleased with the book-ends and she unwrapped his present to find a soft cashmere scarf and gloves. The evening ended with cards and Backgammon. It was after midnight when Averill threw down her last hand and conceded defeat to the brilliant duo of Dale and Colleen. Reife fetched her coat while she made the round of good-byes and thank-you's to her host and hostess. Reife walked her out to her car. He took her keys from her hand and unlocked the door for her.

"Call me when you get home," he said. "I want to know that you made it down the mountain safely. It can be rather treacherous at night. I wish you had let me come and get you."

"I'll be fine. Thank you for the lovely scarf and gloves."

"You'll see your book-ends in my office. I have just the spot in mind."

He drew her to him. "I enjoyed having you here for Christmas so much," he murmured. "Thanks for the piano performance. My family appreciated it."

Her heart stuck in her throat. She murmured into his shoulder, "I enjoyed meeting them all. They're lovely—all of them. You're so lucky not to be an only child."

"It makes for chaos sometimes, but I wouldn't have it any other way."

He pulled back to kiss her and, impulsively, she wrapped her arms around him. "You're so lovely. So sweet," he breathed, and then, "You're cold. You're trembling."

"No. I'm all right. You're a little overwhelming," she said, her voice shaky, her will power deserting her.

He raised one eyebrow and he was—with effort—suppressing a smile. "Am I being too 'friendly'? Drive carefully," he said and released her and opened the car door for her. Once inside, she started the motor and waved to him. She skillfully maneuvered the car on the crowded driveway and made her way home under cold skies from which flurries of snow began to descend.

Chapter 17

It was a week before the second *Friends of Britain Variety Show* slated for the last Friday of January when Joan Conover entered the Braddock offices and, ignoring Averill, walked into Reife's office unannounced. Minutes later Reife buzzed her on her intercom and asked, "Averill, could you come in here a minute?"

She entered the office with steno pad and pencil. "Good morning, Mrs. Conover," Averill said to the seated woman. Joan Conover nodded curtly and took a puff on her cigarette.

Reife said, "Sit down, Averill. Something has come up regarding the variety show. Joan has heard rumors that it will be picketed by anti-war demonstrators." He picked up a pencil and see-sawed it back and forth with his thumb and forefinger, tapping the table first with the lead and then with the eraser. "I want your opinion as to whether or not we should cancel the performance. What do you think?"

"Where did you hear these rumors?" Averill asked mildly, turning to Joan.

Joan studied her cigarette and said, "They come from my husband's business contacts. I may say that they have been verified by other sources."

"I shouldn't think that a few signs and banners would intimidate many people. On the contrary, it might stiffen the resolve of Chattanooga to pack the house out," Averill replied.

Joan flicked her cigarette ash into a nearby ashtray with an annoyed gesture. "What would be your response if I were to tell you that some of the local feed and hardware stores are reporting a run on supplies that are known to be useful in making bombs?" she asked.

"I would contact the police and, most probably, the FBI to find out those customers' names and investigate. Most businesses have ways of tracking sales."

"You realize, of course, that with all these precautions we are still endangering people's lives," Joan pointed out.

"We can't cower in fear and let terrorists control our lives. The police have bomb-sniffing dogs. They could check out the hall the afternoon of the show and then post police officers. This event is to help with food and armaments for people whose backs are up against the wall. The English people are living in fear every day with the German Luftwaffe bombing their homes. How can we back down because of a few idle threats?"

"They are not idle threats. Anyway, whatever is happening in Europe has nothing to do with us. It's not our war," replied Joan, testily.

"There I will disagree with you. We owe a lot to Britain. Are we to be frightened off by a handful of Nazi sympathizers?"

"How are you sure it's only a handful?" Joan asked turning to smash her cigarette in a nearby ashtray.

"It always is," Averill said.

Reife broke in. "Averill, would you contact the police and ask for their cooperation? If the FBI needs to be brought in, the police will take care of it. I agree with you. We should go on with the plans for the show."

"I'll get right on it," replied Averill.

Joan watched Averill move to the door. "I'll say this for you," she said to her, "you have guts."

"Thank you," Averill said, opening the door and turning to look at her. "That's a nice compliment."

Joan gave her a reluctant smile and Averill carefully closed the door behind her.

The police force and undercover officers had turned out in full force the night of the variety show. Despite her brave words, Averill was a bundle of nerves.

"What does the crowd look like?" Henrietta asked, making last-minute notes on a paper whereupon was printed the small drama in which she would take part.

Russ Higgins, who would once again serve as emcee, spoke up, "It's packed. More people than last time. The canine unit is keeping the dogs out of sight but they're there all right. The police force is mostly in civilian clothes, so there haven't been any questions about the extra security."

"I saw a good number of blind people with seeing eye dogs. Would those be some of the canine corps?" asked Henrietta.

Russ smiled a dry smile and said, "It does seem that we have more blind individuals attending than usual."

Suddenly it was time to begin. A local minister opened the program with prayer, and the Central High School Glee Club began with the Star-Spangled Banner, after which Russ exploded onto the stage and, with a mixture of quips and showmanship, had the audience involved in the evening's program.

Henrietta, with perfect cockney accents, portrayed an English char complaining to the mistress of the house, Lady Boomsa Daisy, that Lord Daisy's romantic attentions were most unwelcome. Pris Quigley's response in haughty aristocratic accents brought down the house, "My dear, I couldn't agree with you more," as she replaced her lorgnette and bent once more to her letter writing.

The children were again a success, and proud parents and relatives clapped enthusiastically. The small boy who had lost his dinner at the previous show repeated that performance—this time on stage. Averill matter-of-factly walked onto the stage with a towel and led him off. He went on later and received a standing ovation from the sympathetic audience.

In the wings a sudden attack of nerves had descended upon Averill. Reife, nearby was quick to notice and, slipping an arm around her whispered, "Steady." He smiled down at her and with easy comfort pulled her to him. When a minute later she walked out onto the stage in white blouse and long black velvet skirt and launched into Beethoven's Moonlight Sonata, she met with prolonged applause and was greeted with 'Encore, encore!'. She rose and approached the microphone and said, "May I tell you the background of the piece I will play for an encore? Its title is *White Cliffs of Dover*.

"When England first became convinced that war was inevitable, the first thing they did was to get their most precious treasure—their children—out of harm's way. They knew that the town of Dover on the coast with its chalky cliffs was one of many that would serve as a target for the German bombers. They evacuated all their children from London and the eastern coast along the English Channel to homes deep in the countryside.

Many, many thousands of parents had to wave goodbye to children who they expected might be separated from them for perhaps years. This song is about that event and I dedicate it to those courageous parents who endured separation from their children and turned their energies to winning the war. May I read the lyrics before I play? And she read the beautiful words written by the American, Nat Burton."[1]

To a hushed audience she performed a simple arrangement of the melody without accompaniment from the orchestra. When the last note faded, Averill rose from the piano and with tears streaming down her face greeted the thunderous applause from a crowd on its feet.

For the rest of her life she was never to forget the look in Reife's eyes as she left the stage and entered the wings. He held out his arms; she walked into them and his arms closed around her, enfolding her. Unheeded by them, singers filed past them onto the stage for the closing number and led the audience in a stirring rendition of *My Country 'Tis of Thee*, The crowd held aloft their small American and British flags and waved in time to the music. Unexpectedly and spontaneously, the audience broke into singing, *God Bless America.*

Some of the first to reach Averill backstage were Joan and Peter Conover. When Joan reached her side, she whispered simply, "I'm glad you stuck to your guns."

"Me, too," responded Averill with a grin, and was soon separated from them by members of the audience ascending to the stage and engulfing her and the rest of

---

[1] Author's note: No permission was granted to the author to use the copyrighted words.

the performers with hugs and tears from the women and enthusiastic handshakes and backslapping from the men.

Her mother, with Fortuna in tow, fought her way through the crowd and gathered her daughter in a huge embrace saying over and over, "I'm so proud of you," and then stopping open-mouthed. "Why, what is wrong with Reife?"

Averill turned in time to see a white-faced Reife snatch his coat and hat and run off the stage, the unmistakable yellow of a telegram in his hand, followed a minute later by Russ Higgins. "What is it? What has happened?" she asked, suddenly afraid. A pall settled on the backstage and, while some quietly slipped into coats and scarves and left, others milled about amid the confusion.

Averill finally reached Peter. "Peter, what happened?"

"I don't know, but if I had to make a guess, it has something to do with the factory," he replied grimly. "I'm going over there. Joan. Joan. Where's Joan?"

"I'm here, Peter," Joan said, coming to his side.

"Let's get out of here," Peter said and pulled her along as she struggled into her coat.

"I'm going, too," said Averill. "Mother, you go on home. I'll come along directly."

Fortuna said quietly, "I'll drop your mother off and then I'll come to the factory."

Averill's car was stopped by a police barricade when she approached the environs of the factory. She jumped from her car and ran to a police officer. "What has happened?"

"Don't know for sure, Ma'am. Please stand back."

"I work here. Couldn't you let me through?"

"I have my orders, little lady. No one gets near the building."

She looked around for Joan and Peter. The crowd was growing and she threaded her way through it looking for someone she knew. After scouring the crowd again and again she returned to her car and sat and waited.

Presently, Fortuna arrived with Pris Quigley. Pris exclaimed, "Oh, Averill. We just heard it on the radio. There's been an explosion."

Chapter 18

"An explosion? Where? Inside the offices or down in the factory?"

"Inside the buildings; no one seems to know any more than that."

"There are forty men working in the factory and a night-watchman in the office. Oh, dear God, let them be safe," Averill cried, as she reached for Pris's hand and held tight. In the absence of official announcements, the speculations and fears from the bystanders served to fuel her terror.

After an hour of waiting Fortuna said, "Come, Averill, you may as well go home. You'll catch cold. People may have called your house and they can't reach you sitting here. Come on, Pris, I'll drive you home."

Reluctantly, Averill drove home. Her mother met her at the door.

"I heard the news," she said. "Reife's been calling. He's worried about you."

"He's worried about me? I'm worried about him. I've been sitting outside the plant for almost two hours waiting until he came out. They wouldn't let me inside."

"He said he'd call back."

Averill got ready for bed and put a robe on and went downstairs to read in the living room. Eventually, she laid down her book and rested her head on the back of the chair. She was startled awake by the phone's ring. It was Reife. The FBI had arrived on the scene. His office safe's door had been blown and the plans and designs of the new tank that Braddock's was working on were gone.

"We have duplicates, of a sort, but they have not been kept current. The originals have all our annotations," said Reife. "We don't know if the thieves just scooped out everything or if they were targeting the plans and designs, specifically. If it's the tank designs they were after, it's sabotage."

"What does the FBI think?"

"They always take worst-case scenario. They think it's sabotage. If so, it's most likely an inside job. I'll tell you more when I see you."

"Inside job! That puts everyone under suspicion."

"I'm afraid so. Me included. Don't worry about it, Averill. Get some sleep."

"They would suspect you?"

"The FBI has suspicious minds, Averill. I'll be tied up with the FBI all weekend. My office is unusable. Your desk got clobbered, but everything else is not so bad."

"Where will you work?"

"I'll set up office in the library."

"I'll come in tomorrow and do some cleaning."

"No, don't do that. The repair crew will be here. Everything will be in chaos until they finish. Just come in on Monday and we'll go from there."

Monday morning there was confusion in the offices, but the factory went on as usual. Reife had set up office in the library and was meeting with the FBI. Averill spent much of her time in the wrecked offices trying to create some kind of order by filing in boxes any papers that were salvageable until new file cabinets could be delivered. Reife appeared now and again to rummage through the mess, trying to locate papers he needed for his on-going conference with the FBI agents.

By mid-week, she had all the papers temporarily filed and the FBI agents had finished their investigation. Workmen worked through Wednesday night repairing structural damage to the office. On Thursday, Reife moved back into his office and the library was returned to its business of providing research materials and housing archives. On Friday, there appeared new file cabinets, bookcases; there were new desks for her and Reife, two magnificent couches, one very long burgundy leather for Reife's office, the other a loveseat in a spicy nutmeg color for the waiting area across from Averill's desk. Fittings for new window coverings were taken for the offices, and in the elongated area of the waiting room, Gertie Braddock had purloined from her widowed mother's home a magnificent antique mahogany credenza with rounded drawers and beveled mirror.

Friday afternoon Averill unpacked the last box of files that were usable and filed them in new file cabinets. Running a final dusting cloth over a small table, she turned to Reife who had moved to the door to view the finished effects of the last of the pictures hung and asked, "Are we finished?"

"No, not quite. Why don't I pick you up around seven and we'll go out to dinner?" His eyes were tired, his slim figure now almost scrawny, but he smiled his one-sided smile that could be so devastating to her resolutions.

"I hope we can summon the energy," she said, as she shoved the dust cloth into a drawer, too tired to take it to the laundry in the basement.

"You look like you need pampering a bit." His eyes took in her crumpled blouse, the run in her hosiery, her hair escaping from its snood. She knew she had a habit of rubbing her face when she was deciding where to file things, and wondered if perhaps her face was one big smudge from the carbon copies of the letters she had organized.

"Nothing sounds as good right now as a nice, hot bath," she said, straightening her skirt.

"That goes ditto for me. See you at seven."

"I'll leave now and come in tomorrow and transcribe the letters, if that's all right with you."

"Hang the letters. They can go out on Monday."

After a long, hot, fragrant bath in lavender oil, she stood at her mirror considering what to wear. She wondered if she had time to wash her hair, but decided that she didn't have time for it to dry, even if she hung it over the furnace register. She considered pulling up a chair in front of an open oven, but she wouldn't have time to set it even if it would dry. Instead, she brushed it until it shone and piled it on top of her head, anchoring it with a tortoise shell comb. 'Rats', which consisted of parting the hair in the middle and taking the front part on each side and rolling it and securing it with bobby pins, were in fashion; she decided to try them. When finished she decided they looked smart, although she had her doubts about whether they suited her or not. Eventually, she decided against them, energetically shaking them loose and incorporating them into the rest of her hair. Still she was dissatisfied and ended up jerking out the comb and letting her hair plummet free in a waterfall around her face.

She looked at her bedside clock. She had wasted so much time with her hair; she only had a few minutes left to dress. She rummaged in her closet, finally deciding on a dress in soft caramel colors that brought out flashes of amber from her hair. She buckled the dress's slender belt around her waist where the knit clung to her body from bust to hips gathering at her hips with fullness until it reached her knees. She thought the boat neck called for pearls and fastened her Grandmother's necklace of matched globules around her neck and clipped on matching pearl earrings. Now came a delicate cobwebby pair of stockings, which she lovingly lifted out of a Loveman's box and coaxed them to mid-thigh where they fastened to her garter belt. Makeup was minimal: Vaseline on her eyelashes, a little rouge, soft lipstick, and lastly she reached for shoes, high-heeled pumps which she knew displayed her legs to advantage.

She perched a hat slantwise on her head, the brim highlighting her eyes and eyebrows, and picked up her bag and the cashmere gloves Reife had given her for Christmas. Following a last look at herself in the long mirror to check her seams, she began descending the steps into the living room where she would wait for Reife.

She had not heard him ring the doorbell but he was standing at the bottom of the stairs studying a framed needlework that a great great and possibly another great grandmother had done almost a hundred years ago. Hearing her steps he looked up and she read in them a look of admiration and an expression she could only interpret as stunned awareness. He smiled and held her eyes in the soft gloaming, the house stilled where outside the twilight was dying, and the usually unheard click the furnace made to re-start the fan sounded like a muffled cannon blast.

He took her hands when she reached the bottom of the stairs, let go of one after a long minute and reached for her coat on the coat rack and remarked prosaically, breaking the spell, "It's turned off nippy tonight. You'll need a scarf."

She tried for the stance of friendship mixed with a slight playfulness. "Thanks to you I have one to match my gloves. It's in the pocket of my coat."

"So it is. Here, let me help you with your coat. Now there, that's good. I'll help you with the scarf." He looped the scarf round the back of her neck and threw one end over her shoulder. "Shall we go?" He smiled a happy smile with one lifted eyebrow.

Seated at their favorite eating-place, the Read House, a hotel and restaurant, originally the old Crutchfield House across from Union Station, Reife ordered for them the House's famous beef and vegetable soup to be followed by T-bones with green peas freshly shelled by the chef that day, salad, and hot rolls.

While they waited for their food, he told her what the police and FBI had determined about the explosion that had destroyed the safe in his office. "The theft from the safe was done by someone—or at the behest of someone—who knew exactly where the designs were and what time security was lax. He knew the night watchman was taking his dinner break and would be down in the factory in the lunch room with the night crew."

"Do they have any suspects?" she asked.

"None, as far as I know."

After a minute she said, "We made $5,000 for Friends of Britain."

"No kidding? That's great. I haven't had time to thank you for all the work you did. You did a great job."

"Thank you. It was actually rather fun."

"We'll do another one soon if you'll take it on. England's Ambassador, Lord Halifax, has half-promised to attend."

Averill smiled a one-sided smile. "That means—at its best—he'll plead a crisis in Washington at the last minute."

"My, aren't we cynical?" His eyes were teasing. Their soup and salad were served by the waiter. "What do you hear from your father?" he asked when the waiter had wheeled his butler's cart from their table.

"Blake brought me a letter from him. He was to spend Christmas with my Grandmother Lowe in Maine, then back to England. I don't know whether ...that woman went with him to Maine or not."

"You haven't heard from him since he's been back in England?" he asked, scooping up a spoonful of soup.

She shook her head. Steaks and the peas appeared, personally selected by the chef early that morning from the local Farmers Market, colloquially known as the Curb Market. The staff could have told them they were buttered from fresh cream churned at a nearby dairy that morning at sunup. Yeasty cloverleaf rolls were brought wrapped in a napkin on a plate.

"You say Blake brought you the letter from your father?" asked Reife as he cut into his steak.

"Yes. When he came to your office in December."

"I see." His voice was grim.

She looked up at his tone, but he added nothing else. She began to cut her meat and was later to remember that the meal was almost finished before he casually mentioned that he was catching a train for Washington the next morning.

"Because of what happened at the plant?" she asked, surprised.

"Yes, among other things."

"Reife, you can trust me. I'm not going to ask you to betray any classified information which you may have…"

He interrupted, "Classified information?"

"Reife, I'm not stupid. I know you see people at the very highest levels in Washington."

He said nothing.

"I can't help but think you have a suspect in mind for the break-in. Is it my father?"

"Good God, no. Where did you get that idea?"

"Then who?"

"I was going to tell you anyway. Several things point to one person—Blake. He knew where the designs were kept. He knew about the *Friends of Britain Variety Show* and that many of the workforce would be absent that night. He didn't want to maim or kill; his motive was strictly to gain possession of the tank plans. When he was here at Christmas he made a big pretence of leaving to go back to England, but I don't think he left until after the burglary." Reife carefully placed his napkin beside his plate and added thoughtfully, "The FBI doesn't think he did the actual break-in. Some local hired gun did that, but they believe Blake planned it, took the stolen designs, and hightailed it out of America." Here Reife paused then added, "They are quite certain that there's an accomplice within our company that we don't know about yet."

"Oh, Reife. I can hardly believe it's one of the employees!"

"Nevertheless, it's almost certainly true," he said, shifting his eyes to study the outside crowd of shoppers through the window. "It was possibly someone who was at the variety show but who had lined up the whole thing beforehand. Do you want dessert?"

"No, do you?"

He laid bills on the little tray with the check that the waiter had discreetly laid on the table. "Come on, let's get you bundled up."

As they drove up in front of her house she asked, "Will you come in?"

"No. My train leaves early and I'm not finished packing."

"Do you know when you'll be back?"

"No, but I'll send you a telegram from Washington," he said as he lifted her chin, brushed her lips with his, and took her door key from her to unlock the door. They stepped inside the entrance hall. He drew her into his arms. She hesitated, and then impulsively wrapped her arms around him. His arms tightened.

He lifted her chin and looked into her eyes as if searching for something. Apparently, he found it because he smiled into her eyes. Then suddenly, he released her. "Keep the home fires burning," he said, and was gone.

Chapter 19

Reife called from Washington in the middle of the week to ask Averill to consult his appointment book and give him the dates Blake had visited him at the office. He sounded preoccupied, not offering any information except to say he expected to be back in the office by Monday.

On the next day, Valentine's Day, a blustery, cold Friday dawned. Averill arrived at her office and was shrugging out of her coat when Anita at the switchboard rang to say that Joan Conover was on the line.

"Yes, Joan?" she flung down her handbag on the desk which skidded into her in-basket and in turn toppled the mail which caused the tray to bounce on the wooden floor until it came to a stop against a door, scattering mail in every direction.

"What a great clatter! Did you knock something over?" Joan's voice held a laugh.

"Just the mail tray. They were mostly bills."

"Good! Best place for them. Hey, would you have lunch today with me at the Olympian Restaurant? They make a great chili despite being Greek."

Averill stepped from an entryway where bare concrete floor and plain white walls opened into a long, narrow room whose floors were weathered oak. Grecian artifacts, anonymous pictures of ancestors in Grecian dress, and what looked to be small everyday kitchen tools from the past hung thick on the walls. This array so successfully covered the walls that only with determined focus could one see the background of rich cobalt blue. A small snack bar held customers perched on tapestry-upholstered stools; beyond that there were tables covered with white tablecloths, each centered with a small vase holding wildflowers, while further on, a partial wall emerged into view and beyond that a curved line of booths. The room was buttressed overhead by thick heavy beams, which appeared to be discolored by years of open fires.

Her eyes dwelt on a smallish blue- and white-tiled fireplace crackling with flames tucked into the wall as the hostess led her past the snack bar, onward through the close-placed tables and around the half-wall into the booth area. Joan was settled into one of these, wire-rimmed reading glasses balanced on her nose, perusing the morning's newspaper; across from her and beyond the narrow walkway, another small fireplace burned with great vigor.

"I've ordered chili and salad for both of us. That okay?" Joan asked, laying aside her paper as Averill slid into the booth across from her.

"Chili sounds wonderful. I'm glad you called." said Averill, removing her gloves to unbutton her coat and slide it from her shoulders.

"Are you settled in your new office yet?" Joan asked.

"Yes. It's still a little disorganized, but I have more space than I did."

"I'm glad something good came out of that appalling explosion. I still find it hard to believe that no one was injured or killed."

Averill said reflectively, "I think I agree with Reife that the goal was simply to steal the plans while making a conscious effort to see that no one was injured or killed."

"You mean because it was done when the security guard was on his lunch break?"

"Yes, that and the fact that so many of the staff and workers were attending the *Friends of Britain Variety Show*.

"If Nick Fahrenheit weren't in prison, I'd say he did it. He certainly didn't have any scruples about causing bodily harm," said Joan.

The waitress appeared with a huge tray balanced on one hand and with the other deftly unloaded salads and chili. "It's a busy day for you, isn't it, Delphi?" Joan commented to the dark-eyed server whose crisp blue denim dress with white apron was the standard apparel for The Olympian's staff.

"I'm run off my legs here these days what with the cold weather and everybody wanting chili to warm them up. Good to see you, Mrs. Conover," Delphi slipped the empty tray under her arm perching it on one hip. "Haven't seen you in here for awhile. She looked over her shoulder to a customer who called out, "Hey, Del, how's about a warm-up?" and sang back, "Hang on to your shirt, Morris."

She picked up their menus, stooping to pick up a fallen napkin. "Be back to check on you," she promised and departed, apron strings swinging.

Averill took a bite of chili and hastily reached for her water.

"Careful, it's hot," Joan warned, rather late in the day. Then abruptly, she said, "Averill, I just want to tell you that in one way I was wrong about the variety show and you were right. Of course, in another way my fears were justified. The person or persons who broke into the company office took advantage of the variety show and chose that time on purpose."

"They would have found another time maybe not so safe," Averill agreed.

Joan chased a piece of tomato across her salad plate, speared it, and chomped meditatively. "Reife has told you who he suspects, hasn't he?"

"Yes." Averill said, and added, "I never did like that man."

"Me, either. Anyway, just for the record I wanted you to know that I think you did a marvelous job of the organization for the variety show and Peter and I enjoyed your piano solos very much."

"Thank you. That's kind of you to say so." A glowing end of log crumbled into the fire with a whisper during a moment of sudden quietness in the dining room.

In self-conscious silence, they once more gave attention to their food. Before the silence could become strained Joan resumed, "I was just reading about how Roosevelt is pushing Congress relentlessly for the Lend-Lease bill."

"It would certainly ease the drain on England's finances," remarked Averill, breaking off a piece of cornbread from one of the muffins placed on the table in a napkin-lined basket and popping it into her mouth.

"It will be a lifesaver for them," Joan pronounced firmly. "Instead of them having to pay cash for supplies we could give them whatever they need on credit."

"Good old FDR," said Averill. "He has been a pleasant surprise to those of us who think that America will be forced into this war and need to prepare for it."

"Yes," said Joan. "That wily blueblood is secretly moving heaven and earth to be a friend to England during her dark days. Churchill must be on his knees praying daily that Roosevelt comes to England's rescue with military aid," she added, squeezing a wedge of lemon into her iced tea.

"Do you think the United States will declare war?"

"I personally don't think so unless we are attacked. My fear is for Peter. He flies, you know, and wants to go into the Army Air Force and train to be a fighter pilot."

Averill considered this in sympathetic silence. Then she offered, "I've heard it said that war to women is the fate of one man, but I think that's changing now. More and more women are going into the services." She nibbled on a scrap of lettuce, a faraway look in her eyes and added, "If I enlisted, I think I'd choose the WAVEs. They get to wear such cute little suits."

"Now that's a very feminine reason to choose a branch of service," laughed Joan. "You know, I never come into The Olympian without remembering that this is where I met Peter."

"Oh? How did that happen?" Averill asked, buttering a muffin.

"I was eating lunch with friends and he was sitting across the aisle with a couple of buddies. One of the girls knew them and asked if they wanted to bring their food over and eat with us. Consequently, they squished in beside us with Peter landing almost in my lap; I found I didn't mind at all."

Averill gave her a slow companionable smile. "That was romantic."

Joan's eyes grew soft with remembrance. "Yes, wasn't it? It was love at first sight for both of us."

"What happened then?" asked Averill, intrigued and flattered that Joan would confide in her.

"We just kidded around and the other girls flirted a bit…"

"…and you joined in," Averill teased, pushing aside her empty chili bowl and positioning her iced tea in front of her.

"Well, yes. After a while, everyone was gone but Peter and me. We sat there, it must have been two or three hours, and just talked. He asked me out and we never looked back. We were both dating someone else at the time but that didn't matter. They were instant history. I don't think Lloyd Summers ever forgave me. He was my boyfriend at the time. To this day he is very stiff and formal around me."

"Did he eventually marry?" Averill asked, sipping her tea.

"No, as a matter of fact, he didn't."

"To think you broke someone's heart that badly. It must make a person mad with power," she teased.

"Oh, it does, it does," she grinned at Averill and took her last spoonful of chili then observed, "Peter is ten years older than I, and my parents—and I think his—had reservations; but he's the only man for me. We've been very happy. The only fly in the ointment is that we've never had children. We both want them but it just never happens."

"Would you consider adoption?"

"Possibly. How about you? Have you ever thought about marriage and having a family?"

"Occasionally," Averill said, in a neutral voice. She wondered what Joan would say if she spoke aloud her thoughts: *only after meeting your brother.* She took a long drink of tea and said, "College kept me pretty busy, and I always wanted to get into teaching, and then of course, there was my music so I really never gave much thought to it."

Joan chewed on her lemon meditatively and then offered, "I always hoped Reife and Lyneire Dubuq would make a match of it but now I'm not so sure she's the woman for him."

"Why is that?" asked Averill, carefully.

"Well, for one thing, I don't think he's in love with her." Joan gave Averill a shuttered look while a faint smile tugged at her lips.

When Averill didn't comment Joan dropped her eyes to the menu that Delphi had dropped on their table in passing and said briskly, "Would you like dessert? There are Greek pastries. Their baklava is heavenly."

"No, I don't think so. I have letters to write for Reife. What about you?"

"Not if you don't. I don't like to eat dessert alone. That's why I don't eat them much. Peter doesn't like sweets."

"Now that's hard to imagine."

"Yes, isn't it?"

"This has been enjoyable," said Joan, reaching for her coat. "Shall we go?"

The workweek ended with no word from Reife. As Averill was covering her typewriter, Henrietta telephoned and asked her to go bowling the next afternoon. "I have something to tell you," she enthused, her voice more breathless than normal.

"Tell me now."

"No, I want to see your face when I tell you."

Averill arrived first at the bowling alley and went to their favorite alley, which was vacant. Shrugging off her coat and throwing it into a corner, she hiked up her plaid pleated skirt with its baggy 'Sloppy Joe' sweater atop, and changed into her bowling shoes. Henrietta arrived and tossed off a U.S. Navy pea jacket covering an old high school cheerleading sweater, thick cream wool emblazoned with a purple 'C'. For Henrietta, leading cheers and being voted "Miss Central High" in her senior year had been the zenith of her life until Klaus. She plopped down a heavy bag with her bowling ball and breathlessly announced, "Guess what?"

"I give up."

She stepped back a step and watched Averill's face. "That last week of December when I told you I was visiting my grandmother, I really went to Washington to see Klaus and we were married by the Chaplain there. I'm pregnant!"

"Henrietta, you're joking!"

"No, it's true. I'm so happy I think I'll go tap dance on Walnut Street Bridge. Isn't it wonderful? I never thought it would turn out like this. At one time I truly believed it was over for us."

Privately, Averill was aghast, but rallied a somewhat ambivalent response. She hugged Henrietta. "I'm happy if you are. Really, I am." Then she said. "When is the baby due?"

"In late September." He wants me to visit him in a couple of weeks at Fort Sill in Oklahoma, and," she paused for maximum effect, "I'm going!"

After a pause Averill managed, "But...how about school?"

"How about it? That's what substitutes are for, isn't it?" Henrietta dimpled in happiness, swung her ball rather wildly, whereupon it landed in the gutter halfway down the lane and rolled harmlessly into the well behind the pins. "What a rotten way to begin. I must be hungrier than I thought. Let's hurry and finish our game so we can eat."

"Grab a package of crackers and something to drink. Now that I'm here, I'm in the mood to bowl. We can eat later at Town and Country," protested Averill.

"Bossy," Henrietta said, happily heading for the snack bar.

Two hours later they collapsed onto the bench after some extremely lack-luster bowling the scores of which they cheerfully dismissed. "Now I'm ready for food," declared Averill. "My treat."

Over lunch, Henrietta chattered non-stop. Her plans were to take the Greyhound Express Bus Service to Oklahoma City and ride a local bus to Fort Sill, Oklahoma.

"At least with the express you won't stop at every fork in the road," Averill commented. "Where will you stay when you arrive?"

"Klaus has a friend in prison whose sister will let me stay with her. She is going to pick me up at the bus station in Fort Sill."

"What is your mother saying about all this?" Averill wanted to know.

"Oh, same as you. Wholeheartedly against it," replied Henrietta and gave her a sly look.

So she had noticed Averill's unspoken reservations.

"I'm sorry it was so obvious."

"To be perfectly frank, Averill, Klaus said you especially would be against him because…" Henrietta stopped abruptly.

"Because of what?"

She hesitated and finished brutally, "Because he accused your father of defrauding the government."

Averill was silent. She pushed her half-eaten hamburger away and pulled her coffee cup in front of her.

"Averill, please don't be hurt."

"I'm not hurt. It's just that my father was cleared." *And Klaus wasn't*, the unsaid tag hung over them. "I'm sorry, Henrietta. I have no business raining on your parade."

Monday morning at breakfast Annie said, "It's odd that Fortuna hasn't been back to his room since he left Saturday morning. Did he say he was going to be out of town this weekend?

"No. He'll have to re-surface this morning, because of his job," she answered, disinterestedly.

But as the day advanced, there was no Fortuna. Averill called her mother from work and asked her to check his room.

"He's not here, Averill," her mother rang back to say.

That afternoon her phone rang; it was Edward.

"Edward! How nice to speak with you. Are you in town?"

"For a short time. Will you have dinner with me tonight?"

"I'd love to."

"I'll pick you up at six-thirty. That okay?"

"Very okay."

Settled in a booth at The Blue Plate, Averill said, "Tell me all about what you've been doing since I left you in Washington. I thought you were going back to England."

"I had to stay for Klaus's trial. After that was over, I needed to tie up some loose ends. You look wonderful. Did you get my Christmas card?"

"Yes. Thank you."

"I saw Reife in Washington. Ran into him on the street, as a matter of fact. He told me about the explosion you had here."

"It happened the night of the *Friends of Britain Variety Show*. Most of the company who weren't working the second shift were at the show."

"Have they caught who did it?"

"No. The police and FBI are working on it."

He nodded and cut his meat thoughtfully, then changed the subject. "How is Henrietta?"

She told him about Henrietta and Klaus's marriage. His face grew solemn and he said slowly and evenly, "She's a little fool. He's not only a crook, but now there's some suspicion that he's been spying for Germany."

"Spying? On the British."

"I'm afraid so. And maybe against America, too."

There floated through Averill's mind a stupendous thought. Had Klaus been working with whoever stole the tank plans? Were both he and Blake responsible for the theft? She wanted to ask Edward what he thought, but she couldn't betray Reife's confidence. She twirled her glass around and around.

Edward reached into his pocket. "Forget about Ernst. I have something for you." He drew out a small box wrapped in shiny red with a white bow. "It's a late Valentine for you."

"Edward, how sweet."

She peeled off the paper, lifted the engraved lid, 'Kay's Jewelers', delved into the tissue and cotton, and pulled out a bracelet of linked amethysts.

"It's beautiful, but Edward…"

"Don't say a word. I wanted to do it. If nothing else, think of it as a friendship bracelet. Here, let me help you put it on."

As he turned her wrist over to fasten the bracelet, she thought with some regret how she and Edward had a lot more in common than she and Reife. Why couldn't she have fallen in love with him? It would have been a comfortable love and would have pleased both families. Love, she thought ruefully, when she again took up her napkin and watched the bracelet flash violet sparks under the low lights, never happened in well-organized ways.

Dinner over, Edward drove Averill home. He pulled up in front of her house and parked his car behind another in the driveway.

"Whose car?" he asked.

"I have no idea. Will you come in?" Averill asked. "Mother wasn't here when you came for me. I know she'd love to see you."

"I'd like that."

Upon entering, they saw the U.S. Army Officer's coat and cap hanging on the coat rack. A male voice was rising and falling with her mother's quieter voice interspersed at intervals. She stepped to the kitchen door, Edward close behind. There, sitting at the kitchen table were her mother and father. Her mother had been crying.

Chapter 20

Averill felt nailed to the living room hardwood floor. It took a few seconds to orient herself to the fact that her father was here instead of in England.

"Hello, Dad," she finally managed to say, and she stepped into the kitchen to hug him.

"Hello, Averill."

She turned quickly to her mother. "Mom, are you all right?"

Annie Lowe cleared her face of tears with her napkin and said firmly, "I'm fine." She rose and held out her hand to Edward. "It's good to see you again, Edward. We're having cherry pie. Have you and Averill had dessert already?"

"Yes," replied Edward who had regained his aplomb more quickly than Averill, "but it wasn't your pie."

"I won't have any right now, Mom," said Averill.

"Well, sit down, both of you. Averill, there's coffee. Why don't you pour yourselves cups?"

Averill knew her mother well enough to know that she was ill at ease but trying to hide it. Annie served a piece of the cherry pie to Edward. "Will you have another piece, Bernard?" she asked her husband.

"No, thanks, Annie."

Her father's eyes had been fastened on the table, the walls, anywhere but on Averill. Now he looked at her and asked, "Reife told me about the bombing at Braddock. How are things?"

"Reife's and my office received the damage. The plant, thank God, escaped."

He nodded and went back to studying the table cloth.

"Did you come from England to ask about Braddock Engineering?" Averill asked and immediately realized it might sound sarcastic considering her feelings the last time she saw him. She added a smile to buffer any sting.

"That and other things," her father said, equably. "I didn't get to England, as a matter of fact. I've been in the states since I saw you in Washington."

"You have?"

"That's the other reason I came to see you and Annie. I want to tell you why I was detained in Washington." With a desperate determination, he plunged into the tale about the suspicions of fraud leveled at him by Klaus Ernst and the sabotage charges leveled at him because of his relationship with Jo Blake. "Our latest information is that Blake is on the run," he finished after telling them of the guilty verdict against Klaus.

"Blake was up to his neck in it all the time," nodded Averill, with satisfaction.

"Mr. Blake is most probably on the high seas by now," responded Col. Lowe.

"Mr. Blake?" asked Annie, who had said not a word until now.

"He's no more a group captain than I am."

Averill restrained herself from asking where all this put Jo Blake as Blake's sister, but she wouldn't do that to her mother. Edward's suspicion of Klaus sprang to her mind. "Is Ernst a member of this ring, Dad, as well as being a thief?"

"We don't know. He's been convicted of fraud only up to this point."

"My friend, Henrietta, has married him."

"What? Marry Ernst? She'll rue the day."

"She won't listen to anything said against him."

"The few times I saw him in England I noticed he has a way with women," Lowe said dryly.

Averill suddenly got up and slid closed the kitchen pocket door.

"Are you afraid your boarder, Medina, may overhear?" smiled her father, turning to her as she resumed her seat. "If so, I can rest your mind on that. He was arrested Saturday morning at his barber's."

"Arrested? Why?" asked Averill, astonished.

Her mother gasped and exclaimed, "Fortuna? He wouldn't hurt a fly."

"I'm afraid you're wrong there, Annie. He would hurt whole swarms of flies. He has a violent past." Lowe turned to Averill and asked, "Your former employee, Nick Fahrenheit, is in prison, isn't he?"

"Yes. He went berserk and attacked our accountant. He claims he only wanted to injure her so she couldn't work for a few days; but she developed complications and died in the hospital."

Lowe said, "When Fortuna was employed at Braddock they then had an operative inside to gain the combination to the safe where the tank designs were held." Lowe took a sip of coffee and continued. "In the end, they blew the safe after Fortuna failed to get the combination."

"Fortuna was colossally thick-headed to expect he'd be given access to the safe. Reife would never have allowed that information to an accountant."

"So he discovered. The break-in no doubt was faked. Fortuna had a key to the front entrance he could give his accomplices. It had to look like forced entry for his alibi."

"Yes, he was conveniently backstage at the benefit helping with things during the burglary," said Averill.

"Oh, I almost forgot." Lowe reached to an inner pocket of his uniform and pulled out an envelope. "Reife asked me to give this to you." Beside her, Edward made an involuntary movement.

Averill placed the envelope on the table with its single word, 'Averill,' written in Reife's sprawling handwriting. Fervently, she wished she were alone so she could read it but assumed a casual air. "The first thing I'd better see to is hiring a temporary replacement for our accounting department. If I don't, I'll have to do it myself and I haven't the time."

Edward rose to his feet. "Thanks for the pie, Mrs. Lowe. I must be off." Averill walked with him to the entrance of the house. "I'll call you," he said, gave her a quick one-armed hug, pulled on his coat, reached for his hat, and was gone. She re-entered the kitchen where her mother and father sat, and in that short absence there had been words spoken which left no doubt that this was far from a reconciliation. Her mother was barely holding her anger in check and on her father's face she saw guilt mixed with what she could only term as sulky resolve. He turned to Averill and said, "Your mother earlier talked about financial matters having to do with the divorce. I want her to have the house and of course I'll see that she has money."

"You don't have to talk about me as if I weren't sitting here, Bernard," Annie said in a voice choked with furious tears. "I'll tell Averill what we've talked about. Now, go."

Lowe rose, walked to the front entrance, and lifted his coat and cap off the coat rack. He turned to Averill who had followed him and said, "I'll be in touch."

Averill nodded. From the kitchen, she heard her mother begin to sob.

Chapter 21

Averill settled her mother in bed with hot milk and then read the letter from Reife. It was short and to the point. He estimated he would be another ten days in Washington and asked her to see about hiring someone for the accounting position. One of her first calls of the day the next morning was from Joan Conover, her voice concerned. "Averill, I heard about Fortuna Medina. That leaves you in the same spot you were in before you hired him, doesn't it? Do you need help with the bookkeeping?"

"I talked with Leahy's Placement Service. They're sending someone for us to interview tomorrow."

"Would you like me to take over the books until you get a permanent replacement? I majored in accounting at the University."

"Joan, that would be great. I've been wrestling with debits and credits trying to at least get the bills out and keep track of the payroll but it's certainly not my forté. Can you come in tomorrow?"

"Be there first thing in the morning."

The days that Reife spent in Washington stretched into three weeks. On a Thursday mid-morning as Joan joined her for coffee, she told Averill, "Reife is coming in tonight or rather early morning. His train will arrive around two a.m."

Averill's heart turned over and she reached for a napkin to hide her expression. Why didn't he call or telegram her? Why did she have to get the news second-hand?

She said, "Oh, really? Nice of him to let his secretary know."

Joan said, "He only called us because he wanted to talk to Peter about a point to be cleared up before he left Washington."

"Did he find Blake?"

"He has left the country. He's been tracked as far as Casablanca."

"Does he know whether Blake has the tank designs?"

"Peter didn't say."

When Averill arrived at the office the next morning, Reife was already in his office with the door closed. She was dealing with the mail when he came out, dark circles under his eyes. "Hi there," he said, leaning against the doorjamb and running a hand across his eyes.

"Hi, yourself," Averill replied, carefully neutral.

"Ready for dictation?"

She gathered her pen and pad and followed him inside the office. He took his seat behind the desk and watched her take her customary seat to his side. She had dressed with care that morning but he said nothing and his eyes dropped to his desk. "Ready?" he asked, picking up a sheaf of papers.

Averill replied coolly, "Of course."

He flashed her a quick glance, smiled; she relaxed and smiled back. The first letter was to an address in Cairo asking that England's MI6 keep an eye open for one Group Captain Blake, posing as an English officer with stolen property in his possession. Letter followed letter, and after that several interoffice memos. Joan popped her head in. "Leahy has sent an applicant for the accounting position."

"That's the lot for now," Reife said, nodding at Joan. "Send him in when you return to your desk, will you, Averill?"

As Averill passed her going out Joan grinned and suggested, "That might be a little hard to do. He's a she."

Averill found a very thin woman with sausage-like curls packed from the top of her head down the sides of her hairline. The rest of her hair was pulled tightly in a bun in the back. Her face was devoid of color except for a startling gash of red lipstick. Hanging on her almost emaciated frame was a neatly pressed suit and a starched white blouse fitted over her small chest as devoid of a woman's curves as a man's. She introduced herself as Miss Blanche White. She emphasized the Miss.

"How nice to see you, Miss White. Do you have a résumé?" Averill asked.

The woman indicated a letter-sized leather portfolio in her hand. "Yes, of course."

"Mr. Braddock will see you now."

Twenty minutes later the woman emerged from Reife's office and swept out the door, her face grim. Reife was behind her and shook his head mutely. Averill reached for the phone to dial the agency but it rang before she could pick it up.

Her father was on the line. "Averill, I'm leaving tomorrow to return to Washington. Can you meet me at Mrs. McLaughlin's for supper? I've been staying here, you know."

"Sure, Dad. What time do you want me there?"

"I'll pick you up from work. She serves dinner at six."

"I have my car here. Why don't I just meet you there?"

"Fine. See you at six."

At noon, Averill poked her head in Reife's door and asked him if she could bring him back a sandwich from Kaplan's. "Can you pick up a ham and cheese on rye?" he asked. Averill could, and she left for the corner lunch counter. She saw Miss White waiting at the bus stop and spoke pleasantly to her. Miss White grunted a reply. The wind was cold and Averill could pity any woman some years past her prime who had boarded a bus on a cold February day with a hopeful heart and was now going home to a possibly bleak rented room and no work. The job market was still struggling in February of 1941.

Back at her desk she finished typing up the morning's dictation, her mind occupied with thoughts that it was today that Henrietta was leaving for Fort Sill to visit Klaus. She stamped the last envelope and rose from her desk to lean against a window. Outside a lone birdfoot violet was pushing its way through a crack in the pavement of the parking lot. Brave little flower, she thought. Maybe Henrietta was right. Maybe she and Klaus could make their marriage work even though there were walls of obstacles stacked against them. And there was the baby. A sudden stab of envy surprised her. *Lucky Henrietta going to have a baby.* She turned and went to work.

Reife had a luncheon meeting with the Iron Workers United at the Read House. Passing her desk he paused. "Will you have dinner with me tomorrow night?"

"Yes. Yes, that would be lovely."

"Good. I'll look forward to it." Smiling into her eyes Averill saw his pupils widen and the flame behind the cobalt blue eyes appear. All the waiting, all the anxiety, all the fear she had that he might feel differently when he returned from Washington vanished. He rapped the desk with his knuckles lightly and replied, "See you in the morning," and left, coat tails flying. She looked after him. What a weakling she was! If she had any willpower she would quit her job—not pretend to herself that she and Reife could remain only friends.

Then came another night spent tossing in bed, determining to be detached, unmoved in his presence, exercising caution and restraint. She would not let herself fall in love with him. She would quit her job first. She would…

No, not quit her job. That wasn't an option. She was doing vital work and the United States was headed into fateful days as a nation. She couldn't leave a company who was producing the armaments the nation would need if it went to war. Toward the early hours of the morning she slept.

After Averill and her father had eaten with the rest of the boarders at Mrs. McLaughlin's boarding house, Col. Lowe led her into the little conservatory off the main living room. "Let's sit here, Averill. This room is rarely used. Maybe later you'll play for me," he added, gesturing to a spinet piano in the corner of the room.

Averill sank into a cushiony wing chair that flanked the unlit fireplace. She shivered with the cold.

"Why don't I make a fire? You're cold."

"Please."

Her father crumpled some old newspapers that lay beside the fireplace for that purpose, stooped, and piled up the logs. She watched him work and asked, "What time does your train leave tomorrow?"

"Early."

"I'll come and take you to the station."

"There's no use for that. I'll take a taxi."

"It's no trouble."

"No. Let's say our goodbyes tonight."

"All right, Dad. Maybe that would be better."

Col. Lowe reached for more paper, stood and took a long match from a vase on the mantel, lit the fire, and dusted his hands together. "I saw Reife at the Century Group meeting today. Has he had a chance to talk with you about all that happened in Washington?"

"A little."

He appeared lost in thought for a minute and then said, "Blake's been seen in Egypt."

"Why do you suppose he's in Egypt?"

Col. Lowe reached for the poker, and prodded the fire. He rose, dropped the poker in its holder, strode to the window, shoved his hands into his pockets, and went after the question in an oblique manner. "After trouncing Italy in North Africa, the English have chased them out of Egypt and across Libya and destroyed almost 500 of their tanks. Now, the Germans have formed the Afrika Corps and appointed German Field Marshall Rommel their commander. We believe Blake is attempting to smuggle Braddock's tank designs to him. We think Rommel has plans to set up a factory near the battlefield in pre-fabricated buildings flown in by cargo planes with the raw material needed, use the stolen designs to lathe the tank parts, and assemble his tanks onsite. This will give him a huge advantage in his goal to seize Egypt for the Nazis."

"Quite an ambitious undertaking," Averill commented thoughtfully, "and dangerously ingenious if they could manage to pull it off."

"We must manage to see that they don't."

"How did Fortuna Medina get involved?"

"Medina was always in sympathy with Fascist Italy and the Nazis—professing, of course, just the opposite."

She said, "That reminds me. One Sunday I saw Blake at church and he asked me to have lunch with him. Afterwards, when he was dropping me off at home he saw our boarder coming out of our house. I got the faintest of impressions that Fortuna checked himself in astonishment at the sight of Blake."

"He no doubt was bowled over. Here was his controller on his doorstep. It must have given him an unpleasant moment."

"That was the day that Blake told me Klaus Ernst's father was a Nazi and he spoke so vehemently against their regime. He seemed so credible in his anger."

"Yes. Well, he would, wouldn't he? There's a very good reason he knew about Ernst's father. We have information that Blake was his former aide."

After a pause she asked, "Will you be returning to England soon?"

"Yes, quite soon."

Mrs. McLaughlin poked her head around the corner of the door. "Col. Lowe," she said, holding out a newspaper, "you asked to let you know when your evening newspaper arrived. They were late with it—some late-breaking news someone said. Anyway, here it is."

Lowe glanced at the headlines of the *Chattanooga News-Free Press*, took his seat, and spread out the newspaper. "Roosevelt has signed the Lend-Lease bill," he said, scanning the lead story.

"The program where we are allowed to extend credit to England for war equipment?" asked Averill.

"Yep. We've just helped save England. They've been fighting all alone for over a year. They couldn't have held out much longer without our supplies. This is great news. This is the next best thing we can do for them."

"And the best thing?"

"Declare war on Germany, of course, and help England fight the Nazis. It's going to come to that in the end, anyway."

"Americans will never accept that."

"Not unless we're provoked. There could be an incident similar to the sinking of the *Lusitania*, the vessel Germany sank with American passengers aboard, which brought the U.S. into World War I against the Germans. Or Japan could conceivably attack Hawaii."

"Japan? Attack Hawaii? But, why?"

"They need more land for their growing population. Their factories need imported oil and other raw materials for their war against Manchuria and China because they don't have them in that small island nation. If the United States should slap an embargo of oil on them for their aggression in China, which Congress has threatened to do, they will certainly declare war."

"I remember way back when I first met Klaus as a fellow teacher. He said much the same thing even then. It seems we are teetering on the edge of a second world war, Dad."

"I'm afraid so. The history of Western Civilization may be hanging in the balance."

"I can't help but think of what Mordecai said to Esther in the Old Testament, '...who knoweth whether thou art come to the kingdom for such a time as this?'" reflected Averill, who had been reading about women in the Bible. "Maybe 1776 gave birth to a nation that will play its part in saving the world."

"I've never been a religious man, but you may have something there, Averill."

"If you had been, maybe you would never have become involved with Jo Blake," Averill said on impulse.

Her father stiffened in his chair. Then he asked softly, "Did you have to ruin the last night we have?"

"Dad, sometimes I think you're a little boy. Don't you understand at all what the intrusion of this woman into your life has done to mother and me?"

"No, to be frank I guess I don't. All I can see is what she has brought into my life."

"At least you're honest," Averill said, rose, and held out her hand to her father. "Have a good trip, Dad. Let me hear from you."

"You're going now?"

"I think so."

"I wanted to hear you play," Col. Lowe said, gesturing to the piano.

"What would you like to hear?"

"Anything you like, for as long as you like."

She began with some of *Hungarian Dance Number 5* by Brahms who she knew was one of her father's favorites, played a jazzy rendition of *After You're Gone*, and finished with a boogie-woogie classic, *The Charleston Rag*. She rose from the bench.

Her father threw out his hand and said, "Wait. Do you know *White Cliffs of Dover*?

"Of course." She played the arrangement she had done for the *Friends of Britain Variety Show*. She finished with the last note, looked over at her father, and asked, "Okay?"

"Sing the words, Averill."

She played the simple tune again and sang the words. She looked over at her father and saw tears running down his cheeks. She rose from the piano bench, stepped over, and hugged him. She bent down with her cheek against his and his tears splashed onto her neck. After a minute, he reached for his handkerchief and said, "Forgive me, Averill."

"It's all right, Dad. I cried the night I performed it for the variety show."

"Not only that... but for....everything." He struggled to his feet and they walked to the front door together.

"Goodbye, Dad. Stay safe."

"Goodbye, Averill."

She got into her car and the last thing she saw before she turned the corner was her father standing on the porch of the boarding house watching her as she drove out of sight.

Chapter 22

On March 11, 1941 the Lend-Lease bill was signed by FDR which offered, as Churchill put it, "The loan of a fire hose to a neighbor whose house is on fire." Now, instead of waiting for the British to sail into New York Harbor with cash payments, U.S. ships conveyed the goods to Reykjavík, Iceland where the British transports met the ships and loaded the goods into their holds. Then they started the treacherous 1,000-mile voyage to Liverpool, England through waters infested with German submarines and ships. Germany protested U.S. presence in the neutral shipping lanes around Iceland by threatening and harassing the U.S. ships. America responded by hoards volunteering for these hazardous sea duties in spite of the fact that shortly after the bill for Lend-Lease was passed German U-Boats began attacking and sinking the U.S. convoys.

In June Averill and Pris were having a working lunch at her desk when the radio on Pris's desk suddenly broke off playing music and announced Germany had declared war on Soviet Russia.

"How can that be?" Pris asked. "Germany and Russia are allies. They have a non-aggression pact with each other."

"You know what they say, Pris," said Averill taking a bite of her toasted cheese sandwich, "there's no honor among thieves."

Later Reife told Averill, "Stalin's intelligence agency, the NKVD, has known for weeks that Germany's troops were massing at the Russian border, but he wouldn't believe that Hitler would attack him. He was caught totally unprepared, and now the Russians will have to fight for their lives. Just watch. He'll start whining that the U.S. share the Lend-Lease goodies with him and ask us to provide materials to help him fight his former buddy." He picked up a scrawled memo, preparatory to dictating a letter. "Still—it's great news for the Allies. With Russia fighting against Germany, she can't be fighting with Hitler against Great Britain and her Empire."

In the coming days Averill watched Reife, who she knew would not ask of his workers anything that he would not do himself, walk around with eyes that had permanent black circles under them while he offered double shifts and overtime to any machinist who could stay awake. After the July 1941 blockade of oil shipments to Japan, American citizens watched Germany and Japan engineer ingredients for all-out war. The United States was nudged into their gunsights, and its factories stepped up production, although anti-war sentiment was still strong. The small round table in the corner of Reife's office was permanently occupied by Findley Braddock or foremen poring over blueprints.

Averill began working nights and Saturdays and, on occasion, a Sunday to keep the executive offices running smoothly, coming home too exhausted to eat. Braddock senior—in his mid-seventies—began a sixty-hour workweek, and his voluminous correspondence was added to Averill's duties.

On the first evening of August, Reife and Averill were seated in a secluded booth at the Read House dining room where they ordered the famous Read House Beef Stew with salads and began to talk about their childhoods. Tucking into her salad, Averill talked about her fluent Arabic. "I was so young when we lived in Egypt that it was a close second to English as a native tongue. I learned to bargain with the shop owners in the bazaars by watching my father haggle, and, in the process, picked up quite a lot of street Arabic. Mother, on the other hand, insulated herself by clinging to the little enclave of English-speaking military and never attempted to learn Arabic."

"Your father's knowledge of Arabic is one of the reasons why the military has sent him to North Africa on this special mission. Didn't he tell you?" Reife added clumsily, after observing the leap of surprise into her eyes.

"No." Averill paused midway in lifting her fork to her mouth and stared at Reife.

"Perhaps he was afraid you would beg him not to go and make it harder for him to leave."

"I think he knows me better than that. If he's needed he should go; of course he should."

"The United States and England are desperate to keep the plans Blake stole from falling into the hands of the Germans," said Reife "Your father's job will be to find Blake before this happens. I'm afraid this will be a bit of a shock to you because your father hasn't prepared you or your mother for this, but, well, he leaves tonight on a Swedish freighter bound for the North African coast and Cairo."

Averill froze. "Oh, Reife," she cried. "Vichy France, Italy, and Germany all have their sights set on Gibraltar. Any ship will have to pass through the Straits to get to North Africa. To say nothing of getting there across the Atlantic Ocean swarming with German U-boats spreading across the water from the New England coast to Iceland and down to Cherbourg."

"Yes, but he'll be sailing under the neutral flag of Sweden, and the English have not been driven off Gibraltar and are defending the Strait at all costs."

"You're saying he's going to spy for America and England?"

"In a manner of speaking, yes."

"Why was he chosen for such a dangerous mission?"

"Your father will be a wily opponent. Not only does he speak Arabic like a native, he has absorbed some of the character and essence of the Egyptian culture. He is one of the few Americans I've known who thinks like an Arab. He'll wear the Egyptian *djellabah* and *keffiyeh* and live with former friends of your family as a domestic and will have a fair chance of pulling it off. Actually, I think he's excited about getting to play spy. He'll come through all right, Averill." Reife reached across the table for her hand, held it, and moved his thumb over the soft part of her hand where the thumb and forefinger joined. "The Allies must win this war, else..."

"Else we'll live to one day see the Nazis dominate the world. We have to work like the Three Furies to keep these tank designs out of their hands, don't we?" Averill tightened her hand on his, glad of Reife's comforting presence when she thought of her father and the terrible danger he would encounter.

Reife studied her. "He once said you have a high amount of courage."

"I don't know that it's more than anyone else's courage, but I do know that having courage doesn't mean you're not scared."

"No," Reife replied thoughtfully, "it means you stand and fight even though you're frightened."

Averill positioned her fork carefully at the side of her plate and sat back. Her appetite was gone.

Reife continued. "Your father reminisces quite a bit about your childhood. He once said he always pitied the bullies on the block when you sallied forth waving your shield and sword in support of the underdog."

"As I recall it was mainly swinging a jump rope in their direction, or failing that, rock-throwing. I never could abide any kind of mistreatment or injustice. My knees might be knocking but I'd wade in—both fists flailing. Really, it must have been a rather pathetic sight," she said, laughing, as she reached for her coffee cup.

"Col. Lowe said he was sitting on the porch one day when a bully yelled that you were a coward and dared you to jump from a flower stand over the hedge onto the sidewalk. Before your father could stop you, you jumped."

"And cracked my skull. It's a wonder I didn't break my neck."

Reife ordered a refill of coffee and the waiter asked Averill, "Would you like another, Ma'am?"

"No, thank you." She looked out the window at the shoppers enjoying the evening breeze blowing off the Tennessee River some blocks away. In a change of subject she said, "I've always thought it a pity that Chattanooga didn't take more advantage of its Tennessee River. Many cities glory in their river. They build landscaped river walks with shopping and palladiums for concerts. They make their rivers a drawing card. Our riverbanks are littered with trash and the water is polluted with chemical waste. It's such a pity."

"There is some talk of revitalizing that area, but city government has been slow to commit the money."

"It perhaps needs the steel spine of one of Chattanooga's southern belles such as Mrs. Hedges or Mrs. Patten to get it started," suggested Averill.

"I can see your mind ticking over and Lady Averill to the rescue. Move over, city government," said Reife, laughing at her.

"I might at that. But first, we need to help England win this war or it won't matter whether our river area is a thing of beauty or not."

"Want to see a movie, or just walk awhile?"

"Let's walk."

They made their way along Broad Street to the river. The moonlight threw gauze over the river and turned its muddy surface into silver ripples. Three blocks east from where they paused at river's edge, stood the Walnut Street Bridge stretching across the river connecting downtown Chattanooga with North Chattanooga and Signal Mountain. Traffic was light, and, aside from any derelict that might inhabit one of the falling-down sheds, they were alone. In the distance they could see Jim Braddock's small skiff riding at anchor down the bank from Braddock Engineering's night-shrouded bricks and belching chimneys. They ambled back to the main part of town to where Reife parked the car and passed the deserted concrete cubicle where the attendant for the lot had closed down for the night.

"Averill," said Reife as he turned to her.

"What is it?"

"Nothing. Only..." and before she could react, he pulled her against him, held her against the bricks, and kissed her with increasing passion. With mindless response, she wrapped her arms around him and pulled him close. At that moment her world drew its boundaries around a square yard of ground near a dark Chattanooga parking lot. Gradually, he released her, looked down at her and murmured, "My little love." Taking a step back, he said hoarsely, "I couldn't help that; somehow I don't think you minded."

Averill's answer was low and shaken. "You know I didn't."

"After this war...," he said and stopped. Then he stepped back, pulled her into an encircled arm, and led her to where he had parked his car. "Everything must wait until this war is won."

All through August Averill heard nothing from Col. Lowe and now Chattanoogans were coming back into the city from their summer retreats around Chickamauga Dam, cottages in Summertown on Walden's Ridge, and beaches in Florida. It was toward the end of the first week in September after Reife had ended a telephone call from Lord Halifax that Averill entered his office to find him standing at his window lost in thought. He turned. "The English and Egyptian military have apprehended Blake. He has agreed to turn over the tank designs in return for British Sterling and free passage to Berlin. They need me to come to Egypt to verify that the designs that Blake turns over are genuine. I leave tonight on a military transport out of Fort Oglethorpe."

"Reife, I lived there for ten years. Let me go too," Averill said. "Please."

"Certainly not."

"I could be of great help to you inside Egypt. One of my childhood friends is Chief of Police in Cairo."

"It will be a straight-forward transfer of the blueprints for payment. Your father and I will confront Blake, take possession of the stolen plans, and return. We should be home within the week. I need you here, Averill. I am depending on you, my father, and Russ to keep everything together while I'm gone."

That evening Reife boarded a U. S. military plane from Fort Oglethorpe, Georgia bound for Iceland where he would transfer to a British cargo ship headed for the Mediterranean and Cairo. They would enter hostile territory as soon as they sailed out of the neutral territorial waters of Reykjavík. Goering's Luftwaffe and Germany's U-boats were picking off England's ships with deadly accuracy. Averill was convinced she would never see Reife again. She cried herself to sleep.

Chapter 23

Sunday morning Averill sat in church and joined with the congregation as it sang the hymn, *O God, Our Help in Ages Past*. The familiar, comforting words seeped into her troubled heart; and during the ensuing sermon by the pastor she felt a peace descend upon her anxious mind to which she clung, trusting that God would protect both Reife and her father.

A week after Reife lifted off from the airfield at Fort Oglethorpe, she took a call from the Hamilton County Prison. Nick Fahrenheit, the worker who had killed Viola Smetts, was on the line. "Miss Lowe, you may not believe me, seeing as where I am and what I've done, but if you want to save Reife Braddock's life you will listen real good."

"I'm listening."

"First I want you to know I think about that lady I killed every hour of the day. I went crazy, Miss Lowe. That's the God's honest truth. I thought I'd been cheated out of my honest pay and I groused about it in front of that rotten no-good Nazi spy, Blake, and he asked me to just hurt Miss Smetts enough to make her miss some work. I thought he was some high-up English military man. I didn't know he was a traitor. I just wanted the money that was rightfully mine and was right riled up when I swung that hammer. But I didn't mean to kill her. It was an accident, I swear to God."

Averill said nothing. The words poured out of Fahrenheit once more. "Now, you may not believe what I'm going to tell you, but you need to listen to me. I love my country and you should know that Mr. Braddock is headed into a trap in Egypt. Blake's men are waiting for him. He needs to be warned…unless it's already too late."

This last sank through the dread that had gradually engulfed her as he spoke and chilled the very marrow in her bones. She managed to keep her voice calm. "Where did you get your information?" she asked.

"Never you mind. We on the inside have ways the outside don't know about. Just mark my words, that devil, Blake, is waiting for Mr. Braddock in Egypt and he don't have no good interest at heart except his own pocketbook. Your father ain't gonna fare too well out of all this, neither."

"My father? Where does he come into it?"

"Well, he's been in Egypt lookin' for him, ain't he?"

This was such top-secret information that only a few in Washington knew about it and, here in relatively small Chattanooga, an inmate of a local prison knew it. For a long minute she was speechless. She recalled a quote of Churchill that in wartime truth was so precious that it must be attended by a bodyguard of lies. She forced herself to speak calmly. "The last time I heard from my father he was complaining of a very boring desk job in England."

"Yeah, and Churchill's on the French Riviera frolicking with Eleanor Roosevelt. Miss Lowe, I'm tellin' you the truth here. I ain't dropped so low that I want that little German worm with the toothbrush mustache to beat the Brits to a pulp. Mr. Braddock is walking into a trap. You gotta believe me. My time's up and I hafta go. G'bye, Miss Lowe."

Averill listened to the dial tone and slowly hung up the phone. Could it be true? Even if there was the slightest chance that it was, she had to do something. But what? Could Edward help her? He was in England but she hadn't the slightest idea where; she had no idea how to contact Reife. Nor her father, for that matter. To whom could she talk? Both Reife and her father had friends in high places in Washington, but she didn't know who they were. Or did she? She thought of the top-secret correspondence in the locked files. There were names there. She ran to get the keys and unlocked the filing cabinets. She flipped through the files and read some of the names: Henry (Hap) Arnold, Bonita Bachmann, Arthur T. Harris, Averell Harriman, Harry Hopkins, Cordell Hull, Clare B. Luce, Henry Morganthau Jr., and Lord Louis Mountbatten ...who among these illustrious gentlemen and ladies would listen to her? Especially if they knew she got her information from an incarcerated, convicted killer? It was hopeless...unless...

She reached her party after two hours of wrangling with overseas operators and, by dint of her knowledge of the Arabic language, greeted her long-ago playmate in Cairo with: "Sami! This is Averill Lowe in America. Averill. Averill Lowe. Yes, it's really me. Remember the time we traveled to Luxor with my parents? We had our first camel ride. Remember the day I got lost in the bazaar and you found me at the perfume shop?"

Sami Al-Hamid responded with a profusion of staccato Arabic. Of course he remembered her. She was his dear friend. How was she doing? How could he help her?

Averill answered, "Sami, I need a place to stay in Cairo for a few days. May I stay with you and Susan?"

Of course she could stay, he returned in rapid Arabic. Then he switched to English. "I will ask no questions. You may tell me all when you get here, is not this best?"

"Yes. I will explain when I arrive. I will come to police headquarters. Would this be all right?"

"Of course, of course. It will be good to see you. We will have good times again, is this not true?"

"Yes. We'll have good times, Sami." As she hung up the phone she wondered at her own *chutzpa* in placing all her chips on an outrageous gambit to get to Cairo. To the rest of the world, she was traveling—however ill advised—to her childhood home for a visit with old friends. To only a few would it be known to be the embarkation on a dangerous trip, the outcome of which could possibly be fatal for her and the two men she loved. She picked up the phone and placed a long-distance call to Bonita Bachmann, a native of Chattanooga, and had become, through marriage, an intimate of the inner circle in Washington. She had met Bonita in Washington the year before when she and Reife were there and anytime he heard by mail from Bonita about more serious matters she had always enclosed a hand-written note to Averill containing any tittle-tattle about the Lookout Mountain and Missionary Ridge social sets to which Bonita was privy. The vivacious Bonita was a born gossip—with the exception of the security of America: there she was as silent as the loft of a cathedral at three o'clock in the morning.

Averill was never to know how Bonita arranged it, but within two days she was aboard a military plane and taking off from Fort Oglethorpe en route to Cairo, Egypt.

Part 2

September 17, 1941 – December 19, 1941

Chapter 24

The Cairo plane terminal was the same as she remembered. Men still ran around in *djellabahs* guiding huge carts piled with sweets, fruit, and pastry and aggressively challenging any who were in their way. Cries to the mercy of Allah sounded; effusive curses were heaped upon those whose hapless path intersected with theirs, even though later such trespasses might be forgotten with exuberant kisses on cheeks and a cup of mint tea enjoyed in tranquil friendliness. Shouts of "Welcome, welcome," assaulting the ears of the deplaning passengers all bore testimony that she was indeed back in Egypt. As she passed through the fence-barricaded exit, she spotted a man holding up a cardboard sign reading, 'Averill.' The man introduced himself as Torquo, a friend of Sami. Torquo pushed aside the boy who was trundling her luggage, swung it in the trunk of a dilapidated Ford, saw that she was comfortably seated in the back seat, and departed the curb in a swirl of dust. There was the familiar screech of brakes, screamed deprecations hurled out the window at other drivers, and fragrances of jasmine, cumin, sandalwood, cardamom, coriander, and oregano drifted through the open window. Nowhere did she see any existence of rules of the road as western civilization knew them.

After a stomach-churning drive through the outskirts of Cairo and finally into the city itself, they perforce drew up in front of a dirty white building whose doors stood open to the weather. Torquo escorted her from the car, leaving it where it stood, and together they advanced upon the building, avoiding almost at the very front door a huge pothole where nestled several discarded cigarette wrappers, dried orange peelings, and what looked to be the remains of someone's lunch. Ah, another sign she was in Egypt. No matter what happened, it was good to be back.

She entered a large room where it was at least ten degrees hotter than outside and what few windows existed did so at the very tops of the walls and were exceedingly small by Western standards. The stifling heat of mid-September attacked her and she stopped for a minute to get her bearings. A young man with a very dirty *djellabah* approached her with an offer to sell her beads, and Torquo pushed him away rudely. "Very ahnchant, very valuable antiquities, Missy Sahib," the man persisted at the end of Torquo's long arm. "Get lost," Torquo shouted and she, more politely, replied in Arabic, "Thank you, no." The boy jerked to attention and looked at her with new regard at hearing this American speak his language. Torquo led her past a sign reading, 'Monsieur de Legión', whose anteroom held benches filled with men passing the time of day who stopped their discussions to examine Averill with unrestrained interest but with none of the salacious once-overs she might undergo in the States. She and Torquo were waved inside a room by a guard dispassionately cleaning his fingernails with a long-bladed knife. As she entered the crowded office—all men—she was struck as of old with the lack of body odor, which she had always found idiomatic to Egyptians. There was a great clacking on decrepit typewriters on the part of some, while a larger group seemed to be engaged in whittling wooden objects with the ever-present knife or gathered around three-legged tables drinking thick Turkish coffee.

She immediately recognized her childhood friend, Sami Al-Hamid, who sat at a corner desk wearing a splendid uniform. There were evidences of Susan's loving care in the sharp creases that her iron had placed in his shirt and trousers. Dressed in a rich display of braid and gold stripes, Sami looked up as she approached. Immediately he pushed his chair from the desk, circled it, and took her hand and pressed it to his forehead with a slight bow.

"Ah, my little friend, Averill. Such a funny little name to fit such a grand woman as you have become. It is good to see you. Come; let us go into the courtyard. It is cooler there, no?"

It was quiet in the small, almost hidden, walled refuge from the bustle of the police station. A fountain of water threw sprays into the air, redolent of jasmine, spearmint, and what she guessed might be chamomile. Averill drew a deep breath. Yes, she was truly in Egypt. Sami guided her to a stone bench and they sat. In rapid-fire Arabic Sami talked of his two young sons and of his wife, Susan, who, like her, was the product of an American military family.

"She is preparing many good things to eat, Averill. Do you still like the food of your old country?"

"I adore it, Sami. It is what I miss most."

"Ah, then, you shall have it." He returned to his favorite subject: his two young sons. "They are in the

English school, you mark. Yes, they are going to the finest of English schools. They are top of the class."

At length Averill approached the subject of the reason for her visit. Sami listened carefully and thoughtfully. For such a voluminous talker, he was a surprisingly good listener.

"So there you have it, Sami," she said. "I only have the word of a prison inmate to go on, but if my employer and father are in trouble, I will need all the help I can get to find them. Would it be possible to see Blake wherever he's being held?"

"Ah. It is bad. Yes, very bad. I will do what I can to help. I did not link this Col. Lowe with the Lieutenant Lowe I knew so many years ago until your trunk call from America. This Blake. I read many dispatches concerning him, all bad, but he has escape, yes it is true, and Col. Lowe and your employer disappear. The English military search and search, and we help." He sighed as if a burden shifted on his shoulders.

"He escaped?" Averill slumped on the stone bench and there followed the polite silence which mid-eastern decorum dictates to be present after the conveyance of bad news. Presently, she lifted her chin in determination. "Sami, is there anyone you can place at my disposal to drive me around the city?"

"That can be arranged. Yes, that is easy. The hard part will be in knowing where to start. There are many dark corners in Cairo, as you well know. Some of these corners hold men who are good men who can be trusted. Some hold not so good men who would as soon slit your throat for a piaster." Averill nodded as he resumed, "I protect you as best I can. Torquo will never leave you. It would be better you wear the Egyptian clothes. Not Muslim clothes, but clothes of Coptic Christians. Our Christian women do not wear the veil. Memsahib Susan will help you. She lend you clothes that do not offend our men. The clothes you wear now announce to the world that you are rich American. You, how do you say, protrude from the crowd."

"But I'm not rich," protested Averill.

"Ah, all Americans are rich in Cairo," stated Sami. He snapped his fingers and out of nowhere there appeared a *djellabah*-gowned boy. Sami gave him rapid instructions in Arabic and the boy trotted off. "You may of course have Torquo at your discretion," said Sami and here he paused to signal to Torquo who stepped from his half-hidden spot behind a vine. "He's born in Egypt but schooled in England. He will be good guide. Yes, he will do very deli-cate-ly." To Torquo he said, "You be Miss Averill's guide while she comes to Egypt. She shall stay with us. You unload her at night and appear in mornings."

"Very good, *Effendi*," replied Torquo and turned and made a small bow to Averill.

Averill said, "I will be delighted to have you accompany me, Torquo. Thank you."

"As you say, Madam," replied Torquo.

The three of them then discussed the possibilities of starting the search in certain shops in the bazaar. Averill showed them both pictures of Reife and of her father. "There are things that call for my attention," Sami told her as he rose and turned to go. "I leave you and Torquo for now. Later, he will travel you to our house."

Presently the minion Sami had dispatched earlier appeared with a tray of sandwiches of cucumbers and spiced chicken resting on fragrant home-baked bread accompanied by glasses of mint tea ensconced in silver holders and two pristine white damask napkins laid out upon an equally spotless luncheon cloth. Averill recognized the colorful peacocks on the linens as being those of Susan's handiwork. As a girl Susan had already become proficient in the art of embroidery. She had taught Averill the rudiments, but Averill knew she would never be as good as her teacher.

Torquo, dedicated to the happy axiom that any visiting American lady was to be waited upon, spread out the feast and they chatted like longtime friends. Torquo had been educated at Oxford and had returned to his homeland only months before.

"This madman, Hitler, dreams he will rule the world, Miss Averill. The English have been holding him at bay, but eventually America will have to come into the war, or Europe will be overrun. The English foiled his dream of a quick victory in the Battle of Britain a year ago and now he has broken his treaty with the Soviet Union and thinks to add their military resources to his and turn once again and squash England for good." Torquo helped himself to another sandwich. "They are gallant people, the English, but they will be no match for a Germany who has overrun all of Europe and forced the conquered to aid his war machine. Your United States will not be safe, either. When he has conquered England, it will only be a matter of time until the Nazis turn their eyes across the Atlantic."

Averill shivered in the heat. The thought was too horrible to entertain. "In America, we have heard rumors of Hitler's hatred for Jews. Is this true?"

"Ah, yes. We, too, hear terrible tidings of what is happening to the Jews of Europe. Everything is done in darkness, you see, but we know that little children are banned from school, their parents' businesses and synagogues burned, their homes confiscated, and they are shot in the streets," replied Torquo. "It is a terrible time to be a Jew."

"Dear God," murmured Averill.

"So many unbelievable things are happening in Europe and Africa. The Germans conquered Morocco and now march eastward toward the borders of Egypt. As we speak, they are attacking an army made up of English, Canadian, Indian, and Egyptian soldiers, defending our frontier. So far they have not crossed our fortifications. God help Egypt if they do."

Averill sat for some minutes in silence contemplating the awful picture of the continent of Africa being conquered by the Axis powers. If Germany planned a world of Anglo-Saxon and northern Europeans as a master race with other nationalities relegated to his slaves, then that meant that not only the Jewish people but the Arab countries, the African people, the Slavic population, even the Orientals would eventually fall victim to Hitler's rabid racial hatred. No matter that at present Germany is allied with Japan. That without question would change in the future. His rambling, poorly written book, *Mien Kampf*, penned from prison that spewed bigotry and frustrated rage at the fate of Germany after World War I had laid it all out almost twenty years before.

Torquo wiped his mouth and brought her back to the present by saying, "Miss Averill, tomorrow we will visit the shop of Subri Gur-Aryeh. He is a friend of my late father and is of Moroccan paternity with a Jewish mother. That is where we'll start our hunt for your father and friend. Is this not all right with you?"

"Yes, of course, Torquo."

"Very good. I leave you for a time. The *Effendi* Al-Hamid calls." In somewhat like the manner of an Arabian Nights Jinni, Torquo disappeared through a door in the wall of the courtyard. Weary from her long trip and lulled by the sound of the fountain and the torpor of a late Egyptian September afternoon, Averill drowsed. She was awakened by Torquo standing before her.

"We go now," he said. The tray with its remains of sandwiches and tea had been removed and the sun was lower in the horizon. Averill jumped up, brushed herself off. She remarked dreamily, "It's so peaceful here. It's hard to believe that busy Cairo is just meters away."

"That is the mystery of the East," responded Torquo. "Nothing is as it appears to be."

She was to remember his words later.

Chapter 25

Upon entering Susan's and Sami's house, Susan rushed at her like the schoolgirl she had once been. "Averill! I can't believe it's you. How long has it been?" After a wild hug she led her into the interior, "Come in, come in. Does Torquo have your luggage?" She peered out the door. "No, here he comes with it. He'll take it to the guest room. Ayman, tell your father Averill's here. Oh, it's so good to see you! Please come into the kitchen. This is Kesir, who helps me cook." A young Egyptian man, dressed in a striped *djellabah* and holding a ceramic bowl filled with fresh fruit, bowed. "Oh, and these are our boys: Ayman and Yusif," she continued in an excited rush flinging her hands from boy to boy. "Ayman started school this year and Yusif is three. Say 'Hello' to Miss Averill, boys."

Averill stooped in front of the two boys self-consciously lined in front of her. "Hello, Ayman. Hi, Yusif. What a pretty kitten you have. What's its name?"

Yusif mumbled something with his head down. Ayman spoke up, "Her name is Shalimar. She's three months old."

"She's got a beautiful coat. What do you feed her?"

Yusif kept his head tucked but Ayman spoke up, "Mostly fish heads. But sometimes she eats what we eat."

"Boys, take that cat out and then wash your hands. We are almost ready to eat. Come with me, Averill, and we'll talk while I finish up this sauce. Kesir will attend to setting the table. Sami is tending the meat outside on the spit. It should be just about done."

Averill followed Susan into her kitchen, the air oppressively hot to Averill but seemingly of little concern to Susan. Averill glanced up at the windows set high in the walls where little warm air seemed to escape and even less fresh entered, and watched while Susan bustled around in the dim kitchen, oblivious to any handicap. Sami came in from the outside with individual wild ducks on spits. Susan held out a wide, long platter and Sami piled the ducks on it. "It smells delicious. Isn't it strange how aromas can bring back memories as words and scenes don't?" Averill observed, as Susan set out dishes of olives and mysterious dishes with Arabic breads tucked beside them. Bowls of watermelon, oranges, slices of fried eggplant piled high and dripping with savory sauce, fresh figs, and cheeses crowded cheek to jowl on the laden table.

"Where did Torquo go?" Susan asked of Sami. "I thought he was eating with us."

"He had somewhere else he goes."

When all was ready, they sat on cushions around a low-rising table. Sounds of donkeys, men shouting, and the screaming of children came through the open window. It was cooler in the small eating area because a door was open onto a patio where a hammock was hung and where were dispersed a scattering of chaise lounges all piled high with varicolored cushions. Averill settled into contentment that she had not felt for a long time. Oh, it was like coming home. Why had she waited so long before coming back to Cairo? She said this aloud and Sami smiled and said, "It is good that you have not forgotten old friends."

Then came the comfortable and easy talk that gushes forth when visiting those with whom one grew up. They talked of the pyramids at Giza being heavily guarded now and the absence of tourists. "Cairo is riddled with German agents, dear friend," Sami told her sadly. "German armies are at our borders. They have retaken land they gave up only weeks ago. The Desert Fox, the cunning German Field Marshall Rommel, still has many tricks up his sleeve, I fear."

"If I get a boy cat, I'm going to name him Rommel," spoke up Ayman.

"One cat is enough, Son," said Sami and tousled Ayman's hair.

"War is so tiresome," said Susan. "One has to deal with the black market in order to have any meat at all."

"I didn't hear that," said Sami, disapprovingly.

Susan made a face at him. "Well, it's true. And the garbage they're selling in the bazaars these days. I don't know where the good stuff is going, but we're not seeing it here in our markets. But Kesir helps me with my garden and we grow most of our own vegetables and melons."

"I imagine the military is taking the best for the fighting men," said Averill. "That's what usually happens in wartime."

The languid, spice-laden, fragrant air caused Averill to feel her fatigue. She found herself fighting to stay awake.

"You're tired, Averill. Forgive us. We've forgotten you travel long and lose much time," said Sami with concern.

"I'm sorry. Was it that obvious?"

"You must take a nice hot bath and then straight to bed," commanded Susan. "In the morning you'll feel much better." She was led to her room where a copper tub sat filled with steaming water with a fat, creamy bar of soap and several thick Turkish towels resting on an inlaid table beside the tub. The single iron bed was turned down and wonder, of wonder, an electric fan moved the air so that in here it was cooler than the rest of the house. After bathing she slipped between the cool Egyptian cotton sheets and the sounds of a comforting clatter from the kitchen were the last things she heard before falling asleep.

After warm yeast rolls, butter, jam, coffee and tea that comprised their Egyptian breakfast, Torquo arrived and she took her leave of Susan. Navigating the crooked streets he announced, "We will go first to meet the man of whom I spoke. If Subri doesn't know about Col. Lowe and your friend, it will mean he has lost his wits, and he will lose his fat stomach before he loses that." He turned to grin at Averill, "Nothing proceeds in Cairo without his knowledge. He is reliable…as far as his own interests permit." Torquo amended with a wry smile and a sideways glance at her. "Subri's interests and Egypt's interests are not always the same." He adroitly evaded a pothole in which a chicken was pecking at debris. "He is a good friend of the English and Americans but, too, only when their interests happen to be the same as his. This, of course, he would not say to you, but I will tell you."

They drove through streets dodging stolid plodding donkeys stoically pulling overflowing carts; street vendors carrying large trays on their head piled high with fruit and pastries carelessly stepped into their path, and ancient motorized vehicles that looked to be held together with a bit of string and a lot of hope, pressing relentlessly forward, scattering humans, dogs, and chickens. There was quite a lot of fatalistic Arabic 'Inshallah' bandied about which Averill knew was a nebulous translation of 'Allah willing'. Torquo drew up in front of a shop that looked like hundreds of others of its neighbors. A score of *djellabahs* hung outside its storefront along with unfashionable footwear on display that one stumbled over to get in the door, and outmoded merchandise of the industrial West rose in stacks behind flyspecked windows. Inside, it was surprisingly cool. The walls were insulated with Oriental rugs hanging from the rafters. Carved wooden tables were scattered about, some with bronze coffee sets containing porcelain insets. From behind worn velvet curtains a man emerged dressed in a sparkling clean white *djellabah* decorated with gold designs on the edge of sleeves and hem. He bowed to Averill and came forward to greet Torquo with the familiar Eastern ritual of a kiss on either cheek. "Ah, Torquo, my friend, and the *Aneesa* Averill," he said, turning to Averill, "pray be seated." He drew forward an elaborately carved chair, which he indicated that she occupy. He clapped his hands and a young boy appeared. "Tea, Basrah." The boy bowed and disappeared behind the curtains. Subri stepped to the front of the store and issued staccato commands to two men squatting outside. He could not have more effectively hung a 'closed' sign on his shop door. No one came in for the balance of the time they visited.

Unwilling that her knowledge of Arabic be known, Averill had cautioned Torquo to not disclose it unless she began speaking it. Torquo began, in his vaguely upper-class English accent, to lay out the facts of Averill's visit to Cairo. Subri listened without speaking. The boy, Basrah, glided in quietly and deposited a tray on a low table and unobtrusively departed. Finally, Torquo fell silent. For some time Subri moved between the curtains and the door. Suddenly he whirled and addressed Averill. "The *aneesa*, do you not realize what danger you are entering? This…" and here he drew off his Turkish slipper and hurled it across the room, "this rogue, Blake, escaped his captors and in turn is holding captive the *effendis* Col. Lowe and Braddock, along with an Englishman."

"An Englishman?"

"But yes. He holds a good hand does this Blake. Of course, that is not his real name. But no matter, we will call him Blake."

Averill replied, "As Torquo has told you, this Blake, or whatever his name is, has stolen critical plans and designs of armaments from my company in the United States, drawings of battle artillery that were to be shipped to Britain as part of the United States' Lend Lease program. However, that takes second place to the fact that my father and Mr. Braddock may be tortured and killed."

Subri studied Averill. Somewhere in his distant past was French blood and there was a love for the romantic lurking. A knowing gleam came into his eyes and it was, Averill thought, conceivable that he perceived that Reife was somewhat more than an employer. Smiling slightly he answered, "I understand." He paused to ponder something then said quietly, "I will help you. You are brave, *aneesa*; I think you may succeed." He paused to clap his hands and Basrah appeared. "Chairs for the *effendi* Torquo and myself. And bring food. We have much to say." He reached under a counter, pulled out a Western-type yellow legal pad, reached into his voluminous robes, and extracted a fountain pen. Basrah brought two highly decorative chairs forth from the regions behind the curtain. Subri signaled to Torquo to sit as he himself did, and he uncapped the pen and began to write.

Several plates of fruit and dainties were eaten, numerous pots of tea were consumed, and the sun was almost directly overhead when Subri finished his instructions to Torquo and Averill. "My men will be present wherever you go today. You will perhaps not see them and Blake's men will certainly not spot them, but they will be there."

Ignoring the interested gaze of the lookouts squatted outside the shop, they took their leave of Subri and walked the narrow streets back to a wider part of the road where they had left their nondescript car. They drove to the police station and, after conferring with Sami, they exchanged it for a clearly marked police car with Torquo as driver, now dressed in police uniform.

They arrived in Heliopolis within half an hour. The house they approached backed onto the Cairo International Airport. The noise of approaching and departing planes made it difficult for Averill to hear Torquo's quiet instructions. She was carrying no weapon but she had seen the knives Torquo had slipped into his boots and belt. He knocked commandingly on the blue door of the stone building with the shuttered windows.

"Yes?" A man in a striped *djellabah* wearing a *keffiyeh* opened the door. Torquo produced credentials and demanded to see the *Effendi* Blake. Before the man could respond, curtains parted and a man appeared. Averill suppressed a gasp. It was Blake.

"Good afternoon, Miss Lowe. Good afternoon, Mr. Mansur. It's all right, Khalid; bring us tea. Please sit down," Blake invited, waving Torquo and Averill toward a couch.

"This isn't a social visit," responded Torquo, who did not seem surprised at the sudden appearance of Blake. "I am on police business. I will collect Col. Lowe, Mr. Braddock and the Englishman. There is also a matter of designs for armaments that were stolen from an American engineering firm."

Blake raised his eyebrows and smiled slightly. "How much *effectif?*"

Swinging from his hand was a briefcase that Torquo handed to Blake to examine. Blake opened the case, glanced at papers inside, swiftly counted the sterling grouped by count in canvas bags, and closed the briefcase with a decisive snap. "Where's the rest?" he snarled, pretending great indignation.

"You will get the rest when the hostages are released, as you well know," said Torquo dismissively.

Blake glared at him but only said, "If you come back this evening—with the money, of course—the men will be ready."

Averill opened her mouth, felt a nudge from Torquo, and bit back a protest at the delay. Blake saw the gesture, and smiled unpleasantly. "I am so glad to renew our friendship, Miss Lowe." She saw the malice in his eyes and wondered if her disinterest in his admiring advances in America had nettled him more than she had realized. A rejected lover could not have displayed more injured vanity.

Torquo warned, "Your house is under surveillance, Blake. In case you plan a double cross, know that funds have been frozen in various accounts in the United States until the hostages are safely home."

Blake's countenance turned ugly. "If deposits belonging to the Third Reich are stolen, the German government most certainly will lodge protests and perhaps contemplate a nasty surprise for Miss Lowe."

Averill turned pale but didn't flinch. Torquo said savagely, "Save your threats, Blake; just have Col. Lowe, Reife Braddock, and the Englishman ready to leave at nine o'clock tonight."

Khalid appeared with a tray on which rested demitasse cups of hot steaming tea. An aroma of spearmint filled the air. Blake's eyes were mutinous as Torquo said politely, "Good day, Mr. Blake—or should I say Herr Beck."

The anger in Blake's face was quickly replaced by a smooth mask. "You no doubt have me confused with someone else. Good day." Khalid hurriedly placed the tray on a table and sprang to open the door for them, but they were already outside.

Chapter 26

During 1941 a drama played out on the Mediterranean coast of Libya, which Mussolini, the Fascist leader of Italy, had declared a colony of Italy prior to the outbreak of the war. Digging into the desert sands, less than 500 miles west of Cairo, Italian and German forces were spread on the coast from Morocco to the Egyptian border; and English, New Zealand, Australian, and Indian Allies were poised to begin an offense to wrest control of the territory. These opponents were fighting for the prize of a main port on the Mediterranean and the main supply road between Tobruk and Cairo. Hitler's plans were to make it the gateway through which he would achieve the conquest of Egypt. Italian control of Tobruk fell to the Allies at the beginning of the year, but in the spring Erwin Rommel's Afrika Korps entered the war and the complexion of the battle changed mightily with his superior tank forces; however, in September of 1941 the Australians still held the town.

Some weeks before Averill arrived in Cairo, Blake had arrived in Egypt and began scouting both sides of the war for the highest bidder for the tank designs he had stolen from Braddock. Berlin was offering German marks and England was willing to pay in sterling, but before he had negotiated with either side Blake purchased insurance by hiring thugs to ambush Reife, Col. Lowe, and a British agent—known in the highest circles of British intelligence by the code name of 'Valiance'—in a dark Cairo street. After a shootout with injuries but no deaths, Blake took the three men hostage.

Now in the desert west of Cairo, Torquo and Averill arrived at a house a few miles from Cairo Airport carrying bearer bonds for British sterling for the balance owed to Blake in exchange for the stolen plans and the release of the hostages. It was just after nine in the evening when the door to the little isolated stone house was opened by Blake himself.

"Good evening, Mr. Blake," Torquo said, equably. "I must remind you that we are under surveillance at all times. You will not see them but I forewarn you they are there. I would not try to sabotage this exchange."

Blake responded suavely, "Of course. That is understood. I will take you to them." He caught sight of Averill's disappointed face. "You did not think I kept them here?" he jeered. Then he shook his finger at her. "Little girls should not try to play spy games," he added, chuckling at the suppressed fury that stiffened her figure. She held her tongue.

They rode in a dipping and swaying top-heavy van and followed Blake and his men, armed, on horses with no sight of the Egyptian forces that Torquo assured Averill were hidden in brush along the way after they left the outskirts of Heliopolis. In an hour's time they had left Greater Cairo and were traveling the trackless desert, the air so clear she could hear the distant echoes of a battle for another tiny Egyptian outpost. She lost track of time as the convoy lumbered over miles of sandy, scrubby landscape slowing only when a lookout party of gunmen materialized. After a guttural exchange of staccato Arabic with Blake, they were waved on each time. Palm trees and patches of green at last began to appear with large stones hedging a rutted area that could not be called a road but was somewhat better off for travel than the rocky path whereupon they had bumped. Ahead was a small guard station with a barricade over the ruts and they ground to a stop, submitting to a search by men wearing camouflage and balaclavas. Torquo, Averill noted, had left his knives behind.

A small knoll was in front of them, an abandoned Tell, Averill guessed, around which they circled and came to halt in front of a trio of small buildings. They watched a woman, wearing a burqa, emerge from the main building, and greet Blake as the horses and van drew up. Blake beckoned them to leave the van, and Averill disembarked, stiff from the cold desert air and hugging her thin coat against the unexpected wind.

"Stay here," Blake commanded. He proceeded on to an inner door and disappeared behind it. The woman, her kohl-outlined eyes flashing hatred through the grill in her burqa, stepped to the door and barred entrance.

Averill openly studied her. Finally she spoke. "So...you went over to the other side, did you Jo?"

Chapter 27

There was no answer from the figure.

Averill turned to Torquo and asked, "Did you know that Jo would be here?"

"I suspected it," Torquo answered. "We have been watching Miss Blake for some while."

"You understand nothing! Nothing!" cried Jo with snarling vehemence.

Through the inner door they heard the shuffling of feet; the door opened and her father emerged carrying one end of a litter upon which rested a figure with a bandaged leg, blood-soaked and dirty. Averill ran to hug her father then bent over the figure lying on the carrier. "Reife! They've hurt you."

"Hello, Averill," Reife grinned up at her. "It's just a scratch."

"He's got a leg wound that's become septic," said her father. "He needs sulfanilamide."

"Come, Averill, let's get them in the car. No, wait, look over the designs first." Torquo began unwrapping the long tubed parcel that Blake thrust toward him.

Against a reflexive protest from Col. Lowe, Reife reared up from the litter. He reached and thumbed through the blueprints with the dexterity of familiarity, and dropped back on the litter as if all his energy had been expended into that one act. "They're all there," he whispered.

Torquo handed over a briefcase to Blake. "I hope you choke on it," he growled, followed by an impressive, if rude, Arabic word. "Take your thirty pieces of silver and be hanged!" He moved the van, opened the rear doors and said, "Steady on, chaps," and helped Lowe move his end up into the interior and then around to the rear saying, "Mind the pothole." Only then did Averill recognize the man who was on the other end of the litter carrying the wounded Reife. Edward! She stared, transfixed.

"Later," he silently mouthed.

After they eased Reife into the back of the van, Averill knelt beside him on the floorboard. Col. Lowe and Edward slid into the front seat while Torquo started the engine and pulled out onto the desert and headed toward Cairo, the van threatening once again to topple onto its side with every pothole.

"Please drink a little water, Reife." Averill lifted a flask to Reife's lips. "You have fever. Can you eat some dates?"

"I'll be all right. Don't fuss," He drank but pushed away the dates, closing his eyes to drift in and out of consciousness. Periodically, she bathed his forehead with water from the flask. Finally, the nightmarish return trek ended. Torquo, Sami, Susan, and Averill settled Reife into a room in the rear of the Al-Hamid home where a bed, freshly made with clean linens, awaited. The four posters held mosquito netting suspended above the mattress, clean towels hung on racks beside a washstand, a pitcher of water with glasses in silver retainers rested on a nearby table beside a bowl of fruit, and on another table a fresh pot of tea with pastries newly out of the oven. After Sami administered an adept warm sponge bath, Averill and Susan tucked Reife, dressed in fresh pajamas, into his bed after coaxing a few sips from a cup of tea into him. He murmured, "Nice," smiled at them, and faded into sleep.

"Drop Edward and me off at Shepheards Hotel," Col. Lowe had directed Torquo as they entered Cairo. "I'll send a doctor around."

"Good night, Dad," she had said tenderly to her father when they dropped him and Edward off at the hotel. The look on her father's face when he passed Jo in the little house on his way out to freedom had gone to her heart. He had turned to his former lover with an angry, baffled hurt that found no words. Jo had maintained a stoical silence and met his look with defiance, and Averill had sorrowed for her father. To throw away his marriage for a love that turned out to be based on such treachery must have hurt dreadfully. She turned to Edward. "Good night," she said to her friend whom she now comprehended with incredulity was the fabled English agent, 'Valiance'.

Later, Averill could remember little of the hot days that followed during which Reife became delirious and the English military doctor came two and three times a day to attend him. She kept his forehead bathed in cool water, held water to his parched lips, and tried to conceal her alarm at his worsening condition. Day after day, she stayed by his bedside listening to his feverish ramblings and prayed. Then came the day when she was bathing his head and his eyes opened and he looked at her in recognition and his words were halting.

"You must ...go home. Leave me... please."

"But why?"

"... heard the doctor. He wants... amputate my leg. Don't want you. Please... go."

"You're going to get well, Reife. You're much, much better. Yes, he did talk of amputating, but you are out of danger now. It won't be necessary."

"He talked...today."

"No, that's the fever. It was last week when he talked of it." She stroked his wet hair.

"Don't... touch. Go." He turned his head away from her.

Averill leaned over him and her tears dripped onto his face. "Please let me stay."

"No."

"All right, I'll go. But you're not going to lose your leg, I promise you that. I'm going," she added hastily when, in the recesses of the pillow, with surprising energy he had swiveled his head angrily toward her. She slipped out of the room.

Susan came into the room and sat beside him. Reife kept his eyes closed. She said, "Averill is so worried about you and you've wounded her. You're better. You're not going to lose a leg."

He opened his eyes. "... don't believe...it."

"No. It's true. You're out of danger."

"No."

His attitude brought despair to Averill and angry frustration to Susan. Oddly enough, the military doctor, Dr. Norton, seemed pleased with his patient's progress.

"He is facing the worst and acclimating himself to it. He's a courageous man."

For the next few days, Averill could only get news second-hand, for Reife refused to let her into his room.

One day as Susan changed his towels for clean ones, he turned to her and asked with surprising firmness, "When will I be able to go home?"

"In a few days. You must gain strength. Then you'll go home. Maybe by ship. Maybe by airplane. It hasn't been decided yet. You've lost a lot of blood and must build up your strength. You have refused all the good food I've been preparing for you for weeks. How do you think that makes me feel?" She came to the side of his bed and reached for his hand.

"I feel a little hungry now."

"That's a good sign. I'll get you some food."

"Susan?"

"Yes?"

"Send Averill in with it."

"You got it."

She prepared a tray of food and with it Averill tiptoed into Reife's darkened room. Reife's eyes were shut and she placed the tray on a low table that held his medicines. "Averill." No one could say that word like Reife, she thought.

"Yes?"

"I'm glad…you didn't leave."

"So am I."

Several days later Reife was able to sit in the garden and Averill brought their lunch, set it on the glass-topped table in front of his chair, and took the one beside him. He ignored it and turned to her. "When we were held captive I had a lot of time to think." He stopped to watch a hummingbird land on a flower and make his helicopter lift-off for a bush some yards away as the cat, Shalimar, hove into view. Averill saw moisture on his lashes. He drew a deep breath. He began speaking swiftly as if he had hoarded energy.

"I think you ought to know that in that windowless, unbearably hot, and smelly room in the desert miles away from civilization, your father and I asked Christ into our lives."

"Oh, Reife, did you?"

"Yes.

"While we were held in that hot dark room, thinking we would be killed at any minute, we spoke of things that otherwise might not be mentioned. Your father told me how you handled your anger at others when you were growing up. He said you never forgot, and certainly never forgave. He was expecting the Averill who treated those who crossed her with arrogant contempt. He was not prepared for you to forgive him when he saw you last year in Washington. He was so afraid to meet you; he thought you would ostracize, cut him out of your life forever."

"Afraid of me? I never knew. He seemed to be almost defiant."

"Fear turns to anger inside some men and then we pull a curtain, afraid of what we'll say, what we might do. Didn't you see his hands at the Willard? They were shaking so badly, he could hardly handle his cup."

Averill recalled the bitter resentment that she would have carried to her grave had she not learned that, for Christ to forgive her, she must forgive others. She said softly, "That's true. My father knows me very well." They sat in contented silence and watched Shalimar stretch luxuriously as Reife scratched her tummy.

"I didn't know I could be so happy," she said at length, leaning over to kiss his forehead. An indignant cat stalked off after being cavalierly thrust aside and with a surprisingly strong grip, Reife pulled her close and their lips met. She was pulled out of her chair and into an onslaught of emotion she never before had experienced. He drew her into his own need and ignited a yearning in her as ardent as a desert for water. Her hands cradled his face and entwined in his hair as she returned kiss for kiss. Finally, gasping for air, she released herself and straightened.

"This can't be good for you," she said, out of breath.

"*Au contraire*," Reife said smiling but wincing where she inadvertently jostled his leg, "it's just what the doctor ordered."

"No, it's not. Look, your wound is bleeding again. Eat something before the food grows cold and then I'll dress your leg."

It was only later, when he went in to take his nap, did she realize that the word 'love' was never mentioned.

Chapter 28

Col. Lowe and Edward stayed at Shepheards Hotel in the center of Cairo where they worked with Cairo police and England's MI6 to close down the Blake network operating in Egypt while Reife recovered at the Al-Hamid's on the outskirts of the city. Averill and her father were seated at a table in the courtyard of Shepheards, when he told her, "The tank designs which Blake stole have been transferred to the British military. They will now be able to assemble tanks on-site with the supplies that Braddock has been sending them. This may help end this interminable morass of bloodletting the North African campaign has become. By the way, Edward is leaving for Washington tomorrow."

Averill took a sip of mint tea, and asked, "Are you staying on?"

"For the time being."

"Is it too painful to talk about Jo?"

Her father looked out into the distance and didn't answer.

"I'm sorry, Dad. There are unanswered questions that you perhaps know that would help me understand exactly what happened here."

"Is it so necessary for you to know?" Her father asked, his eyes still focused in the distance.

"Not if you'd rather not talk about it."

Her father shifted his eyes to her. Averill saw pain in them and reached to put her hand on his, "I'm so sorry, Dad." She added, "You've been betrayed, too. Blake was her brother and she must have felt pulled from both sides. We don't have to talk about it now."

They sat in the garden with the smell of honeysuckle and jasmine perfuming the air. A bee droned nearby. At length, her father spoke, "Jo knew what the Nazis stood for, and she was part of it from the first. There's no whitewashing it, Averill. She never loved me; it was all a lie from first to last." Averill thought her father looked ten years older than when she had seen him last. She reached out, put her hand on top of his, and squeezed it.

"When I saw her at that God-forsaken outpost only ten miles from the fighting… all the time thinking she was back in England waiting for me…" Col. Lowe left his sentence unfinished as Edward approached through a small stand of sycamore trees from the rear of the hotel.

"It must have made your world crumble." Averill surprised herself with the flash of swift compassion that swept over her in the presence of her father's pain. "Any news about Blake?" asked Averill as Edward approached their small table.

He pulled out a chair, ordered a coffee, and commented, "The worst thing about this is that we had to let them escape into Berlin."

Averill cried, "They were allowed to get away?"

"That was part of the agreement for our return," answered Edward.

"Part?"

"Another part was the money for the surrender of the stolen designs, of course."

"Was there more?"

Edward looked at Col. Lowe.

"Another demand was that he give the names of spies working in the United States. Those that Blake knew about, of course," Lowe said.

"And some of these names you recognized; is that it? Tell me, that's it, isn't it. Perhaps you realize that I will know them, too."

"Tell her. She has a right to know. He's in custody, so it can't harm the operation, Edward," her father said.

Edward turned to Averill. "Klaus Ernst was picked up two days ago in Chattanooga on espionage charges."

Averill sat very still. Then she asked, "And Henrietta?"

"Henrietta knew nothing about it. She very possibly will never see her husband free again. Too bad for her baby girl."

"Her baby girl? She had her baby?"

"Yes," said Edward. "It was born prematurely last week. Sorry to say, they arrested Klaus at Erlanger Hospital when he was visiting his wife."

"Yes," her father reflected. "Poor, silly, credulous Henrietta."

"She was always impetuous," observed Averill, "but that was part of her charm."

Edward addressed Averill, "Why don't you leave with me tomorrow? Braddock is recovering and surely your work needs you back home."

Averill said, "No, not yet."

Edward gave her a searching look, but said nothing else.

"Is that your final answer, Averill?" Her father asked in the silence.

"Yes."

"I wrote your mother," he said.

"About…Jo?"

He nodded.

"I'm glad," Averill said. "She still loves you."

Her father fidgeted a bit, and cleared his throat. "I didn't know that," he finally said.

"Oh, Dad," said Averill quietly.

Her father dropped his head into his hands and didn't reply.

"Well," Averill said and gathered her purse and gloves, "I guess this is good-bye for now, Edward. Torquo is waiting to take me back to Susan and Sami's house."

"I'll walk you to your ride," he said and threw some coins on the table.

She leaned to kiss her father, "I'll see you later, Dad." He nodded.

Edward held her arm as they traversed the pebbled walkway around to the front of the hotel where Torquo was sitting in an unmarked police car reading a newspaper. When he saw her he jumped out and opened the door of the car. Averill turned to Edward and said, "Will you do something for me?"

"If I can."

"When you get back to Chattanooga will you get in touch with Henrietta and find out how she's doing?"

"I'll do that."

Averill rose on tiptoe and kissed him on the cheek. "Good-bye, then."

Edward stepped back to let Torquo help her into the car and when she looked back as they drove away, he was still standing there watching.

Reife was recuperating. Each day he made astounding leaps toward wholeness. He walked with Averill to the bazaars almost every day where he could indulge his love of bargaining. They returned each day with an item for Susan's household. One day it was a fluffy sheepskin rug. Another time it was a set of copper mixing bowls for her kitchen. They picked up fresh vegetables and fruits at the market for her, thus saving her the trip. One day they returned with a steaming, dripping package and unwrapped grilled lamb with peppers and onions on skewers. From the capacious bag they retrieved a container of caramel custard and sautéed eggplant with a savory marinade. "We don't want you to cook tonight," Averill announced. "It's much too hot. We brought back the evening meal."

"How divine!" Susan exclaimed. "That will give me time to finish the book I borrowed from you, Averill. I thought I was never going to find time to read it."

"You're going to put up your feet and start reading right now," Averill declared. "Reife needs a nap, and I am going to play soccer with Ayman and Yusif."

"You treat me as if I were an old woman," grumbled Reife, but he disappeared into his bedroom for what Averill suspected was for him a welcome rest.

Later, when Averill had bathed and changed clothes she found Susan in the garden tying up some tomatoes. Averill plopped on a chaise lounge. "Did you finish the book?"

"Yes, and I would never have guessed the killer. Agatha Christie always keeps you guessing clear to the end, doesn't she?"

"She does indeed," responded Averill, stretching luxuriously.

Susan glanced toward Reife's window and lowered her voice. "You and Reife are very much in love, aren't you?"

"I'm in love with him, and I think he is with me, but he has never said so."

"Some men have trouble saying those three little words," said Susan.

"I wonder why," reflected Averill.

"Does it bother you much?"

"No. Well, yes. Oh, I don't know. We can't get married as things stand now anyway."

"How do things stand?"

"You know—the war which will start any day now."

"To some people, that would be a reason to get married. To grab happiness while it's possible."

"That isn't the way Reife thinks."

"Is it the way you think?"

"I guess it is."

"I thought so. Most women would feel the same way," Susan said, tucking her hair up under the hat she wore for gardening.

"There isn't anything I can do about it, so I try not to think about it," said Averill. "I just remind myself of those long nights when I worried if he was dead or alive and I was trying to bargain with God and I promised Him I would never ask for another thing…"

"And now you remind yourself that God spared his life, don't you? You feel you don't have a right to expect anything more."

"You're right. I do think that."

Susan sat on the edge of the chaise, cupped her head in her hands, and watched Shalimar bat at a butterfly. Then she said, "Well, I don't think that's what God is like. I think He enjoys our asking for things."

Averill was silent.

"Remember the scripture where Jesus is talking about how as earthly fathers we enjoy giving good things to our children and told us that was how our Heavenly Father enjoys giving good things to His children when they ask."

"It sounds too much like we're pestering God when we keep on asking for the same thing," Averill objected.

"I don't think so. I believe God may even give us hardships so that we will stay in touch with him. I think He likes to be pestered."

"You do? I hadn't thought of it in that way."

"Well," suggested Susan as she jumped up to go into the house, "maybe you should. It's perfectly true. How do you think I got my Sami?"

After she left, Averill thought about what Susan had said. She got up, went into her room, got out her Bible, and found the passage in Luke's gospel. She closed the Bible thoughtfully and went into the kitchen where Reife was sitting on a stool eating an orange. He looked up as she entered. He smiled a slow companionable smile.

"I'll keep asking," she told herself, went to the cupboard, and started taking down dinner dishes with which to set the table.

248

Chapter 29

Later, Averill was to look back at these languid 1941 fall days in Cairo as the calm before the storm. She and Reife spent happy hours sailing on the Nile, shopping in the bazaars, playing Backgammon and chess under the shade trees in the Al Hamid's garden. There were lively games of Monopoly at night when Sami came home from work. The boys would join them, and Ayman would end up with Park Place and all the railroads. In the mornings after Ayman left for kindergarten, Sami for the office, and Reife with Torquo to make the rounds of government offices on business, she and Susan would have a leisurely brunch on the terrace. Yusif quietly played beside them on the stone floor with his set of Legos that the Danish Ambassador to Egypt had given him, while Shalimar chased water pipits up and down the garden. Presently, Torquo would drive Reife home and he, Averill, Susan, and Yusif would stroll down to the Nile River that was just a few blocks from the Al Hamid home. There was a vegetable market close by and Susan would buy fresh produce for the next few days. Lunch would be something from the vendors and eaten on the banks of the Nile: hot, flat breads stuffed with hummus, skewers of lamb and grilled vegetables, or a sandwich with rice, beans, and mutton. Back home there were short naps in the shaded garden lying on chaise lounges. Kesir would feed them *kahk* filled with date paste or hot scones dripping with honey for their tea and they would forget for a few minutes that a few hundred miles in the distance they were being protected from the Nazis by Allied troops.

One night there came an ominous quiet over the city. In the far distance there could be heard the distant thunder of artillery. "How close are they?" Reife asked Sami.

"It's a German or Italian raiding party that found an ammunition dump," he replied. "Our people will find them. It sounds worse than it is."

"It's time for us to go home, Averill," said Reife. "The business needs me. I'm finished here."

And so, despite the protests of the Al-Hamids, the next week Averill and Reife packed and said their goodbyes and headed on the first lap of their journey down the Nile to a port on the Mediterranean. There they were met by a freighter flying the neutral Spanish flag, and were taken aboard as the only civilian passengers, aware that the Axis were sinking Spanish ships, too, as suspected conveyers of war matériel to the Allies.

Both were given spacious rooms that had hastily been cleared of military gear. Reife, exhausted from the trip, sank down on a couch in a surprisingly comfortable lounge, and Averill brought him tea from the galley and dressed his leg. At night back in her room she drew out a biography of Napoleon she spotted on a dusty bookshelf and settled in to read before falling asleep. There were daily drills in case of attack from sea or air, and at dusk heavy curtains were pulled across her windows blacking out any light.

On their third day out they were shelled by an Italian ship. All the shells missed except one which landed on the deck, unexploded. A demolition squad disarmed it and, zigzagging, the captain steamed westward heading toward the neutral waters of Lisbon, Portugal.

Averill became violently ill. A ship's seaman who served as medic attended her for three days, during which she ran a high fever and ate nothing. On the night before they were to land at Lisbon, Reife helped her to the dining room where she ate a meal of greasy pasta. For the first time Averill realized the soothing effects of grease upon a disrupted tummy. "It's the most delicious thing I've ever eaten," she told Reife who watched, frowning with disgust at the swimming strands of spaghetti. "No, I mean it. It feels wonderful on my stomach."

"It looks loathsome. I'm glad you're feeling better, anyway. We have to disembark tomorrow and I was wondering if we would have to have an ambulance meet us."

"Nonsense. I can walk. What about you?"

"I'm fine."

That evening she and Reife walked up and down the deck watching the lights of Lisbon drawing nearer and nearer. "After being closeted in that room for days, the air smells heavenly," she told Reife.

"Doesn't it?" They found army blankets under some canvas rigging and as the air grew cooler Reife scrounged about for more blankets and tucked them over her before spreading one over himself. "When we arrive at Lisbon, we'll stay at the American Embassy. The Ambassador is an old friend of my father's from Georgia Tech."

The night was in thick darkness as they entered International waters off Portugal. Neutral the country might be, but gone was the gem-like string of lights that once greeted its coastal commerce. Patrol boats criss-crossed its waters and the freighter slowed and approached the dock at Lisbon at four knots an hour, Reife estimated. After the cold nights of the desert the night air felt almost balmy with a promise of rain in the air.

Reife brought his hand out from under the army blanket and reached out to touch her. She brought her imprisoned arm up under her blanket, freed it, and reached out for his hand. He said, "If we get back safely, I mean to work even harder in getting Braddock's armaments to the battlefronts. When those Italian shells were exploding all around us I thought we'd be hit and still can't believe we weren't. Maybe God has spared me for a reason. There are still hundreds of tanks needed."

"And I'm going to help you."

"You've worked alongside me, never minding that you don't get enough sleep and that you don't have a life like all the other girls around who are going to parties and being taken out on dates."

"The only man I want to party with or go out on dates is working like seven demons turning out tanks for Britain. I am so proud of what you have done. I'm thankful I had a chance to be a part of it."

Reife leaned over and Averill looked up into the black shadow that loomed large above her. The shadow came closer and she felt his lips on hers and suddenly his arms imprisoned her and he was kissing her. Her one free hand pulled his head close to her. A hand slipped behind her and she was being pulled half out of the chair with the intensity of the movement. I can't breathe, she thought, just let up for a minute… never let up. She struggled for air and he let her go, and sat back. His hand still stroked her face and finally he said huskily, "That's for all those days at Sami's when I wanted to kiss you, but barely had enough energy to live."

She laughed, shaken to her core. "You certainly made up for lost time."

A door opened somewhere behind them and a seaman appeared beside them.

"So sorry, Mr. Braddock. The Captain wishes to see you. We're approaching Lisbon now. Miss, you may want to get your things together. We'll be docking under cover of darkness in about an hour."

As guests of diplomats, Reife and Averill took up residence in the American Embassy and awaited transport to America. Lisbon, she was to learn, was a hotbed of rumors and intrigue. As a neutral nation, it was home to Axis agents as well as to Allied agents, and in many cases enemy agents were well known to the other side. Averill, with the Ambassador's wife, enjoyed sight-seeing and shopping, while every day found Reife in various offices trying to find passage to the United States. Eventually he succeeded and they boarded a U.S. Merchant Marine freighter and began their perilous journey across the North Atlantic.

Day after day rough seas forced Averill to her room trying to hold onto her meals. There was no news from the outside since the ship was maintaining radio silence in fear of the U-boats prowling the waters. About a week into the journey, their ship was signaled to allow a boarding party from a German U-boat. The cold-eyed men inspected their cargo, and, finding it empty except for several hundred butts of amontillado wine which the roguish merchant seamen had procured for their own private use, they allowed the ship to continue on her journey, after relieving them of the wine. Later, Averill was to learn that had the search taken place only six days later, Germany would have been at war with the United States and the outcome might have been devastatingly different. They docked in New York the Friday before Christmas, December 19, Averill's twenty-third birthday, and learned their country was at war.

Part 3

January 1942 – Autumn 1944

Chapter 30

"What Reife's office needs," Joan said, one very busy day after the new year, "is numbered queue tickets for visitors." Averill could have told her that some were too important to take a number as many were from the Office of Strategic Services (OSS) that had been born during the tumultuous days preceding Pearl Harbor, the FBI serving as reluctant midwife. Only the grim danger confronting the U.S. from Imperial Japan and Nazi Germany could have persuaded J. Edgar Hoover, head of the FBI, to relinquish power to an organization, which would, after the war, become the CIA.

Late one afternoon Averill took an overseas call where the voice sounded as if it came over a line where several housewives had hung their washing. The voice spoke in upper class English with an indistinguishable foreign accent and identified himself as Subri Gur-Aryeh.

"Subri! Are you calling from Cairo?"

"I am indeed. How are you Miss Lowe?"

"I'm fine. And you?"

"Ah, I am a father in need of a big favor from you, Miss Lowe," he began.

"Of course. Tell me what it is."

"It is my daughter, Erica. She is a graduate student in your University of Chattanooga. She is doing research there."

"Yes. How can I help you?"

A boom followed by a dull thud came over the line.

"Are you there?" asked Averill, frantically.

Subri's voice was weaker. "Yes, yes. Just visit her. She is homesick for Cairo but is unable to come home. Will you look her up at the university? A grateful papa would thank you."

"I would be delighted."

"Give her my love."

"I most certainly will. I'd love to meet her."

More thumping and crashes followed by a high intermittent electronic squeal.

"Thank you, Miss Lowe. I must disconnect now."

"I understand. Goodbye, Subri."

The next day Averill left work early and found the dormitory room of Erica Gur-Aryeh on the university campus. A young Middle-Eastern girl met her at the door. "Are you Erica Gur-Aryeh?" Averill asked, checking a scrap of paper with a hastily sketched-out map.

"Yes," the girl answered hesitantly.

"I am a friend of your father's. May I come in?"

"Please." She waved to the room behind her where a large desk dominated the room. It was scattered with blueprints, compasses, blue-squared engineering paper, slide rules, and a couple of notebooks open to what looked like a lab report and a page of calculations. In the corner there was a drafting table with drafting tape, drafting brush, straight edge, triangles, pencils, and a pencil sharpener. Strewn on the bed were textbooks whose titles included the words physics, calculus, and thermodynamics. Erica impatiently pushed aside the textbooks and sat on the bed while motioning for Averill to sit on the stool in front of the drafting table.

"You bring bad news of my father?" asked Erica, her slender graceful figure bending forward. The black eyes held fear.

"No, no." Averill told her about meeting her father in Cairo and his subsequent call to her.

"Papa is a meddling old pet," Erica said relaxing with an indulgent smile. "I'm fine. My studies here are very interesting to me, and I have little time to be homesick. It is very kind of you to visit me. Americans are like that, I have found."

"Yes. I'm afraid our desire for everyone to be happy can sometimes be seen as intrusion," Averill said, with an apologetic smile.

"Oh, no, not at all," Erica protested, "It's one of the things that I like most about Americans."

"Well, that's all right, then. Would you allow me to take you out to an early supper? Or have you already eaten?" The room contained no signs of snack foods or drinks except a thermos sitting on an end table near a lamp. Other than the study materials, it was exceedingly neat.

"I have an appointment to meet my professor, Dr. Aksel Hjördís. Why do you not join us? He is a most interesting man." At this Erica, who had been sitting Indian fashion, un-crisscrossed her long olive legs, slid them off the bed, and stabbed her feet into loafers.

They entered the dining hall of the university and Erica led Averill to a corner where sat a young blond-haired man with fairly thick glasses reading a book. He looked up at their arrival and stood to his feet.

"Aksel, meet Averill Lowe. She is a friend of my father's." Averill did not miss the familiar given name with which Erica addressed her mentor and wondered if their relationship was something more.

The young Dr. Hjördís bowed with a theatrical Continental gesture and, instead of shaking the hand that Averill extended, he kissed it.

"What will you eat, Aksel?" Erica asked as they seated themselves.

"Something you, as a good Jewish girl, possibly won't have: a pork sandwich."

Averill started with surprise. She had forgotten that Sami had said that Subri Gur-Aryeh, a Moroccan Arab, had immigrated to Egypt and married a Jewess who died in childbirth.

Erica turned to her. "There are a few Jews in Cairo, Miss Lowe. Possibly you already knew that?"

"Yes. I visited various synagogues with my father when I lived there as a child; and please call me 'Averill'."

"And I am 'Aksel'," he responded, with a boyish grin.

The waitress approached and he asked, "Well then, Averill. What will you have to eat?"

"I'll have the Reuben."

"The Reubens are always tasteful. Or do you say 'tasty'?"

"Tasty, I think," answered Averill. Hjördís beamed at her.

Revealing that she was at least partially Americanized, Erica told the waitress, "I'll have a grilled cheese on rye and French fries."

While they waited for their food, Aksel talked about his native Norway and the teaching position that had brought him to the States. "I wanted to have a complete change of weather, culture, and scenery," he said, in answer to the question Averill asked as to what brought him so far from home. "And of course, not live under a Nazi regime." He paused to look out a window nearby. "The only things that are familiar are the hills. You Tennesseans call them mountains but to a Norwegian, they are hills."

"Well, to a Cairo native," said Erica, "they are positively the Alps. The weather can be cruelly cold, too."

"All the way down to minus 8.3 degrees Celsius or, seventeen degrees, Fahrenheit, as you would say, Averill," Aksel told her. "A cool spring in my country."

After a few minutes of conversation Averill realized that Aksel and Erica were not comfortable discussing the research they were doing and when they asked her about her visit to Cairo, she gave a carefully abridged account of it and easily steered the conversation to the stories of the garrulous Aksel. He told them how his parents were living under Nazi occupation in Norway and recounted how he had, with some luck and skill, escaped after the German invasion and made his way to the U.S. in a fishing vessel, dodging German U-boats. He told how he was befriended when he landed in New York by a Chattanoogan and had subsequently applied for a job at the University of Chattanooga. There he had met Erica.

Several pots of tea and cups of coffee later Averill caught sight through a window of a storm approaching and their pleasant talk was brought to an abrupt halt. Averill dashed through the parking lot of cars, mopeds, and bicycle racks to reach her car just before the rain began in earnest. It was too late to go back to the office, but the next day she told Reife about Subri's phone call and her subsequent visit with Erica and Aksel. He looked thunderstruck. "You met Aksel Hjördís?"

"Yes, and he wants to meet you."

"I'd like to meet him."

Toward the end of the week Joan returned from a week's visit to Peter at his air force base and dropped by Averill's office.

"You look rested, Joan," said Averill after Joan had flung herself in a chair, kicked off her shoes, and stretched out her legs. "And here I felt guilty about leaving you with all this."

"I just about killed myself in this sweatshop while you were swanning around Egypt chasing spies." She inspected her stockings in dismay. "Will you look at that? I paid a dollar and a half for this hosiery that is supposed to be run-proof. The saleswoman even took a toothpick and demonstrated with it. Ran it up and down the stocking. And now look at that run, spread toe to heel." She jerked herself up. "Oh, I almost forgot. Jim and Frank got their orders and both left for training this morning."

"Are they going in as seamen or midshipmen?"

"They're taking the tests for midshipmen and are practically sleeping with Naval Ordnance manuals. Only the top two thirds who pass make it to midshipmen; if they do, when they're assigned to a ship they'll be Ensigns, reserve of course."

Joan looked ruefully at her leg. "I think I'll go around with black lines painted up my bare legs from now on."

"I did that a lot when I was a teacher."

The conversation soon turned to the topic of Peter's training. "He says flying a B-17 isn't all that much different from flying a Piper Cub except it doubles the engines and is, of course, a bomber. He's terribly excited about going into combat."

"When will he be ready for combat?"

"It'll be toward the end of the year. Let's see, ten months from today...what is today, anyway?"

"January twenty-second."

"Oh, yes, 1942 already. Anyway, his training will last ten months so he'll be deployed toward the end of the year."

Mid-morning the next day Aksel Hjördís appeared in front of Averill's desk and smiled. "You are Mr. Braddock's secretary? I hadn't realized that the other day when I talked with you. I thought perhaps you worked on the factory floor."

"No, I sit here all day at his beck and call. Does he have an appointment with you?"

"But yes. It is convenient?"

"Of course. I'll tell him you're here." She pressed the intercom button, announced his arrival, and walked to Reife's door to open it. Reife had circled his desk and was on his way to the door.

"Come in Dr. Hjördís. So good of you to come. Sorry I didn't tell you about this, Averill. Can you see we're not disturbed?"

A few minutes after he had closed the door on Hjördís, Pris Quigley brought her lunch from the accounting department. She dragged a chair over to Averill's desk, and they spread out their lunches.

"I've just talked with Henrietta," announced Pris, biting into her egg salad sandwich.

"I've been trying to reach her."

"She and her mother left town and took the baby to visit her grandmother, but they're home now. She wants you and me to come over and see the baby."

"Let's do it. She didn't mention Klaus, I suppose."

"Not a word."

"Reife says he is in prison but didn't say where. He was arrested as a German agent while we were in Cairo. That's the extent of my knowledge."

"Mine, too. She sounds very tired. Not like her usual chirpy self. That's to be expected, I imagine. Babies must be exhausting."

"At least she has her mother to help her."

"She says Mrs. Drayson is in heaven having a baby around the house."

Thirty minutes later Pris stashed her lunch debris in the wastebasket and went back to her 'bills payable'. Averill brushed the crumbs from the desk, tossed her empty carton of cottage cheese into the trash, and whipped a letterhead into the typewriter and began working.

The door behind them opened and Aksel Hjördís and Reife emerged. Hjördís caught sight of her and smiled. "Good-day, Averill. How extremely agreeable it is to see you again." When other exchanged pleasantries were finished, Reife escorted him to the entry hall.

"I need to get some letters in the afternoon mail, Averill. Grab your shorthand pad," said Reife as he re-entered the office.

Averill raised her eyebrows when he began to dictate. Later, she was to realize it was the first time she heard the terms, 'heavy water', 'atomic reactor', and the name of a small town not far from Chattanooga—Oak Ridge, Tennessee.

Chapter 31

Henrietta's mother met them at the door, hugged them, and ushered them in to a house smelling of baby powder and the sound of a baby crying. "Henrietta will be so glad to see you. The baby is a darling. Come on, you must see little Janice."

Following Camille they passed a French door leading out to the backyard. Through the door, Averill saw clotheslines holding dazzling white diapers, shirts, vests, and a home-quilted small blanket of blue and pink squares whipping in the cold breeze. They entered a back bedroom, and, there in a rocking chair, Henrietta had just quieted her baby by guiding it to a breast. Her hair was pulled back in a chignon, and although her dress was fresh from the ironing board, it was a sedate housedress and quite unlike the clothes the vibrant, evanescent Henrietta of only last year would have worn. Henrietta lifted a face that was lined with a year of heartbreak and the new maturity that a baby had brought into her life. Averill searched the face for traces of the old Henrietta. She was gone.

"Come in, Averill, Pris. Momma, will you move those clothes off the loveseat? I've just got her feeding, and don't want to rock the boat."

"Of course, Darling. You just go ahead and feed little Janice. There you are, girls, have a seat," her mother said as she swept some little duds from the sofa with her large capable hands. Camille Drayson was a large woman and from the first minute Averill had met her she thought how well suited those big hands were to such a figure.

"She's been fussy all morning. I thought it was because my milk wasn't satisfying her, but she seems to be settling down to a feeding frenzy," said Henrietta with a tinkling little laugh that made Averill hope that the old Henrietta was still there under all the layers of worry and possible treachery of Klaus. "I'll let you hold her when she's finished. She looks just like Momma, don't you think?"

"You don't need to lie through your teeth to flatter me," objected Camille. "You know she's the very image of you."

At least, Averill thought, the baby bore no discernible look to that of her father.

"I'm not getting into that discussion," said Pris, laughing. "You're so fortunate to have your mother help you. Taking care of a baby must be overwhelming."

"Pris, when they brought that child to me in the hospital, I had a panic attack. I can't do it, I said to myself. I'll drop it. I won't have enough milk. All kinds of silly things like that. When you have a baby all you need is twenty-four hours of time in which you have absolutely nothing to do, because a baby will use every minute of it. Even poor Momma runs her legs off keeping up with all the extra work."

"Now, you hush your mouth. I love it. I told the girls at my Bridge club they would have to do without me for a bit. I've something more important to do."

"Who wants to play silly old Bridge when they can help take care of this little darling," said Pris airily, not knowing much about either.

"Er…yes, of course you're right about that," said Camille, momentarily flummoxed, finding her beloved card game unconsciously deprecated. "Well, anyway, when Henrietta was packing to visit my mother's to show off the baby, I said I wouldn't know what to do with myself if I didn't go along, so I got on that train, too."

"Poor Granny, Janice's crying almost drove her to drink. She tried not to show it, but she was delighted when I decided to bring the baby home. It was a nice change, though. There's something about Atlanta that's invigorating. It's even more full of soldiers and sailors than Chattanooga. Everyone is so anxious to beat Hitler and Hirohito. All the men talk war and the women spend their days volunteering at the hospital and running canteens for the soldiers who pass through on their way overseas. The young girls our age are having the time of their lives dancing all night at the canteens."

"I'll have to see about starting some canteens here in Chattanooga. It's the least I can do for my country," said Pris, demurely.

Janice had fallen asleep and the nipple slipped from her mouth. Henrietta rose and placed her in the arms of Averill.

"She's light as a feather. Such tiny, perfect little hands," Averill said, enchanted with Henrietta's baby.

"My turn next," said Pris, and leaned over to stroke the sleeping baby's smooth, soft cheek.

Henrietta arranged her clothing and stretched out on the bed and propped her head up on an elbow. She said, "Go on. You're dying to know. Ask me about Klaus."

"Oh, Henrietta," said Camille.

"He's in Washington and he's in prison. They're preparing to try him as a spy. The military sees that he is represented by an attorney, but there will be other legal expenses. Klaus writes and says that Reife Braddock has offered to pay for those."

"Reife?" exclaimed Averill, almost dropping the baby. Pris stared.

"Yes. I could hardly believe it when Klaus told me."

"I think it's marvelous of him," said Camille who sat on a cedar chest folding baby clothes.

"Klaus is innocent. He didn't make a very good husband, and I'm going to file for a divorce when the trial is over, but I don't think he's guilty of espionage."

"What makes you so sure?" asked Pris.

"For one thing—and I hate to say this about my husband—but he doesn't have the nerve for it. He's all talk. I only had to be married to him for a few months before I found that out. He's supposed to have headed up an espionage ring of over a hundred agents here in the U.S. That's just not possible. He couldn't organize his classroom. Averill, you remember how disorganized he always was?"

"I remember that his class was well versed in current events. Some of the parents complained that was all he taught and said their children didn't know their times tables at the end of the year."

"Exactly," said Henrietta. "I rest my case. He just brought the morning paper, and that was the extent of his lesson plans for that day. And a man like this is supposed to head up a highly organized group of over a hundred people? Nonsense, I say."

"Don't get upset, Henrietta. Remember your milk," Camille cautioned.

"If my milk hasn't curdled or dried up by now, it won't do it, Momma. There's something about nursing a baby that calms you down. Anyway, I want to hear about Cairo, Averill."

Averill related her adventures and her friends expressed admiration and awe for her bravery. During her recital Pris had taken the baby from her and had moved to the rocking chair; presently she placed her in her bassinet. The women watched the baby sleep and talked of old times, and at length said their goodbyes. Camille entreated them to stay for supper, but Averill had noticed the spotlessly clean kitchen and no sign of any meal in progress when they passed through it on their way to the bedroom and guessed that it would work an extra hardship on Camille to feed two extra people.

"Thank you, Camille, but I need to get home," said Averill. Pris agreed that she, too, needed to be 'toddling on home'.

Averill dropped Pris off at her house and made her own way home. As she approached her house, she saw Reife's car parked in front. Her heart gave a little leap, and she raced up the steps and threw open the door. Reife was sitting in the living room talking with Annie Lowe.

Reife rose and moved toward her. Annie, as was her wont, disappeared into the back of the house. He helped her off with her coat and hat and hung them on the coat rack in the entry hall beside his own overcoat, woolen scarf, and hat. "I came by to have a talk with my girl," he said, his arm around her leading her back in to the living room.

"As if you didn't see her every day," Averill teased.

"That's my secretary I see. There's a big difference."

"So I notice," she said as he turned her toward him, wrapped his arms around her, bent her to him and kissed her. After a few seconds he tightened his grip and pulled her even closer. He eventually pulled away and looked down at her with darkened eyes. "Come over here and sit beside me." Obediently, she followed him onto the sofa, and sat with his arm around her. "Your mother said you were visiting Henrietta Ernst. How are she and the baby?"

"The baby is a little love, and Mrs. Drayson is having the time of her life taking care of them both. They seem to all be doing fine. We talked girl talk and 'isn't the baby darling' talk."

Reife shuddered. "You women amaze me. A man looks at a baby and decides if it's breathing, what is there to say?"

"I know. That's why baby visits are for women." Averill paused and reached up for Reife's hand over her shoulder and covered it with her own. "Henrietta talked about you a little, though."

"Me? Why?"

"She said you're footing the bill for Klaus's extra legal expenses," she said, turning to look at him. "Are you?"

"Yes, I am. Do you find that surprising?"

"Not surprising, just highly unlikely with all the proof my father says they have against him. Do you believe him innocent?"

"I don't know. I do happen to think that he should have the chance of a good defense, and that means top-flight legal aid."

"When does the trial start?"

"May the twenty-fifth."

"Will you need to go to Washington?"

"I don't think so. I have a man up there arranging for a defense."

"It's a noble thing you're doing, Reife."

"Noble? Not at all. I just don't like to see Henrietta's husband found guilty of something he might not have done. I think it's more than likely he's guilty, but I still want him to have a good defense."

"As I said, you're a very nice man, Reife Braddock," Averill said, lifting her face to his. He bent his face to hers and kissed her again. After quite a long while she got up and found a radio station playing Frank Sinatra, and they sat and talked quietly about their loved-ones going in to harm's way: Col. Lowe, Reife's brothers who were recent Naval recruits and handsome Captain Peter Conover, training to engage the enemy in air battles where the rate of Allied pilots killed was astronomical. She was suddenly afraid for the future.

Chapter 32

Averill arrived at her office one morning in early February to find Aksel Hjördís seated on the couch across from her desk holding a coffee cup with the logo, 'University of Chattanooga' in blue and gold imprinted on its side.

"How is Erica?" asked Averill. "I've been meaning to call her to ask her out for lunch."

"She is most good," he answered. "And you are well?"

"Yes. Reife keeps trying to kill me with overwork, but his plan boomerangs. I just keep feeling better and better."

He smiled and replied, "I like Americans. They have such delightful ways of saying things."

"Americans are not the most popular people in your country right now."

"But yes, they are. Oh, of course, you mean with the Nazis." He made a sound of derision. "What do they matter? We will get rid of them one day."

"You have an underground, I suppose?" Averill asked.

"We will get rid of them," Aksel repeated, more guarded this time but with a decisive nod of his head.

He then buried himself in some papers he had brought in a briefcase.

Presently Reife arrived and the two men adjourned to Reife's office. On his way, Reife stopped by her desk and *sotto voce* he said, "Don't charm him too much. He might start believing it, and you are not available." He looked at her with a smile tugging at his lips under an assumed stern demeanor. He rapped her desk with his knuckles and said to Aksel as they proceeded into Reife's office, "We can refill that cup in my office. I'll make you fresh." Averill smiled to herself. Reife was suggesting that he always made his coffee. This would be his first time, as far as she knew.

That afternoon Averill placed a call to Erica and invited her to see a movie with her the next Saturday. "But yes," said Erica in her lilting English accent, "I would love to."

"Wonderful! I'll pick you up at your dorm at one-thirty."

"Would you mind if I brought Aksel along? He wants to see *Suspicion*."

"That will be great. I'll see if Reife can join us. He adores Joan Fontaine."

"And I like your Cary Grant," replied Erica.

Averill said cautiously, "Reife is a mystery buff and I think he's read the book it's based on and the movie changes the ending. I hope it doesn't spoil the movie for him."

"How did they change it?" asked Erica.

"The ending," said Averill.

Erica, the eternal scientist insisted, "But how?"

"He really does kill his wife. In the book, that is."

"Now you've spoiled it for me," Erica moaned. Averill laughed and said, "Well, you asked."

Reife could, indeed, join them and he did grumble about the ending as Averill predicted while the four made their way to dinner through the theater crowd. At the Read House dining room they were finally seated and all ordered the specialty of the house—a beef soup—as Averill observed, "The U.S. is bound to begin food rationing soon and beef will be the first thing to be rationed."

"Here I will disagree," said Reife. "I think coffee will be first. The English army may march on its tea, but America will fight with a belly full of coffee."

The talk turned, as usual, toward the war. "What a tragedy that Singapore fell to the Japanese. I guess it was inevitable after they sank those British ships off Malaysia," commented Reife as he dipped into the steaming soup. "They say it broke Churchill's heart when he heard the *HMS Prince of Wales* battleship was bombed. It was his pet."

Aksel said, reflectively, "So much breaking of hearts these days. Manila has fallen to the Japanese in the Philippines. President Roosevelt will either have to rescue General MacArthur from Corregidor or lose him to the Japanese as prisoner."

"He'll be rescued," responded Reife. "The Allies can't afford to lose MacArthur." He drank deeply of his coffee and added, "They are not like Hitler who holds in contempt his commanders and sometimes executes them when a mission fails. When Albert Einstein fled Nazi Germany and immigrated to the United States, Hitler's attitude was, 'Let the vermin go. Germany does not need its Jews.'"

Aksel said, "I have a brilliant student who has escaped Nazi-occupied Norway and wants to come to America. He's not Jewish but he has been occupied in underground activities that would surely set him in front of a firing squad by the Nazis if he were ever captured. Fortunately, he escaped from Norway right under the Nazi's noses. If the U.S. grants him asylum he wishes to join me in my work here at the University of Chattanooga."

This was obviously not news to Erica, for she added, "If he comes, he does not wish to stay in a dormitory. Do you know any place where he might board?"

Reife said, "Well, there's Mrs. McLaughlin's boarding house. She serves meals with her rooms. It's on a quiet residential street. The food is very good and the rooms are spacious and immaculate."

Averill protested, "Oh no, he must stay with us in Fortuna Medina's old room. I know Mother would love to have him. She's always complaining that she doesn't have a man to cook for."

"There you are then," said Reife, "we've got your friend's problem solved."

"You're very kind," said Aksel. "I'll convey this message to him." The sound of a closing door could be heard in his voice as he dismissed the subject before they could probe further.

Into the ensuing hush Erica asked, "What movie do you think will do well in this year's Academy Awards? I have heard *Citizen Kane* mentioned." From there the conversation ran along the Hollywood route; Erica was clearly star-struck.

Spring arrived and Averill entered her office wearing a lightweight wool dress that required no coat. She removed her hat—a perky velour number with a brim—and heard muted voices coming from Reife's office. Presently, he and a young man emerged from the office. He wore a foreign-looking tweed coat and carried a matching hat. Reife said, "Olaf, I'd like you to meet Averill Lowe. Averill, this is Olaf Vidar. He is the friend Aksel was telling us about a couple of months ago."

"I'm so glad you had a safe trip, Olaf."

"Yes, thank you. I am gratified I had no great trouble." He smiled a broad smile and he looked at her with eyes that held admiration.

Reife led him out and the two talked in low tones. Reentering the office, he said to Averill, "I gave him your mother's address. I hope you don't mind. He would like to get settled soon."

"No, of course I don't mind. I told Mother about him and she is hoping he will room with us. I'll give her a ring and tell her he has arrived." Reife nodded and went back into his office. He paused at the doorway and looked her over with a lingering glance that he seldom allowed himself at the office.

"New dress?"

"Yes. It's my spring folly."

He smiled and was gone, but there was no mistaking that little flame that had appeared in the back of his eyes. Averill hummed as she dialed the number to her house.

Olaf's move into the upstairs spare bedroom was settled with a minimum of fuss and thereafter, his appearance at the kitchen table always meant a lively discussion. He talked of world events and gave rapturous glimpses of a far away frigid land but whose delightful summers made everything bearable. Olaf talked of sailing the fjords with his father and of skiing before he was four years old. He related short days filled with visits back and forth between neighbors, the hot spicy drink with currants and almonds that was served in every kitchen and was called something that Averill could not pronounce. He never talked about his work with Aksel and Erica, and Averill and her mother never asked.

One afternoon Reife asked Averill to deliver a tube of drawings to Erica at the University. As she prepared to leave, he called her back to inspect the package one more time. "Yes, all here. Thanks, Averill. Take the company car," and tossed her a ring of keys.

Averill found Erica in U of C's lab and delivered her package. There was no time for chitchat as Erica seemed intensely engrossed in her work and said absently, "Thanks, Averill."

Averill had glimpsed the plans in the tube when Reife double-checked its contents. She didn't know a lot about physics but there were diagrams and formulae that weren't like any mechanical design formula she had ever seen. She had noted phrases such as, '…heavy water…D_2O…Uranium 235.' It was unintelligible to her and reminded her of her college freshman year chemistry class where she had relied on her friend and lab mate to prod her through the course where she thankfully pulled a 'C' at the end.

As she climbed into the company car in the University parking lot she followed a dark green Buick to the exit. She noted that its license number, 4-22395, was their phone number without the four. That evening as she walked to her car in Braddock's parking lot the same car was parked a few slots down. A dark-haired man was sitting in the driver's seat watching her intently.

Toward the end of April, Annie Lowe called Averill at work and spoke through the wheeze of sobs. "Oh, Averill, come home, please."

"Mother! What has happened?"

"I was out shopping…came…home…front…door open…don't know… what's been taken."

"Are you saying our house has been burgled?"

"Yes, oh, please come."

She and Reife arrived straightway and found police on the scene. Upstairs-upholstered armchairs had been overturned and disemboweled, drawers emptied of their contents, and Annie's diamond engagement ring had been taken. Averill's room had been rifled and some jewelry taken. She mourned her necklace and bracelet of cameos that her father had sent her from Naples, Italy, but the rest was in a safe that the burglar had not had time to discover.

"What about Olaf's room?" Averill then asked.

"I haven't checked it yet," said Annie, rubbing her arms in a nervous gesture and Reife leaped for the stairs with Annie and Averill following. Opening the door to the room in the attic, they saw that here the damage was complete. The floor was piled with overturned furniture and their contents scattered like so many Spillikins. The mattress of the bed was in big tufted clumps.

"Oh. Oh!" Annie sat in a chair and began weeping afresh.

"We'll need to notify Olaf at the lab. I'll just get it from my address book," said Averill and she left to go into her room and get her handbag off her bed. It was then that through the open door from the bedroom, she noticed a towel move on a chrome bar in her bathroom.

"Officer! Officer! Come quickly!" She called. She was brutally pushed aside as a figure leaped from the bathroom. It struggled with the window that looked out upon a small balcony. "No, you don't," she said and grabbed at the man's belt. The burglar turned and gave her a fierce swipe down the side of her face. Reife reached the room first and tackled the man, bringing him to the floor with a tremendous crash. Cuffs were jammed onto his wrists and one police officer said roughly at the spate of curses issuing from his mouth, "That'll be enough of that kind of talk. There are ladies present," and two-stepped him out the door to emerge on Beechwood Lane to interested stares from gathered neighbors.

Upstairs in Averill's bedroom Reife held a washcloth to Averill's head where she had been struck. "You're going to have a black eye, darling, but no other damage that I can see."

The phone rang and her mother, downstairs by now, called up to tell them that Aksel Hjördís was at Braddock Engineering and it was urgent that he talk with Reife. Reife descended the stairs three at a time and pulled out of the circular driveway in a shower of gravel.

Her mother first tended to Averill's face, then both began the cleanup. Neighbors began arriving, and by evening the destruction was cleaned up and the overflowing dust cans set out for collection. Later, that evening, a police officer came to the house and told Averill and her mother that the burglar had been identified from the license plate number that Averill had remembered from the day she delivered the drawings to Erica. He was a naturalized American from Berlin. They were looking into his background and suspected that he may be something more than a common burglar.

Chapter 33

The United States, formerly divided between isolationists and those seeking to aid Britain in the battle of her life, had risen with one voice following the treacherous attack by Japan on the United States naval base at Pearl Harbor on December 7, 1941; both the U.S. and England declared war on Japan the next day and the U.S. on Germany three days later. Following hard on the heels of Japan's sneak attack on Hawaii the Japanese then invaded the islands of the Philippines. The national capital, Manila, was bombed and the U.S. and Filipino defenders eventually withdrew to the Bataan Peninsula under General Edward King while commander of the U.S. Army Forces in the Far East, General Douglas MacArthur, and all diplomatic personnel withdrew to join Commander Colonel Samuel L. Howard and 10,000 naval personnel and marines to the rock fortress of Corregidor on Manila Bay across the strait from Bataan. On March 11 MacArthur was plucked off beleaguered Corregidor in the dead of night by a U.S. PT boat which took him to a base in Mindanao, Philippines where he was flown to Australia by order of President Roosevelt who appointed him Supreme Commander of

Allied Forces in the Southwest Pacific. In Bataan, the American and Filipino troops, starved and disease-ridden, were surrendered by General King to the Japanese on April 9 who then forced them to march on foot for 80 miles without food or drink to a camp where they were packed into facilities built to accommodate only a fraction of the captives. Over a quarter of prisoners died in that unspeakable weeklong march which came ever after to be known as the 'Bataan Death March'. General Wainwright, the successor to MacArthur on Corregidor, held on as long as possible but finally surrendered the fortress on May 6 and all of the Philippines fell. The Pacific war was in disarray. MacArthur and Fleet Admiral Chester Nimitz were soon to change that with the help of the U.S., Australians, New Zealanders, and other troops.

Ensign Frank Braddock had been assigned to the aircraft carrier, the *USS Yorktown*, in January 1942 as a naval surgeon and soon after sailed through the Panama Canal from the Caribbean and traversed the Pacific Ocean in search of the Japanese. His wife, Ellen, went about her duties, outwardly phlegmatic and calm. Dale, the older brother, abandoned his photographic studio, and assumed a large share of management responsibility at the Braddock factory. Divorced, he alternated dropping by Frank's home after work to join in the evening meal with Ellen and her children, AnnaLee and Frankie, or visiting with Colleen and her daughters, Maybelle and Ruth. Ensign Jim Braddock had been assigned to the carrier, *USS Enterprise*, which would become known after the war as the most decorated ship of World War II.

Despite his glib assurance to Averill that he would not be involved in Klaus's defense other than financial, Reife kept the rails warm traveling back and forth between Washington and Chattanooga that May of 1942. Despite his efforts, Klaus was found guilty of espionage. However, as Averill knew from the correspondence that she handled, another reason for Reife's visits to Washington was to meet with the executive committee of the organization, Iron Workers United. He and his colleagues were mostly owners of small and medium businesses whose dedication to winning the war overrode partisanship and instigated a shared technology among former business competitors.

During the first week of May in 1942 the Braddock family was glued to the radio for news of the Battle of the Coral Sea in which Frank's ship was engaged. The ship was severely damaged and for ten days the family heard nothing. Averill put a blubbering Ellen through to Reife one morning in mid-May and went to stand in the open doorway of Reife's office where she could hear Ellen's voice from across the room.

"Ellen," cajoled Reife, "Ellen, just take a deep breath and tell me. Is he alive?"

"Yes…yes. Oh, yes, he's alive, Reife! The *USS Yorktown* is at Pearl Harbor where it's being repaired. It got there under its own steam."

"That's fantastic, Ellen. Was he injured?"

"He was thrown around a little in sick bay where he was working, but he's okay. Just a mild concussion. I have to ring off, Reife. My mother is having an asthma attack." The line went dead.

"Does she need help?" asked Averill from the door.

"No. She'll be all right. It's just the excitement."

Reife threw the receiver on the hook, looked up at Averill, reached in his in-basket and flung its contents in the air. Leaping from his chair, he circled his desk on a run and grabbed Averill who had stood stock-still upon seeing the disciplined and self-controlled Reife in such exuberance. "Whoopee!" he yelled and gathered her into his arms and kissed her long and hard. Breathless, she leaned back enough to ask, "He wasn't injured?"

"Not badly. A bump on the head. He called Ellen from Pearl Harbor."

"Oh, thank God."

"Know what I want to do?"

"No, what?"

"I want to go to church, kneel at the altar and thank God."

"I'll go with you."

Pastor Resterick came out of the office as they arrived and walked to the altar with them. There the good man prayed, thanking God for saving so many lives on the *Yorktown* and for the safe passage of the ship to Pearl Harbor through enemy-infested waters. Last of all, and most fervently, he thanked God for the safety of Ensign Frank Braddock, USNR.

The coming days found Reife abstracted and thoughtful as his workload increased. Almost every weekday night was now spent overnight in the furnace room where there was a shower and cot and where he kept a change of clothes. Some nights Russ Higgins joined him by pulling two chairs together and piling it with pillows. Reife grew a beard to save time shaving and skipped more meals than he should have. Braddock Engineering was now launched all-out for war production and soon was turning out a huge amount of tanks a month.

Dale prowled the assembly lines, sometimes pitching in to help. The custodian, Frederick Jackson, a Negro who had been at Braddock for ten years doing janitorial work, began helping out on the assembly lines and his paycheck jumped thirty percent to his and his wife's delight. Their son, Lincoln, was hired to work alongside Frederick. Joan came in almost every day to help with filing, typing, accounting, and whatever office work needed doing. Her society career suffered; the balls and cotillions that had been her favorite pastime were events of the past. "They're no fun without Peter, anyway," she was to say to Averill.

The worst was not over for the family of Ensign Frank Braddock. During the first week of June of 1942, the *Yorktown* had gone back to the fighting in the Battle of Midway and fatally damaged a Japanese aircraft carrier. In return, however, the *Yorktown* suffered mortal damage itself from a Japanese submarine torpedo. H.V. Kaltenborn led the evening news on June 4 reporting that the ship had been abandoned by all survivors, and on June 7 the family listened as the news was broadcast around the world that after listing badly for some hours it had plunged to the bottom of the Pacific.

The family waited for further news, but none came and there was no published list of survivors. The Braddocks went on with their work but within listening distance of a radio.

Other minor news came from Europe, although most of the world did not know its import until peace was declared in 1945. Reinhard Heydrich, the sadistic and brutal Nazi executor of 'The Final Solution' as the Nazis called their stealthy plan to exterminate the Jews, was assassinated. This did not stop the Nazi extermination juggernaut, however. With Adolph Hitler's Minister of Interior, Heinrich Himmler, the murderous policy against millions of Jews was continued in greater measure culminating in clandestine death camps, their dreadful secrets only to be uncovered by the liberating Allied armies.

"How can a Christian nation such as Germany, ruthlessly attempt to invade the whole of Europe and Britain? What caused her people to follow Hitler?" Averill was to ask Reife one rare day as they lay on blankets beside Harrison Bay, both wet from swimming and boating. Jim's borrowed skiff lay at anchor and their beach picnic was given shade by a huge patio umbrella that had been driven into the sand.

Reife turned on his stomach and looked out across the dun-colored water. "Hitler's Nazi regime has propagandized Germany so thoroughly many think he is the Messiah. Hitler turned the economy around after the widespread unemployment and poverty caused by the terms of the Treaty of Versailles, terms of which demanded restitution from the Germans to the Allies after World War I and bankrupt the country. Hitler's fury toward the nations who had driven Germany to her knees fueled his promised revenge for their destitute financial system, and, to the survivors of the people whose relatives starved after the Armistice, he offered a Germany that will rule the world for the next 1,000 years. That's heady stuff for a humiliated and mortified people who felt they had peace stuffed down their throat which stripped them of all dignity."

Averill's eyes slid over Reife's face. He was too pale and his cobalt-blue eyes stood out markedly against his colorless cheekbones. Above the emaciated cheeks, in the valley below his eyes, there was an unhealthy bruised look which broadcast seven-day workweeks, a passion for life telescoped into a ruthless discipline to carry out a job. Now his beard was coming in gray. She thought he loved her; she also knew that he would never say so until he could foresee a future that they could share.

A despairing little breath escaped her.

"Why the sigh, my love? Do you want to go back to work? Are you tired of my company?" he asked teasingly.

"You know I'm not. I want so much that I cannot have right now. This war brought you into my life and now I'm afraid it will eventually take you someplace where I can't reach you," she added simply, and stroked his arm lying prone on the sand.

He sat up and reached for her. "Where do you think I'll go that you can't reach?"

"I'm afraid of the tide that may carry you into forgetting that there's a life to be lived apart from winning the war. I'm afraid of the undertow that sweeps us apart although we're physically together in our work at the company. I'm afraid that one day you'll be on one shore and I'll be on another and there will be an ocean between us that can't be crossed and we'll find that we've helped saved the world but we have sacrificed the chance of a life together."

Reife abruptly released her, gathered up the empty sandwich wrappers and tossed them toward a trash barrel. Then he reached for his towel. "It's time to go. Let's clean up here and I'll drive the truck down and hitch up the boat." He rose and looked down at a startled Averill who shrank from the look he gave her. "I find that statement self-serving and unconscionable with the state the world is in now," he said, totally unreachable now.

Averill watched him stride toward the parking area without a backward look. With a dully-beating heart, she bent to gather up her things and pack the empty picnic basket with the dirty dishes. The sun disappeared behind dark clouds and a cool breeze sprang up which hinted of a thunderstorm. On the way home, they made minimal conversation. She sat beside him and a black hatred toward him arose in her heart for the way he had bludgeoned her with his sharp words and made her feel like a chastened schoolgirl.

Chapter 34

The next morning Averill typed a dozen resignation letters. Each one was tossed into the wastebasket. While she was typing number thirteen Reife walked through her office on the way to his own. "Good morning," he said, neutrally.

"Good morning," she answered, in the same tone, meeting his eyes coolly. He disappeared into his office and she tore out the latest sheet of paper from the typewriter and flung it into the waste can. She abruptly left her desk, entered the company kitchen, snatched open the door to the refrigerator, seized a Coca Cola, hurled open the door to an outside patio, and flung herself onto a glider to look unseeingly out over the Tennessee River. The rhythmic motion of the glider and the cool drink on her stomach soothed her.

Watching the brown water flowing through the middle of the town, she remembered the history all grade school children had to read of how Chattanooga had grown from a small trading post on the banks of the winding Tennessee River to become the dynamic industrial city whose men had been shaped by wresting the iron ore out of nearby South Pittsburgh, Tennessee.

She thought of this iron ore that had been forged by her grandfather and others into stoves, cooking ware, hot water tanks, manhole covers; and now with wartime, it was being molded into armaments. Just as the city had flexed its muscles and altered its output from dealing in domestic appurtenances to the serious building of machines of war, so had the men who worked in the factories of bowl-shaped Chattanooga, scooped out between Missionary Ridge, Lookout Mountain, Signal Mountain, and the southern terminus of the Cumberland Mountain range of the Appalachians in northern Alabama, put aside lesser things and grasped hold of the eternal duty of a man—that of protecting his household from the marauder. She finished her bottle of Coke and met Joan on the stairs holding a letter in her hand. She thrust it toward Averill. It was hand delivered from Washington, D.C. "This just came for you. I thought you might want to see it right away."

Averill tore open the envelope and pulled out a single sheet.

Dear Averill,
I am asking a friend to deliver a copy of this to you at your office. Kindly let Reife read this. Yesterday, Klaus Ernst was fatally shot trying to escape from prison.
Best to you and your mother,
Dad

"Bad news?" Joan asked.

"Klaus Ernst is dead. Henrietta will need me this afternoon when she gets the news. I must get busy. I'll have to leave work early."

"I'll help you. I've just finished helping Gavin with payroll."

Joan began on some filing. Reife opened the door to his office and poked his head around. "Averill, can you take some letters?"

"Of course." Averill picked up her steno pad and pen and entered his office. Reife gave her no glance but began the dictation striding back and forth behind his desk. His dictation was in rapid, staccato phrases. After some time, the words came so furiously swift that she laid her pad and pencil on her lap and looked at him. His back was to her and after a few minutes, he turned and asked her to read back the last sentence. She obliged, and he exploded. "That's at the very beginning. You've missed the whole letter. What happened?"

"I don't take dictation from the mouth of a machine gun." She looked at him with eyes blazing. In the midst of her anger a cold little hand clutched at her heart. His eyes that once had held warmth and softness were now cold ashes. Averill carefully laid her pad and pencil on his desk and rose. She said slowly and evenly, "There's my steno pad," she said pointing to the wire-bound tablet. "Take down your own letters. And while you're at it, you can type them, too. I'm going to visit Henrietta. Klaus has been killed."

She erupted from Reife's office and snatched up her handbag. She stopped only long enough say, "I'll be gone for the day, Joan." As she pulled open the door she was half turned and saw Reife standing in the doorway of his office with Joan turned from the filing cabinet, both looking as if lightening had struck.

Henrietta answered the door holding a telegram. Wordless they embraced, and Averill felt Henrietta's hot tears on her cheek. Henrietta led her back to her spacious bedroom filled with sunlight and the yeasty smell of baby. Averill sat in a boudoir chair while Henrietta resumed what had obviously been her position before Averill had arrived—face down on her bed. Little Janice was in her bassinet playing with the mobiles strung across the top of her little bed. Her chubby legs pumped with delight as she reached for the swirling, swinging figures.

Averill sat for some minutes in the bedroom listening to the sobbing woman and the gurgling baby. At last Henrietta sat up, her face bloated and eyes streaming. She grabbed Averill and clung to her as fresh sobs beat through her tiny frame. Averill murmured, "I know, I know. Darling Henrietta, it's going to be all right. You have Janice. You have your mom. You have me and Pris. We'll help you get through this."

"Why did he run? He was going to appeal. His lawyer said he had a good chance to overturn the verdict. Why? Why" She beat the bed with her fists.

"I don't know, Henrietta. Sometimes a person is overwhelmed with despair. They feel there's no reason to go on. It'll look better tomorrow. The sun will come up again and it'll be a brand new day. In the meantime is there anything I can help you with? Funeral plans, anything."

"I have mother," she choked out, "and Granny is coming in on tomorrow's train and I have two aunts with their husbands arriving in a couple of days. Mother's gone to the store for groceries. Just stay with me for a spell. Can you hand Janice to me? She's hungry."

Averill ran and scooped up little Janice who had begun to fuss and turned bright-with-tears questing eyes on her before bestowing a melting smile on her. "Oh, you darling," sang out Averill and pressed the baby close. Henrietta held out her arms and Averill placed the baby into them. The baby was soon nursing with Henrietta rocking in the big chair she used for feeding Janice. Averill stayed to help her bathe Janice and had the delight of rubbing baby shampoo into the silky fine dark brown hair on the rosy scalp. Henrietta asked, "Will you stay for lunch, Averill? Momma should be home from the store soon; right now, our cupboard is bare. There's some tea, somewhere, though." Henrietta walked into the kitchen shifting Janice onto one arm, and pulled a teapot off a shelf and began measuring in tea.

"Here, I'll do that," said Averill, relieving her of the tea. "A glass of iced tea is just what we need."

Henrietta relinquished the measuring spoon, ran to the kitchen screen door where it slammed like a bullet behind her because of a broken spring, and sprinted to a patch of mint where Averill could see her pulling up a plant growing near a faucet. Averill put the kettle on and opened the refrigerator and brought out ice trays and located an ice bucket with tongs. She rooted around for sugar and had all this done when Henrietta returned with little Janice rosy and laughing in spite of her jostled journey. The kettle boiled, and Averill poured the steaming water over the little china insert in the Japanese teapot that had been a wedding gift to Daniel and Camille Drayson.

"Oh, that's just what I needed," breathed Henrietta as she took a sip of the cool tea that had been steeped and poured over ice with a sprig of mint added. "When the English say 'tea' they're talking hot tea. When Southerners talk of tea, we mean iced tea, usually with fresh mint."

"I know. When I was in Egypt every time Susan suggested tea I looked at the ice box which always held a big block of ice instead of which Susan would be reaching for the kettle and cups and saucers." And Henrietta laughed—a sound that bespoke of happier days to Averill as she leaned back and ran her hands through her hair and allowed herself to relax. This horrible day was going better than she imagined; then into her head popped the sight of Reife's hard eyes across from her as she threw her steno pad on his desk. She would deal with that later—but not now; next week, perhaps, while she stood in an unemployment line. With vicious discipline she wrenched her thoughts away and focused her attention on the baby who had returned to her nursing.

Camille arrived, carrying bags of groceries in both arms. "Are there more, Mrs. Drayson?" she asked.

"Yes, there's a ten-pound bag of potatoes sitting in the open trunk of the car. Would you mind?"

"Back in a jiff."

Outside there was a young man pushing a cart. "Hot tamales, Miss?"

"Oh, yes. Let me just get my purse." She ran back inside the house. She returned and, to the young man's surprise, bought every tamale on the cart. "Well, thank you Ma'am. I'm much obliged."

"You're welcome." She grabbed the potatoes in her other hand, slamming down the trunk lid with her elbow, swooped to pick up the *Chattanooga News-Free Press* from the lawn adroitly with a free thumb, reentered the kitchen, and dropped everything on the counter. "Don't cook, Camille. Smell these tamales. Aren't they heavenly? Let's have them for lunch."

"Let's," Mrs. Drayson agreed, "it's too hot to cook anyway," and she emptied the table of its last groceries and banged three plates in their places while Averill dug out tableware and napkins. The tea and tamales were delicious and they talked of everything except the fact that Klaus Ernst had died yesterday and his baby was lying tranquilly with its little rump in its mother's hand while that mother scooped up tamales with a fork in her other hand. In her mind's eye Averill could see a cross-stitched motto that had hung in her grandmother's kitchen: 'Breaking bread with friends is a minute in time; sorrow fills hours; let not the two meet.'

When Averill arrived home her mother met her at the door. "Joan wants you to call her," she said, her eyes worried. Averill ran up to her room to the extension telephone she had installed. Mrs. Lowe was sitting in the living room listening to the radio when Averill descended the stairs with heavy steps.

"What is it, Averill?" Annie asked.

"Frank Braddock has been officially classified as missing in action. His ship, the *Yorktown*, was at the Battle of Midway," said Averill and walked into the living room and dropped into a chair.

"The last I remember he was in Pearl Harbor with the ship awaiting repairs," said Annie, her mouth agape with consternation.

"It was repaired and set sail just in time to be engaged at Midway Island. It was heavily damaged on June 4 and the Captain ordered all hands to abandon ship. It was sunk by the Japanese a few days later and went down in three miles of water."

"That's good news, then, isn't it? Surely all the men were saved." Her mother asked anxiously.

"It is if Frank was one of the sailors who abandoned. Some of them couldn't because they died in the attack. We just don't know yet. The Braddocks have heard nothing until today."

Annie reached to switch on the news. H.V. Kaltenborn came on reading from the latest wire service offerings. The Allies were calling Midway a turning point in the war because of the overwhelming defeat of the Japanese at the tiny island. But all knew the end was not in sight.

"Do I still have a job?" Averill asked Reife from her desk when he arrived the next morning.

"Of course. Why not?" he asked raising an eyebrow and continuing on into his office. Averill followed him.

"Reife, I want to apologize about yesterday. It was unforgivable for me to walk out on you like that. I'm so very sorry to hear about Frank."

"Yes, well, let's look on the bright side. A lot of the men got off the ship before it was sunk. It will take days to get it sorted out and word get back here to the States about who survived and who didn't. It's tough on Ellen to have this yo-yo of emotions, poor girl. First his ship is damaged in the Coral Sea and lives are lost. Then she hears Frank's safe. Now, a month later, she's back in the nightmare."

"I know. I'm so sorry."

"Well, we'll know one way or another in time," said Reife, in the dead tone he used when he was keeping his emotions squashed.

Averill turned to leave. "Let me know if I can help you with any letters."

He looked up. "Your steno pad ended up in my trashcan, somehow."

She looked at him and saw his lips twitching. They broke out into a laugh that doubled them up. When she slipped behind her desk a few minutes later she reflected that, although the petulant toss that he must have given her steno pad that landed it in the trash had afforded them much merriment and had cleared the air somewhat, she knew they had lost something that might never return. She wondered if she were destined to join the ranks of women who, after thrust to great heights of happiness with the man they loved, was fated to watch love crash and burn on the altar of a war which had to be fought if civilization were to survive. She made her way to a utility closet and with her mouth pressed up against a disgusting rag that smelled of motor oil, she let the scalding tears flow, and, with a clear-sighted mind, probed the possibility that maybe what happened to them wasn't the war. Perhaps Reife had never loved her, after all.

Chapter 35

The Braddock family did not get word about Frank's fate at Midway Island until the middle of July. He was taken prisoner; but with several others escaped. He came home on an extended furlough to his family's great delight. In August, Bernard Lowe came home on an extended leave, and Annie welcomed him without recriminations and he moved into her bedroom in the big house at 1600 Beechwood Lane. Her father looked thinner, more tired and it seemed to Averill that his shoulders did not stand as erect as they once did. Annie seemed quietly content and Averill looked forward every evening to finding her mother and father in the living room listening to the radio, her father reading the paper or doing its puzzle and her mother knitting baby things for Henrietta's baby. How good God was to let her family be together once again!

Averill never did submit her resignation letter, and Reife was pleasant, although a bit distracted these days. Averill suspected there was someone else in his life and stoically carried on her work, determined to stay because she was persuaded that she was in the best place to help America win the war. Fortunately, the work at Braddock's kept her too busy to do more than work and sleep, and she had little time for dwelling on what she and Reife had lost. It was not unusual for her to arrive home from work after eight in the evening.

Two weeks later Edward Guinn called Averill at the office. "How are things at Braddock?"

"The new tanks rolled off the assembly line yesterday. Next week they'll be on their way to Europe. When did you get back into town?"

"A few days ago. I have a few more days of leave and then I have to go back to Ceylon. I want to see you. "Will you have dinner with me tonight?"

"Love to, but Ceylon, Edward?"

"I've been there for the past few weeks. We'll talk about it tonight when I see you. I'll pick you up about seven-thirty. Is that all right?"

"Great. See you."

That night they settled themselves at an outside table at a little restaurant on the river. Edward looked haggard and tired.

"Edward, what happened?"

"The cyclone which hit the Bay of Bengal in October killed 40,000 people. I was part of an adjunct military team that was assigned with U.S. Seabees to restore order, supply food, and construct temporary housing on Ceylon. Those people lost everything and there was not much time to sleep for those of us who were helping."

"Not exactly tanned and rested from sun and sea, were you?" said Averill.

"Tanned, maybe; rested, no," responded Edward.

"Do you want to talk about it?"

"Not now. I want to hear about what's going on here at home. How are Henrietta and the baby?" Averill told him all the news and he listened with an abstracted air. The two were finishing their dessert when Edward abruptly said, "I have been wrestling for weeks whether to tell you something. I've finally come to the conclusion that your knowing may help keep you safe. Averill, there is a project so hush-hush that very few know about it. America is involved in the development of the ultimate weapon. It's known as nuclear fission where atoms are split and a chain reaction of energy is set off that keeps on going until we don't know yet where it will end."

"A sort of super bomb could be built with it?" Averill's face paled as she looked at Edward's grave face.

"It releases such horrific energy that one bomb could possibly destroy New York City or Tokyo. England was working on it, but they had to transfer it to the United States because of the threat of invasion. We know that the Germans are working on it, too, so now there is a life and death race for the Allies to develop it first. A Norwegian scientist, Bohr, is one of those at the forefront. Two of his associates are Aksel Hjördís and Olaf Vidar. Bohr is in Chicago, but Hjördís and Vidar, are, as you know, at the University of Chattanooga. They will begin to regularly shuttle back and forth between here and Oak Ridge, which is only about a hundred miles north of Chattanooga where more research is being done. Vidar will be gone for weeks at a time but you must not ask him anything about his absences. Will you promise me that?"

"I'm not a fool, Edward," she responded with some asperity.

He took a drink of water and continued. "It's the best guarded secret of the war. There are several places where English and American research is being done. The University of Chattanooga is one location, Chicago is another; Los Alamos in New Mexico and Oak Ridge, Tennessee are two others.

"The burglary at your house and your boarder's ransacked room may well be connected to his work on this weapon." Edward paused and reached over and lifted her chin. "Just be vigilant. Notice everything around you. I know I can trust you not to talk about this."

"Of course," she said, shaking off his hand, irritated by the patronizing gesture.

"Reife Braddock knows because his company is doing some design work for Hjördís. You never suspected anything?"

She shook her head, unable to say anything. It was hard to believe. She was living in the middle of the greatest secret of World War II and she had had no idea, and neither did any of the rest of the inhabitants of Chattanooga.

During the next days Averill met Edward for lunch. In the evenings when she could get away from work, they attended church events, patronized bazaars for the war effort, and took in the occasional concert or movie. They met with friends for badminton or boating trips on Harrison Bay but mostly they talked. On the other hand, Reife now only talked business with her, and Averill was now sure there was another woman, but she had no idea who, someone from the Braddock social set, she assumed. At times she would catch him watching her with thoughtful eyes, and the ache of loss that she worked so hard to vanquish spawned anew.

One day in late November near the end of his leave, Edward arrived at the office to collect Averill for a luncheon date and Reife was standing at her desk discussing an outgoing letter. Edward stopped and waited by the door for him to conclude, after which

Reife—much to Averill's bafflement—gave Edward a curt nod and looked as if he might address him but abruptly checked himself, fairly bolted to his office, and closed the door. Averill gathered up her papers, thrust them in a drawer, and plucked her coat and hat from a coat rack. Edward helped her on with them and they left the office.

Sitting across from her at lunch at The Olympian Restaurant, Edward told her he was leaving the next day to travel to San Francisco and from there he would go back to Ceylon. "Will you answer me something if I ask it?" His brown eyes searched hers as if he could read her thoughts.

"If I can," Averill said, a little hesitantly.

"Has something happened between you and Reife?"

"Always go straight to the point, don't you?" She stirred her iced tea and answered, "Yes, you might say something has happened. It seems I've made a fool of myself over a man who doesn't love me."

"And yet you still work for him."

She gave him a veiled look. "I'm needed, and I'm going to stay. Braddock's is vital to the war. That's all that matters now."

Edward drew a long breath. "Yes, that's all that matters now."

That night when he took her home, he drew her into his arms and kissed her. "Will you write me?"

"Of course I'll write you."

"Well, that's all right then."

The next day he called her from the train terminal. "I just wanted to tell you I still love you. When you told me you weren't seeing Braddock anymore, I had hope for the first time in a long time. Averill, don't say anything; just hear me out. Promise me you will think about it while I'm gone. Will you promise me that?"

"Edward, you're very dear to me. Yes, I will promise that."

Henrietta Ernst went to bed early these days because most nights she was awakened around midnight by Janice's banshee-sharp screams and the one-year-old would take an hour or so before being quieted. Then would follow a day of the monotonous round of feeding and bathing Janice, washing and hanging out baby clothes on the clothesline in the backyard, folding diapers, and ironing scads of little duds. She grabbed a nap sometimes when the active Janice slept.

One noon Averill left the office intending to eat lunch somewhere close; instead, she found herself without much of an appetite and decided to pay Henrietta and the baby a visit. She found Henrietta and her mother sitting down to toasted cheese sandwiches; Camille insisted that she have one, too. The three passed an enjoyable hour taking turns holding little Janice who, in the light of day, was transformed into beguiling angelhood.

"How are you and Reife getting along?" asked Henrietta, seemingly intent on pulling with forefinger and middle a black tuft of hair into a curl on the otherwise hairless pate of Janice.

"We work together. That's the extent of it," Averill said, in unruffled equanimity.

"I expect you've heard that he's dating some socialite from the Lookout Mountain set."

"Henrietta!" her mother said, sharply.

"It's all right, Camille. He's perfectly free to date anyone he chooses," Averill replied. From anyone but Henrietta she might have interpreted the remark as malicious, but these days Henrietta seemed to be almost sleepwalking. Always outspoken, she was even more so now. It was as if grief, the burden of motherhood, loneliness—Averill knew her to be lonely for male company—had leached into a character trait that was part of her charm: her careless impetuosity. Averill had long suspected that on the dark flipside of this attribute lurked the quality of occasional insensitiveness, unrecognized by Henrietta herself and grasped only by those who felt its sting.

From that point, the conversation became strained and Camille attempted with some success to assuage Henrietta's moodiness with lively talk. Presently, Averill glanced at her watch and exclaimed, "Two o'clock! It's been lovely. Thanks for the toasted cheese," and soon took her leave.

She returned to the office to find a statuesque dark-haired woman standing talking with Joan outside the offices. With visible uneasiness, Joan introduced the woman as Lyneire Dubuq, a name with which Averill was already acquainted from the few times she read the society pages. Lyneire acknowledged the greeting with a pleasant "hello" and a smile that did not reach cool, appraising eyes. She ran lavender kid gloves through her hand, tucked a stray curl under her huge-brimmed lavender hat with faultlessly manicured nails and said, "Reife has told me about his efficient secretary. I'm glad to be meeting the paragon," and again smiled a mind-numbingly charming smile which was intended to rob the words of malice.

"I wouldn't use the term, 'paragon' and I doubt if Reife would, either." Averill replied with smiling composure.

Lyneire frowned but didn't pursue it. She asked, "He said you were a former school teacher?"

"No. I *am* a schoolteacher. I'm just not in the classroom right now."

"Of course. My mistake. Well, Joan, it was a lovely lunch. We'll see you tonight then?"

"If I can. My schedule here gets hectic at times."

"I understand. What a bore this war has become."

Averill couldn't stop herself. "Oh, yes. The men walking the Death March from Bataan found it particularly monotonous," she said, irony in her voice. Then almost immediately regretted her sarcasm. It wasn't like her to hurl biting remarks.

Lyneire stared at her with undisguised hostility and said, "I really must fly. Goodbye, Joan. Good day, Miss Lowe."

After she had made her exit, Joan turned to Averill and said, "You didn't know Reife is seeing her, did you, Averill?"

"Not precisely, but it comes as no great surprise."

"I'm sorry. The family at one time expected Lyneire and Reife to make a match of it."

"What happened? Averill asked.

"*You* happened, Averill."

"Well, now things can get back on track for Lyneire. I'm obviously out of the picture."

Joan looked at her unhappily. Then she burst out, "Oh, can't you see? Reife feels such shame for not being overseas fighting, as are Frank and Jim and Peter. It's eating him up. He hates having to be here at Braddock and you're part of that life. It's not fair to you. He knows it, but he can't help it. Just give him time, Averill. He loves you. I know he does."

"No, I don't think he does, Joan," Averill said slowly. "Edward Guinn does, though. He wants to marry me when he returns from Ceylon."

"You don't love Edward, Averill."

"How do you know whom I love, Joan? People change."

Joan stared beyond Averill with widening eyes. Averill turned and saw Reife climbing up from the basement carrying a piece of heavy machinery. He gave an expressionless "thanks" with an unreadable nod as Averill stepped over to open his office door for him. She wondered how much he had heard.

"There's stew in a pan on the stove, Averill," said her mother one night in November when she arrived late.

"Thanks, Mom. I'll have a bowl and go on to bed. Anything in the paper, Dad?"

"Rommel's forces in North Africa are retreating. Looks like we've turned the corner in the battle for North Africa. Listen, Churchill is speaking now on the radio from London." There was a crackle of static and the voice of Winston Churchill, the redoubtable Prime Minister of England, came from the Philco radio:

"We have a new experience. We have victory—a remarkable and definite victory. I have never promised anything but blood, tears, toil, and sweat. Now, however, the bright gleam has caught the helmets of our soldiers, and warmed and cheered all our hearts. Now this is not the end. It is not even the beginning of the end. But it is, perhaps, the end of the beginning."

The listeners at the Lord Mayor's luncheon from where he had spoken in London gave a huge roar of laughter.

Col. Lowe chuckled and reached again for his paper. "Churchill does have a way with words."

"I'm so glad for Sami and Susan and their boys. The threat to Cairo is over. Oh, that is such great news," cried Averill and went into the kitchen to eat lamb stew.

Chapter 36

Spring arrived once more in the Tennessee valley and the dogwoods and azaleas were blooming on Lookout Mountain. Across the bowl that was Chattanooga, Missionary Ridge sat as a southern fortress wall of the coal-blackened city. Here on the slopes of the Ridge descending to Dodd's Avenue, named for D. T. Dodds, a late nineteenth century Illinoisan turned Southerner who bought farm property and developed several communities at the foothills of the Ridge, the Lowe's backyard gave refuge to a riot of green-sprouting pear and cherry trees. The grape arbor on the inclined yard was coming alive with tiny green bullets that would in turn be luscious satin-purple Concord grapes, which would hang on the carefully tended vines. Col. Lowe and Olaf Vidar sat in the kitchen drinking coffee this Saturday morning watching a scarlet tanager flying to and fro above the nets overlaying the cherry trees as Averill entered.

"Hi, Dad, Olaf. What are you two up to?"

"Watching my cherry trees survive an attack by the spring birds. Look at this newspaper article, Averill," her father said as he took his eyes off his backyard and pushed the morning's paper toward her. "The Allies are chasing the Germans out of Africa and Olaf's father had a hand in winning this battle living under the noses of the Nazis."

Olaf explained in answer to Averill's interested look. "It is true. My father owns a shipping business. He—and other boat owners like him—smuggled guns and ammunition to the Allies in this battle." Olaf rose to rinse out his cup.

"That's amazing—and terrifying." Averill poured a cup and settled herself across from them. "What is the punishment if the Nazis uncover this?"

Olaf shrugged. "Not any worse than what the Allies suffer when the Germans fight against them in North Africa. Norway fought the Nazis against tremendous odds and lost, but that doesn't mean we have to submit. My father and others like him will go down fighting."

Averill studied him, thinking of the new knowledge that Edward had shared with her about Olaf's secret work on a weapon that could eventually end the war—depending on which nation got it first. "Are you taking a day off, Olaf?"

Olaf picked up another slice of crumb cake, grabbed his light jacket, and headed for the door. "No, I'm on my way to the lab now," he said, smiling his wide, handsome smile and swung out of the kitchen.

"How was your week, Averill?" her father asked, turning back to survey her.

"Busy. What's the news about Guadalcanal?"

"It's over. We sustained heavy losses but we held on. It's a victory for our side, thank God."

"Isn't Jim on the carrier, *USS Enterprise*?"

"Yes, it was hit by Japanese bombers and suffered loss of life but Colleen heard from Jim in Pearl Harbor and he wasn't injured."

"Thank God," breathed Averill. The doorbell rang and, with coffee in hand, she went to answer it. When she opened the door Pris Quigley was waving goodbye to Olaf Vidar who was pulling out of the driveway. "Who's the good looking man?" she asked Averill.

"Oh! You haven't met our new boarder, have you?"

"I'll say not. I certainly would have remembered him."

"Push your eyeballs back into their sockets, Pris, and come in and have a cup of coffee. I'll introduce you sometime."

"Thank you, girl friend. Both things sound lovely."

Col. Lowe had gone out to work in his vegetable garden, Averill handed Pris a mug, and the two pulled out chairs at the well-worn yellow wooden kitchen table.

"This is such a restful kitchen," and Pris sighed and looked around with pleasure. The window was open and the white curtains rose and settled with the faint breeze that blew through it. The clock above the stove was a cat whose tail marked the tick-tock of time with swishes of its tail. "I'm so glad spring is here. Is there anything more beautiful than a Chattanooga springtime? I'm glad you live up above the hurly burly of the city. It's so peaceful here on the side of Missionary Ridge."

"I enjoy the view from the back yard. When I was a little girl, I used to sit in Dad's grape arbor and look out over the city while I ate myself sick with grapes. I don't think I've ever since felt such serenity."

"Speaking of serenity, after you left yesterday, I worked late and was about to enter Reife's office with some accounting figures when I heard Edward Guinn and Reife having a horrific argument. I thought they would come to blows."

"Edward? In Reife's office? I thought he was in Ceylon. What was the argument about, could you tell?"

"Reife was yelling something about Edward not having the right to tell you about some project. I think he called it 'The Manhattan Project'. Reife pounded his fist on his desk and said it was the biggest secret of the war and that Edward should not have told anyone."

"Oh," said Averill. She guessed what Reife was so angry about. Of course, Edward perhaps shouldn't have told her about the atomic bomb project. She had wondered why he did after she had time to think about it.

Pris pounced. "Why did you say 'Oh' like that? Do you know what Reife was so angry about?"

"Yes, I'm afraid I do. And he's perfectly right to be angry. You know what they say, 'Loose lips sink ships'. Edward was very indiscreet to talk of it."

"I don't suppose you're going to tell me what it is."

"You're right, Pris. I'm not."

"And Edward didn't let you know he was in town?"

"He did not. I received a letter from him postmarked Ceylon just a few days ago. He didn't say anything in it about leaving for America. Did you see Edward or just hear him?"

"I didn't see him. The door was not quite shut when I heard the voices. I put the accounting figures on that little table outside his office and left." She paused to study Averill's face and observed, "It's odd that he hasn't let you know he was in the city."

"Isn't it?" Averill carelessly replied and changed the subject.

The workday was beginning Monday when Lyneire Dubuq entered the office. She wore a figure-hugging little number topped with a short jacket. With determination she sailed past Averill toward Reife's office giving her not so much as a glance. Adroitly intercepting her, Averill kept her voice level and suggested, "Why don't you have a seat, Miss Dubuq? I'll see if Mr. Braddock can see you."

Lyneire attempted to bypass her, but Averill held her ground and her manner was firm. "I don't intend to be rude, but I'm sure you will want me to do my job, and part of it is to announce any visitors. Please, let's not have any unpleasantness," and she held Lyneire's glare with a steady gaze.

Lyneire halted and with lack of grace sighed, "Oh, all right. Have it your way." She waved her hand negligently. Averill's back was to Reife's office but she observed her visitor's face change, her eyes suddenly focusing over Averill's shoulder and sun-lighting with pleasure. She sidestepped Averill and cooed, "Oh, hi there, Darling. I was in the neighborhood. Do you have time for a wee talk?"

Averill wheeled and saw Reife standing just inside his open door and the thought occurred to her that if she were Lyneire, she might not have felt too welcome. The look in his eyes was anything but lover-like, but Lyneire seemed not to notice and flounced toward him as Reife said in a flat tone, "Certainly. Come in, Lyneire." As he was closing the door, Averill said, "Aksel Hjördís called. He wants you to meet him for lunch at the Read House at twelve."

"Give him a ring and tell him it's a date," he replied shortly and shut the door. Averill wondered if Reife had been annoyed at Lyneire's use of the sobriquet, 'darling' in front of her. She thought he had been, but she allowed for the fact that it might have been her own irritation that she registered.

She returned to her desk and began opening the office mail. Without noting the 'Confidential' stamp on the envelope, she opened an envelope from a New York theatrical company. Two tickets for *Oklahoma!* dropped into her lap. She hastily snatched up the envelope and saw her mistake. Obviously, Reife was not too busy with the war effort to keep him from taking Lyneire to see the Broadway musical in New York. She checked the date and saw that it was for the coming Saturday night. She piled it with the other correspondence to be taken in to Reife and tried to ignore the sharp ache the sight of the tickets sent through her stomach. She was fighting an urge to submit her resignation just as Russ Higgins entered the office.

"Morning, Russ, how are things on the factory line?"

"Splendid. Good news, Averill. Rommel is on the run and our tanks are being used in North Africa to chase him back to Casablanca. Rumor has it that Hitler is beside himself with fury and intends to relieve him and possibly have him shot. Any day now, we'll read that the Desert Fox has returned to Berlin 'for health reasons'."

"And shortly afterwards there will be sorrowful bulletins out of Berlin telling of news of his death and an ostentatious state funeral to follow," opined Reife grimly, who had opened his door in time to hear this last, Lyneire by his side.

"Yes," answered Russ, "the world will be told there was a road accident or a serious illness which will unfortunately become fatal."

"Nothing like a bullet in the brain to ruin your day," said Reife dryly. "Has the mail been sorted, Averill?"

She handed him the mail with the envelope of tickets without comment. "Come in, Russ," Reife cocked his thumb in the direction of his office. He turned to

Lyneire. "I'll try to make it, Lyneire, but I can't promise anything."

"Oh, Reife," answered Lyneire, screwing her face into a pout, "you must come. Everyone is counting on it."

"I'll try. Goodbye now."

The sight of those tickets to a Broadway musical had done major damage to Averill's emotions. She knew that her leaving would be a major disruption to Braddock Engineering. What kind of person was she who couldn't put aside her petty little emotional battles and focus on the more important one: that of winning the war? She would stay. She belonged here. If anyone was an interloper, it was Lyneire. And anyway, what was Lyneire doing for the war effort? Nothing, from anything that Averill could see, she thought, unkind emotions in the ascendancy. The woman's presence on the planet was purely cosmetic. She was bone idle, useless. Somehow, all this rationalizing did not help very much and she went about her work not liking her thoughts very much.

She arrived home late that evening to find Olaf sitting on the front porch in the swing. "Come and sit down, Averill," he suggested, patting the seat beside him.

"All right, I will. It's a beautiful night."

"Are all your springs this beautiful?" he asked as she took her place beside him.

"I think so. Maybe this one seems more beautiful because its juxtaposition beside such horror happening elsewhere in the world makes it seem so. I imagine you have lovely springs in Norway, too."

"I try not to think what might be happening in Norway right now. But yes, you're right. Springtime can be spectacular. The weather doesn't warm up until late

April or early May but when it does the people spill out into the parks and it's like being reborn. Easter is especially joyous for us in Norway and it's late this year, as late as it possibly can occur—the weathermen are saying—so that means a warmer Easter."

"I know. I read somewhere that Easter won't come again this late for almost a hundred years," Averill said. "I wonder what the world will be like in a hundred years."

"I hope this war will be the last we have," said Olaf.

"That's what they said after World War I and it didn't happen. Perhaps that's why the Bible says that there will be wars and rumors of war until Christ returns."

"He will bring peace?"

"Yes. He's the only one who can bring peace that will last."

"Amazing," returned Olaf thoughtfully.

"Yes, isn't it?" She quoted softly, "'My peace I give unto you. Not as the world gives.' That's what He said almost two thousand years ago as He was leaving the earth to go back to His Father."

"He said that?"

"Absolutely. Do you have that peace, Olaf?"

"No, but I find peace in science. Does that count?"

"I'm sure it must help. But as I struggle along my own Christian road, I've found that there's no peace like the peace that Jesus gives."

Olaf was silent and moved the swing back and forth. Then he said softly, "I would like that, I guess," he said finally.

"You can have it, Olaf," answered Averill. And there in a swing on a front porch of a home thousands of miles away from his native land Olaf prayed a prayer for forgiveness of sins and accepted Jesus Christ to be

Lord of his life. The young Norwegian was born into the Kingdom of Heaven where there is neither Jew nor Greek nor Ethiopian nor black nor white, but all who would be the Bride of Christ in His coming kingdom on earth are accepted.

Chapter 37

Averill could not find a satisfactory answer to why Edward should have returned to Chattanooga that early spring of 1943 and let her think he was still in Ceylon. Since that morning last November when he called from the train station, he had been writing as if he were on the island of Ceylon. Could Pris have been wrong about hearing Edward's voice having that acrimonious discussion with Reife? Could it have been the voice of another? She entered the kitchen the next Saturday and found her father and Olaf finishing breakfast. Olaf rose swiftly, carried his plate and coffee mug to the sink, rinsed them, and remarked with a glance at the clock, "I'm late for my appointment."

With a sideways look at Averill, Col. Lowe asked, "Is it a meeting with our friend? If it is, I would like to join you."

"Of course."

With a flash of intuition, Averill observed nonchalantly, "Tell Edward he might have called me."

Olaf looked nonplussed and her father betrayed himself with a startled blink of the eye, but then grinned and said, "You're right up there with the Office of Strategic Services, aren't you, my girl?"

"I have my sources," Averill said demurely. Actually, it had been the wildest of shots in the dark.

That night Edward called her and arranged to meet her at Mrs. McLaughlin's boarding house for Sunday dinner. "I can't be seen in church," he said, "even though I've changed my appearance somewhat. Mrs. McLaughlin thinks I'm Dallas Newbury, so perhaps when you come, you'd better call me Mr. Newbury or Dallas."

"My, my. Aren't we all cloak and dagger these days?"

"Don't laugh at something you know nothing about," was the unexpected response from the usually affable Edward.

Averill reflected it was the first time she had ever known Edward to be curt with her. "You're right, Edward. I shouldn't," she replied mildly.

Mrs. McLaughlin came out from the kitchen and greeted her as she entered the living room of the big boarding house. "My dear, so nice to see you. There's a young man waiting for you in the conservatory."

While she was speaking, Edward entered the room and Mrs. McLaughlin left to go back into the kitchen from whence could be heard banging of pans and clamorous voices calling back and forth.

"Edward…," as she was taken into his arms.

"It's been so long," he murmured into her ear.

"Why all the secrecy?" she asked, drawing away and taking his hands in hers.

"Let's eat and then we can talk. Let's forget everything except we're going to eat the best beef brisket in Chattanooga."

"Don't forget her green pepper and cheese casserole and a coconut cake that takes the breath out of you," responded Averill as they entered the dining room where various individuals were eating family style.

After they polished off what Edward said was the best meal he'd ever had, the two went into the empty conservatory and sat down on the sofa. The room had long casement windows over which hung white lace curtains and was vastly over-populated with its old-fashioned furniture, knick-knacks, and curios. A purple-hued Victorian mahogany sideboard sat crowded with its display of old silver and porcelain. The little spinet piano still sat where it had when she and her father had met over two years ago just days before he had left for Egypt where he had encountered Blake and his thugs. The only things that were new were pictures of men in military uniform positioned on various surfaces. Averill surmised they were former boarders with whom Mrs. McLaughlin kept in touch. One picture had a low arrangement of freshly picked white roses from Mrs. McLaughlin's garden tucked beside it. She wondered if the picture was that of a boarder who wouldn't return.

"When I left you," Edward began, "I traveled to Ceylon to work with military staff in the Pacific. I was there until two weeks ago when I was sent here with an urgent message for Aksel Hjördís."

Averill nodded. When he paused, she said, "Go on."

"Did Reife tell you we had a terrific row?"

"No, but Pris told me she heard the two of you arguing in his office."

"You may know that Reife and I have known each other for several years. Iron Workers United, formed in 1939 to prepare for possible war with Germany after England declared war on Hitler, brought us together. When your father suggested to Reife that he employ you as his assistant, it was because we wanted someone who could be trusted; we didn't want to risk loose talk from a secretary's lips."

"I'm glad I got to be a part of something I believe in with all my heart and soul," said Averill. "I love teaching and will probably go back to it someday, but I want to stay with Braddock's until the war is won."

"In spite of having to see Braddock court another woman?" Edward looked at her with a searching eye when he asked this.

"Maybe it doesn't bother me all that much," said Averill, lifting her chin. *Not bother me? Oh, Reife.*

"I wish I could believe that," said Edward.

"It doesn't matter," said Averill. "It's miniscule against all the suffering in the world."

"So you're staying on and will continue to work with Braddock?"

"Of course."

"I wish you didn't see him every day," he muttered. He paced nervously back and forth across the carpet until pausing, he seemed to make up his mind to plunge ahead, and blurted, "I was wrong to tell you about the nuclear secret, the Manhattan Project. I'm bitterly sorry about putting such a critical program in jeopardy," he said. She admired him for looking at her directly when he spoke. "Only a handful of people in the world know about it. They tell me that even the Vice President doesn't know."

Averill thought how, since Cairo, she had realized how little she knew this man. Could any human, locked in three dimensions, fully comprehend another human? "You know I won't say anything to anyone," she answered.

"I know," Edward wandered over to the long casement windows and looked out, "but it was wrong of me to involve you."

"It's all right. Let's not mention it again," Averill said. She could not help but think Reife's anger was justified regarding Edward's indiscretion. Was it a result of the raging jealousy he felt toward Reife? Was the real reason he told her such a monumentally significant secret was that he wanted to 'show off' for Averill? Wasn't that why people told secrets, anyway? A desire to be one up? Underneath the smooth exterior of Edward must have raged intense jealousy and, yes, a kind of spite, in order to betray such a secret. Of his own secret double life he had kept faith: he had never hinted of his role in England's Secret Intelligence Service, popularly known as MI6, and his reputation as the notorious super spy—'Valiance'—until the Egyptian interlude put paid to that part of his life.

Now he turned and walked over to her, cupped her elbows, and bent his lips to hers. "I've wanted to do this ever since you walked through the door," he said and kissed her. She embraced him but almost at once, sensing a lack of passion, he reluctantly pressed her to arm's length and desperately read her eyes, searching for something. Apparently not finding it, he abruptly released her and walked back to the windows to stand and gaze onto the peaceful Sunday scene, one hand rattling change in his pocket. "I have loved you ever since the tenth grade when you walked into the church with your parents for the first time."

Averill said nothing, looked down at the Turkey carpet, and noticed for the first time its design of birds and flowers. An expensive carpet. Mrs. McLaughlin had not always had to take in boarders, she thought irrelevantly. Edward's kiss had not awakened any feelings for him and for that, she was sorry. It would have been wonderful to parade her love for Edward in front of Reife. How lovely it would be to proclaim that she, too, had another love. Her basic honesty shrank from using Edward that way.

"Don't say anything right now that will be hard to take back later," Edward said, as he turned and lifted her chin from her scrutiny of the carpet. "I know you don't love me the way you perhaps still love Reife Braddock. People change, though. Sometimes it takes a while to fall in love with a good friend. That's what I am, isn't it? A good friend?"

"I'm sorry. I know that's not enough for you."

Edward groaned and turned back to the window. "Being good friends is the best way to start a marriage," he said in a muffled, but stubborn, tone.

"Yes, it is. I know that."

He turned again to face her. "I'm leaving tomorrow for Ceylon. This time it may be until the war ends."

"Can you say anything about how you became to be known as 'Valiance'?"

He considered the question. "Yes, I can tell you some of it." He stood, one hand on the mantelpiece, relaxed, but she glimpsed for the first time the underlying grace and confident watchfulness reminiscent of predatory animals apparent in the lean figure. Jolted, she saw her childhood friend with new eyes and could—with utter belief—picture him as the secret agent she now knew him to be. It was unsettling. *Is anyone who we think they are?*

"My parents were divorced in England and my mother and I moved to the United States using her maiden name when we immigrated," Edward continued. "My father, who is fairly high-positioned in England's intelligence community, stayed behind. It was due to him that I was contacted shortly after Germany marched into Poland and recruited for an ultra-secret mission. England was a hair's breath away from defeat when America entered the war, as you know. If Hitler hadn't eased off her in 1941 and turned much of his attention to the war on Russia, the defeat of England might have been a fact of history. Churchill later said his daily prayer during those dark days was that the United States would enter the war and help them defeat the Germans. He told his staff he slept the sleep of the saved when Japan attacked at Pearl Harbor for he knew the U.S. would rouse and engage like a wounded bull.

"To not put too fine a point on it, I lied to you about the year I was in England on research for the University. I was traveling extensively undercover, where I began overseeing infiltration of other agents and performing other essentials of the murky business of 'spying'. Of that, I cannot speak because there are British agents with whom I worked who are still very much active. My cover was blown when Blake took your father, Reife, and me prisoner in Egypt. Only Blake's greediness for British Sterling saved us all."

"Thank God for avarice, then."

Averill sat very still for quite some time; she was shaken to her very bones. Unbidden, into her mind flashed the conversation she had had with Reife in the restaurant of the Hay-Adams Hotel that Thanksgiving week over two years ago when he told her that Valiance's undercover work had, in a large part, resulted in England's Royal Air Force winning the Battle of Britain. With an effort, she threw off the feeling of having just been led on a tightrope over a hitherto unimagined world—startling and unexpected. She rose from her chair to ask, "Would you like coffee? I can get some from the kitchen."

"Do that. I'm going to wait here and pretend that you have changed your mind about us and we're married, the kids are down for naps, and you and I are enjoying a quiet Sunday in our house on a hushed suburban street."

Averill grinned at him. "Edward, you are incorrigible. But while you're fantasizing I wonder: could you conjure up a real fire?" She faked a dramatic shiver and gestured to the cold fireplace as she left the room. "I hate to drink coffee in my coat."

She was later to reflect what a puzzlement it was that under all those sediments of the mystery that was Edward there ran an unsuspected vein of latent romanticism.

Chapter 38

Returning from work the next day, Averill found Olaf on the front porch with the *Chattanooga News-Free Press*. "Sit down and look at this, Averill." Olaf indicated the seat beside him in the swing. "What do you think?" In great banner headlines, the paper trumpeted the death of Admiral Yamamoto, Supreme Commander of the Japanese Naval Fleet. His plane had been shot down while flying him to an observation post. "It will be a miracle," Olaf said, lowering his voice, "if the Japanese don't realize that the Allies have broken their code after this," he finished, tapping the headlines.

"Is that how they knew to fire upon that particular plane?" Averill asked, sitting down beside him in the swing.

"Most assuredly," Olaf answered. Abruptly he asked, "Would you see a movie with me tonight?"

"That would be nice. Shall we eat first? Let's go see what Mom's got for supper."

"An excellent idea," said Olaf. He folded the paper carefully and upon entering the front door and passing through the living room on his way to the kitchen, he placed it on the small table beside Col. Lowe's chair.

Annie had pork chops ready with mashed potatoes and green beans from the garden. After an excellent rhubarb-strawberry pie, Averill and Olaf made short work of the dishes and soon left to see *Casablanca* at the Bijou Theater in downtown Chattanooga.

Humphrey Bogart was saying to Claude Rains, "Louie, this could be a start of a beautiful friendship," when Olaf leaned over so that his lips grazed her ear and whispered, "Shall we go?"

Outside, he took her hand and led her across the busy street to where he had parked his car. Once they were settled, he slanted his head to check his rear-view mirror to pull out of the parking slot. The fair hairs on his hands were blond-red and lay relaxed on the steering wheel as he turned his head to ask, "Did you like the film?"

"Very much. I lost my heart to Paul Henreid."

"Not Humphrey Bogart?"

"No. He always looks scrunched up in the middle like an accordion."

Olaf threw back his head and laughed, then commented, "Ingrid Bergman is certainly easy on the eyes."

"Isn't she the loveliest thing you ever saw?"

"I wouldn't say that," Olaf replied, giving her a sly sideways glance as he navigated through the late night theater traffic. "You're very lovely yourself, you know," he added, reaching over and tilting her head toward him with a finger under her chin.

Averill smiled into his eyes and made no comment.

Olaf drove for a time without speaking then looked over and asked suddenly, "You think I'm too young for you, do you not?"

"I don't believe I've given it any thought."

"There is not that much age difference. What is it—four, five years? I'm old for my age. I entered college at fifteen years."

"You really should be dating college coeds."

"If I wanted to date college coeds, I would."

"Yes, I expect you would," she said, laughing.

"Don't laugh."

"I can't help it. This whole conversation is so ridiculous."

"I don't find it at all ridiculous. I'm in love with you."

"Olaf, you can't mean it," she answered, lightly.

"But I do. Didn't you know I fell in love with you the day I met you? I knew you were Reife's girl so I never said anything. Now, it is different."

"Yes," Averill said a hint of bitterness, "things are different."

"He is a foolish man. To prefer that... bit of fluff to you."

"Is that how you see Lyneire?"

"Bah. She is unimportant, negligible, but you..." He stopped and then exclaimed in exasperation, "Oh, let us not waste words talking of her."

"All right. What do you wish to talk about?"

"I wish to know all about you. Tell me, how do you feel about light-haired men?" He cocked his eyebrow. "I know you find the dark-haired Reife attractive, but do you not like the other kind a little, also?"

She laughed and, seeing that Olaf was serious, she said, "Yes, I do. I think you are immensely attractive."

"Then you will continue seeing me," he said, as if putting the question to rest for good.

"I see no reason why not," she answered, smiling.

He reached over, tucked her left hand up under his right arm, and drove contentedly onward.

In the coming days, Olaf haunted Averill's office. Between his classes and lab work, he found snatches of time to spend sitting on the sofa across from her desk. Little by little Averill became aware that these visits were irritating Reife. Olaf seemed content to sit and watch her work during the busy times, but Reife, alert now as a bird dog to Olaf's visits, seemed to take perverse pleasure in calling her in to his office under various pretexts any time the other man appeared. Joan, watching all this, said to Averill one day, "Peter is coming home on leave next week. I'm giving a little reception. Why don't you bring Olaf along?"

"Do you know, I think I will," said Averill, and felt sudden pleasure.

The black-tie reception was in full swing as Averill and Olaf arrived, she wearing a long slim dress of soft yellow organza over satin and he looking devastatingly handsome in evening clothes. Mingling with the guests, he was at ease in the older adult society, more sophisticated than Averill had seen him. She began to wonder about his family. Perhaps he was used to this sort of life. He never talked much about his background, but he was revealing unexpected *savoir-faire.*

It was Peter's first leave since enlisting and Joan, aglow with happiness, could hardly take her eyes off her Army Air Force husband, handsome in his dress whites. The caterers, it appeared, had let Joan down, delivering the food but not staying to serve it, and family and friends pitched in to keep the food and drink coming. Averill, feeling quite relaxed in leaving this new Olaf to his devices, spent time in the kitchen unpacking supplies from the refrigerator and cabinets and placing them on serving trays. In due time, Olaf appeared in the kitchen and helped ferry the food.

As the evening progressed, Lyneire Dubuq—by now very drunk—jumped onto a table and proposed a toast to Peter. Reife put down his drink in disgust and headed toward the adjoining library. She screamed, "Reife! Stay for the toast!" Averill watched with hot embarrassment for her as Lyneire jumped off the table, ran after Reife, grabbed his arm, and tried to pull him back into the room. Reife whirled and pulled his arm away, snapping, "Take your hands off me," whereupon Lyneire threw her drink at Reife's departing back.

Dale Braddock moved swiftly to Lyneire. He put his long arm around her and pulled her to him. "Let him go, love," he said, "he'll be back eventually, and make the correct apologies." It might have rescued the moment had Lyneire not been past caring, but she demanded loudly, "You can't treat me like this, Reife Braddock. I'll scratch your eyes out, I'll...." to which Dale applied reassuring noises. Joan persuaded Lyneire to sit in a chair and perched on the chair's arm, keeping her arm firmly in place on her shoulders. To distract the uncomfortable guests, Joan lifted her glass and said, "To Peter," caressing her husband across the room with her eyes.

Olaf, standing beside Averill impulsively gathered her to him and kissed her ear. Lyneire, alert to any attention paid to Averill, saw the gesture, and with coquettish interest took the measure of a man whom hitherto she had paid little attention and asked, "Hey, Handsome, how about a refill?"

Olaf gravely took her glass from her, filled it to the brim from a water pitcher, presented it to her, and said in firm, measured tones, "Drink this, and don't... say... another... word."

She gave Olaf a murderous look and deliberately slammed the glass on an end table sending sprays of water onto the polished wood, but, meeting his steady gaze, she held her tongue. Averill slipped over and sat on the other arm of Lyneire's armchair. Joan gave her a grateful look and made her way swiftly to Peter's side, whereupon Peter slipped an arm around his wife's waist and smiling down at her, kissed her, oblivious to the guests. Lyneire ignored Averill and, after a few minutes rose and in an uneven walk made her way to a sofa, threw herself down on it, and fell unattractively asleep.

Reife did not reappear and the ill-at-ease guests began leaving; eventually Averill and Olaf took their leave. Olaf appeared lost in thought as he guided the car down the mountain and Averill sorted out her own reactions to the unpleasant fact that Reife had abandoned his girlfriend to her odious behavior without trying to salvage the evening. Olaf, with his gracious, lovely manners would have, were the two men's situations reversed, she decided. She turned to him when they had descended the mountain and were well on their way to the Lowe's house and said, "You were delightful company tonight. Thank you for going with me."

He reached out and took her hand, saying nothing. Averill contentedly laid her head on his shoulder while the car carried them through the sleeping streets of Chattanooga.

Chapter 39

With three men active in the war being waged in Europe and in the Pacific, the Braddock family was in a state of permanent flux during 1943. Jim Braddock came home when his ship, the *USS Enterprise*, docked in Bremerton, Washington in mid-summer, and her men were given a thirty-day leave. Frank had ended his short leave by beginning duty as a ship's surgeon bound for the South Pacific aboard the *USS Brownson*, a destroyer fresh from the shipyards of Bethlehem Steel on Staten Island; and in November Peter Conover left for an air-base in England.

The war was turning for the Allies, and victories in the Pacific and in Europe were becoming commonplace for everyone except the ones who fought. The casualties on the small islands in the Pacific were grossly disproportionate to their size. The Allies were on the march to Tokyo and every island captured was a stepping-stone in that direction. Sometimes the ground gained was only enough land to erect a takeoff and landing field for U.S. airplanes.

Averill celebrated Christmas 1943 quietly with her parents while over the radio they heard that Dwight D. Eisenhower had been appointed Supreme Commander of Allied Forces in Europe. In the Pacific, U.S. troops continued to fight bloody battles with Japanese troops, whose skill proved formidable. A few days into the new year the Braddocks awoke to the news that the *USS Brownson* had been sunk by an enemy dive-bomber off the coast of New Guinea the day after Christmas. There was as yet no news about Frank for another few days and the family once again waited for news of a missing son. The news when it came was good. Frank was one of a handful of survivors who, under fire by Japanese fighters, had been rescued by a sister ship, the *USS Daly*. The Braddock family breathed easily again.

Olaf and Averill now saw very little of each other since work his work in Oak Ridge, Tennessee had reached high gear, but at every opportunity, he pressed his suit on Averill. He was a young man in love for the first time and was not altogether unsuccessful because Averill's response was very different than that to Edward. Whereas, much as she would have liked to be attracted to Edward, there was nothing but a feeling of friendship; on the other hand, she was attracted to Olaf, despite his youth.

Even though seven-day weeks were now *de rigueur* at Braddock Factories, Averill took Sunday mornings off to attend church and eat dinner with her parents. On such a Sunday, Annie Lowe answered a telephone's ring in the Lowe household. She curved her neck around the door and said, "It's for you, Averill."

It was Joan Conover. A very calm, collected Joan with not a touch of hysteria in her voice. "Averill, I received a telegram from the war department. It's Peter. He's been shot down over Hamburg, Germany."

"I'll come right over, Joan. Was he taken prisoner?"

"No. It's worse. He never had a chance to eject. The plane crashed. There were no survivors."

When Averill arrived at the Conover house, the door was opened by Reife. He said gravely, "Thank you for coming, Averill." He stepped aside to let her enter. In her extreme grief, Averill reached over and laid her hand on his face. "Reife, I'm so sorry." For a long second he stood impassive and unresponsive, then pulled her to him, and held her as if he would never let her go. For a panicked moment, she thought she might suffocate. She fought to turn her head to catch her breath and he caught her mouth with his. When he finally released her, he said hoarsely, "I've been so mixed up, Averill. I think these last months I've lost my mind a little."

She laughed, and her voice had a catch in it. "You can't lose your mind a little. Either you lose it or don't."

Reife gained some measure of control and said, "I'll take you to Joan. She's been asking for you."

The Braddock women were there: Ellen, Frank's wife, and Colleen, Jim's. Gertrude was seated beside Joan on a sofa holding her hand. A tall, willowy dark-haired woman Averill had never seen before arose from her place on the other side of Joan and motioned to Averill to seat herself there. "I'm Jessie, Dale's former wife," she said. "Please sit down. Let me get you something to drink."

"Thank you. Just coffee."

"Oh, Joan, I'm so very, very sorry," Averill said, as she lowered herself onto the couch beside her. The two embraced, and Joan laid her head on Averill's shoulder. Joan wiped her red destroyed eyes with her handkerchief, but her voice remained matter-of-fact. "Averill, I've lost Peter."

"I know, my darling. I know."

The afternoon wore on with friends and family coming and going. Averill helped make sandwiches, pour coffee, and cut cakes for those who came by. She could feel Reife's eyes on her constantly. He talked with the guests but his eyes restlessly sought hers.

Lyneire arrived, threw her short fox fur carelessly on top of a Chinese lacquered chest which stood at the entrance to the living room. A piece of a Lladro nativity set rocked dangerously. She crossed the room, took Reife's arm, and possessively led him over with her to speak to Joan. Averill took an empty tray back into the kitchen and began washing up. When the kitchen was in order, she retrieved her coat and left by a side door.

She found her car and drove down the mountain. The day was drawing to a close and the sun was beginning to set. The trees stood stark and leafless which, Averill thought, befitted such a dreadful day. She rolled down all her windows and a sharp wind clawed her face while she breathed in the smell of a dying year. Nineteen forty-three had brought a turn of the fortunes of war that 1942 had not seen. The Allies were winning the war but at great cost. Peter had died, but Allied B-17s piloted by other brave men still pounded their German targets, and all Germany was becoming a wasteland. Her father told her that Allied fliers had orders to avoid civilian buildings, but she knew that in the heat of war there were bound to be many civilian casualties. She thought of the difference between the tranquil skies above her and those of England and Germany, and she felt shattered. How would it feel to see death falling from the air? Were the people of Hamburg as brave as those of London who didn't let the flames and destruction erode their will to fight on? She thought they probably were.

The phone was ringing when she arrived home. Her mother and father were out. She picked up the phone to hear Reife demand, "Where did you go? Why did you leave without telling me goodbye? You left because of Lyneire, didn't you?"

Suddenly, the day, Peter's death, Reife's acquiescence in the face of Lyneire's astonishing display of ownership all exploded in raw emotion. Her mask slipped and plummeted to the ground with her rush of words. "How dare you let her paw you over like a fur coat? It was obscene! You were obscene to allow it. And after...after your greeting at the door. I think you're despicable. Now excuse me. I'm getting ready to go to evening church service."

"Wait! Forget Lyneire. Averill, I need to see you tonight. Please."

"Only if you come to church because that's where I'll be."

"I'm around the corner at a gasoline station. I'll be at your house within two minutes. We'll go to church. It sounds like a good thing to do."

"Come on in. I'm upstairs changing my clothes."

Reife was waiting for her as she descended the stairs wearing a woolen suit over a rolled-neck silk blouse. She had thrown a plaid cape over her suit and a little feathered hat was perched on her head. The intensity of Reife's gaze forced her to drop her eyes when she arrived at the foot of the stairs. Her heart was behaving in a most irrational manner. Reife took her arm in his old possessive way and led her out to his car.

Later, she was to remember little of the sermon, but the old, traditional hymns of her faith calmed her spirit. She sang "Leaning on the Everlasting Arms" with tears running down her cheeks while Reife's hand stole on top of hers and gripped her wrist and hand with his long fingers. To the end of her days, she was never to forget that moment when God moved into her heart and renewed His age-old promise to be with her always.

She settled back as if onto the bosom of Christ, and her breathing became even and regular.

Afterwards, they drove to her house and she led Reife into the living room. With her parents gone and Olaf in Oak Ridge, the house was quiet. There, Reife took her into his arms and talked about the dead months that had passed.

"I've been out of my mind during these past months. When I blew up at you at Harrison Bay it was because your words reminded me that two of my older brothers and a brother-in-law were fighting this war and I was sitting at home safe."

"You weren't safe all the time," Averill remonstrated. "You went to Egypt to find Blake and were shot in the leg. You could have died trying to make sure that the Allies got the tanks they needed."

Reife shrugged. "That doesn't count."

"It does count."

"Not to me, it doesn't. The thought that I should be over there with my brothers ate at me over these last months. I thought at one point I was going to lose my mind. I think the night of Peter's reception, I almost did. Then, tonight when my family seemed to look to me to keep everything together, I saw with clear eyes what this courageous family has done. Father is seventy-three and he shouldn't be working sixty-hour weeks, but if Braddock doesn't keep going, who will supply the armaments that my brothers and others need to stay alive and defend this country? Most of all, it finally sunk into my thick skull that false modesty and a denial about the necessity of my staying at Braddock Engineering has cost me the one thing I wanted above all—you.

Averill wanted to ask, *Why did you take all this out on me?* but she couldn't bear to add to the guilt he was feeling. Still, there was a corner of her heart that had been unmoved. She said with bitterness, "So you think all you have to do is to say you're sorry and everything is going to be the way it was with us?"

Reife sat back on the couch. "You won't forgive me?"

"I'm sorry, Reife, but I've made a kind of peace with myself during these months, and I need time to readjust to the fact that…that…"

"That I still love you?"

"Yes," she replied, a hot surge of anger rising anew with the knowledge that she had been forced to make him say the words at long last.

"I see. I guess that's a natural reaction. I have to say I didn't anticipate it. More fool, I."

Averill sat looking at her hands.

Reife rose and towered over her. "Do you love that schoolboy?" He asked suddenly with a violence she hadn't expected.

So he had noticed. "Are you talking about Olaf?" she asked, all innocence.

"You know I am."

"Olaf has nothing to do with this."

"He's in love with you. It leaps to the eye anytime I see him with you. You have no idea what I suffered to watch him come to the office and sit drooling at you. It was my fault for throwing you over like I did, but that only made it worse."

He reached down and pulled her up and put his arms around her. She felt numb.

Reife released her, leaned back, and surveyed her with eyes that suddenly become cold. "I see. You're going to punish me," he said, with suppressed anger.

Averill lost her temper. "You are quite the egoist, aren't you? The irresistible Reife Braddock! You thought you would come with your niggling little apologies and I would fall into your arms. You thought I would be thankful and, oh, so grateful to have you back. You can't erase one and a half years, Reife. Even you—in your boundless arrogance—should realize that."

Reife looked at her for a long moment. Then he turned and walked to the entry hall where he gathered his coat from the antique coat rack and, without another word, left.

Chapter 40

"I'm worried about Reife; he's like a car hurtling down a hill without brakes," Russ Higgins, the operations manager, told Averill one day when she was trying to run Reife down to answer an overseas call. They found him on his back on the floor in overalls with a wrench working on a piece of equipment. Averill knew this kind of behavior was what had made him respected among his employees. Too, she knew he did not do it to be respected: he did it because the factory was running twenty-four hours a day seven days a week and Reife had to force his exhausted employees to stay home for a day's rest after grueling shifts without time off and there was so much work to do. The former custodian, Frederick Jackson, had not taken a day off the line in three months, he was so proud to be working on armaments instead of mopping floors. Factory workers were taking turns at cleaning and repairing equipment. Seventy-three-year-old Gertie Braddock was coming in twice a week to clean bathrooms. Averill came in early and dusted offices. Retired Braddock employees came back to help in various capacities—mostly cleaning and repairing machinery. Factory workers took turns sweeping the factory floor. Old barriers came down, and Reife was hiring women to work on the assembly line.

Olaf and Aksel Hjördís, along with Erica Gur-Aryeh, were to be transferred to a mysterious somewhere in the New Mexico desert. Averill guessed it had something to do with the nuclear project.

"Will you wait on me?" Olaf asked Averill.

"Better not; I'm an old prune of twenty-five and you'll be meeting lots of bathing beauties that close to Hollywood."

"I don't think you take me seriously," Olaf said, his eyes darkening with something akin to anger, then the old light came back to his eyes "But someday I'll come back for you. I know I can make you happy. You'll see," he added confidently.

Averill smiled up at him and kissed him. "Yes, we'll see," she said, unable to identify the emotions fighting within her. Olaf had to be content with that.

A wan but self-contained Joan came back to work to help in the accounting department. "Please find something for me to do," she had begged Reife. The overworked bookkeeper welcomed her back and soon she was putting in eight hours of work. When the weather permitted, Averill, Joan, and Pris took their lunches out onto the patio that looked down over the Tennessee River where they ate fried chicken and devoured fried egg sandwiches. Meat and eggs were rationed, but Pris's family lived on a farm in nearby Hixon and farmers were the favored ones in the war. They were raising their own food and that for their neighbors and, naturally, they ate well.

Reife and Averill were courteous to each other at work, but Reife no longer gazed after Averill or smiled the heart-stopping smile she had loved. Soon she came to the bitter realization that her refusal to be taken for granted had been a victory of sorts, but a hollow one. In the night hours, awake and restless, she fought against the knowledge that she still loved him, now that he was lost to her forever.

Lyneire called him at the office from time to time but when Averill put the call through, she noticed Reife was never on the line long. She found a perverse pleasure when one day Joan put Lyneire's call through to Reife and snapped as she slammed down the phone, "Reife has no time to squire that silly, demanding woman hither and yon."

Edward caught typhoid fever in Ceylon and came home bringing as his wife a beautiful black-eyed Eurasian woman who had nursed him through the terrible disease. "You're okay with this, aren't you, Averill? It was pretty sudden."

"Of course I am, Edward. We will always be friends. Nothing can change that," she said, and then went home, slammed stomach-down on her bed and unreasonably burst into tears. "Nerves," she told herself.

It was an autumn morning of 1944 when Averill entered Reife's office and found him slumped over his desk. She leapt for the intercom button. "Russ!" she screamed. "Bring help! Reife is ill!" She pulled him onto the floor and began artificial respiration even though she could not be sure he had stopped breathing. After a minute, Russ Higgins and several others burst into the office, scooped him up, stuffed him into a car, and raced with him to the hospital. At 39, he had suffered a mild heart attack.

The next day she appeared at his hospital door bearing flowers. He took one look at her and she never quite knew how it happened, but suddenly she was grabbed by an arm, intravenous needle and all, and pulled toward him and they were kissing each other as though time had no end. He was almost incoherent but she could hear him saying over and over, "Oh, my little love, my little love," and she was gabbling over and over, "I thought I had lost you." Alas for the flowers. Crushed lilies, daisies, and roses were squished between their bodies.

Reife said, "I want to marry you right away. Do we have to have a big wedding?"

"I don't want a big wedding with the war on," she told him with her head against his and her words punctuated by kisses. "I just want to be Mrs. Braddock as soon as possible."

"And so you shall," he answered, caressing her from eyes to toes with a look that almost stopped her heart.

A Final Word

Many thanks to Betty Benson Robertson, Nita McBride Wade, and Linda Bates Poore Steadman for their early reading of portions and giving me my first encouraging words and suggestions. Years ago, Linda sent me a book on how to write a romance novel. It has long been lost, but I have not lost the delight that her belief in me gave.

Thank you to all the other readers who read this in various stages of preparation: Eydie Benson Bolin, Byron Benson, Dr. Louis Morgan, Neva Wilson Engels, Doris Harder, Debbie Rush, Mari-Ann Nicholson, Margie Curl Ellis, Carol Stahl, Dan Leichty, Mary Alice Bauman, Pat Forney, Ron Benson, Juanita Purinton, Frances Simpson, and Sallie Welch Curl. Linda Lassen, my hairdresser, spent part of an appointment re-telling the story to me, therewith unknowingly giving me the greatest accolade a writer can receive: a vindication that the characters had jumped off the pages to become real.

If you care to do so, please visit me at www.virginiabenson.com where you may write with your comments to virginia@virginiabenson.com. Any forthcoming books will be posted there.